SIMON

PLAYING THE GAME

GerriCon Books Ltd

First published in Great Britain in 2010
by
GerriCon Books Ltd
Orford Green
Suite 1
Warrington
Cheshire
WA2 8PA
www.gerriconbooks.co.uk

Names, characters and related indicia are copyright and trademark
Copyright © 2010 Simon Gould

Simon Gould has asserted his moral rights
to be identified as the author

A CIP Catalogue of this book is available from
the British Library

ISBN: 978-0-9561034-7-5

The places named in this book are real. The fictional events are based
on factual ones but have been changed by the author.
Any similarity between the fictional characters and people in
the public domain are coincidental, and are generated purely
from the imagination of the author.

All rights reserved; no part of this publication may be reproduced or
transmitted by any means, electronic, mechanical, photocopying
or otherwise without the written permission of the publisher.

Cover Photos: ©istockphoto.com

Cover designed and typeset in Sabon
by Chandler Book Design
www.chandlerbookdesign.co.uk

Printed in Great Britain by the
Ashford Colour Press Ltd.

1

Looking blearily across the room, desperately trying to focus on the digital read out of my alarm clock I figured it must be around three in the morning, but that was my best guess. The phone was ringing out for maybe the sixth ring but for all I knew it could have been ringing for hours. I let it ring for another couple of seconds, trying desperately to get myself together. I'd been in bed for around two hours and asleep for less than half of that, despite sinking several beers over a couple of games of pool with a few friends last night. It had been a rare night completely switched off from work. When those nights come around you have to make the most of them. I'd been around long enough to realise that good news seldom arrives at this time of night and I suspected that the call I was about to receive contained no good news at all.

'Yeah, this is Patton', I mumbled, picking up the telephone. As my eyes became more focussed, growing accustomed to the darkness, the familiar outline of my bedroom furniture gave me little comfort. My heart sank as my worst fears were confirmed.

'Hey there, Detective,' I sat upright, trying to shake off the tiredness. 'It's time to play. You want her back, you have to play!'

I recognised the eerie digitised voice straight away, despite only having heard it a couple of times before. For the last four and half weeks, my partner and I had been working a high-profile case that had been driving us insane. In my fifteen or so years working homicide in the LAPD, I had seen all kinds of crazy but nothing like this. I knew that Los Angeles had its fair share of sick bastards but this one must be close to the top of the pile.

So far the individual that the papers had nicknamed 'The Chemist' had struck, and been successful, twice. Up until tonight, The Chemist had kidnapped two girls, injected them with an extremely high dose of a drug called Clozapone and then mailed us the antidote. All we had to do then was to 'play the game' and find the girl. This was girl number three, and we hadn't found the first two in time. We hadn't even been close.

Clozapone, in its prescribed dosage is pretty harmless. It is commonly used to combat schizophrenia or as an anti-depressant. Sure, there are side effects but nothing major. In the dosages that this bastard was prescribing it would gradually decrease the number of white blood cells in the victim's bloodstream then systematically shut down their vital organs. It's not quick and it's not painless. A hell of a way to go – and trust me when I say – you don't want to be the one who finds the body. Not if you want to sleep anytime this century, anyway.

The phone went dead, but it didn't matter. I'd had two of these calls before and I knew the drill by now. Wearily I got out of bed, shivering as the cold night air cascaded over me. I walked to the bathroom and stood for a moment as I filled a glass with water; the alcohol I'd consumed last night had made my mouth dry. My head was pounding although I thought that this was as much to do with the beer last night as the phone call I'd just received. If we stood any chance of getting the girl back, we'd have to be on top of our game today, and would need more than a little luck alongside that. I looked in the mirror as I drank the water, and thought I looked older than my forty-five years. Maybe years of chasing psychopaths like The Chemist had aged me slightly, or just maybe I could no longer sink several beers then be ready to go again after little or no sleep.

For some reason, I was the one getting the initial call and that meant that The Chemist wanted me close to the case. I hadn't figured out why The Chemist wanted me specifically yet, but I knew it was crucial. Most of my first week on this case was spent searching through my past cases histories to see if any of my past 'wins', had been released recently – seeing if it was personal. Nothing so far, but one thing was for certain, I was determined to make this one another win. I had no choice. For me, each case was either win or lose. In my experience no-one ever drew, and I wasn't about to start now.

Wearily, I went through the now all too familiar motions for the third time in just over a month. A call to my partner who sounded a lot worse than I felt, a call to my station captain, who sounded like he never slept whenever I'd had the misfortune to have to call him in the early hours of a morning and, finally, a call to the PD getting them to check for the fax I knew would have arrived seconds after I'd had the telephone call from The Chemist.

After I hung up the final call, I took a moment to savour the sound of absolute quiet. I knew in just about forty-five minutes, at one of the major incident rooms of the PD, I would be once again surrounded in chaos.

2

Considering I live a good forty minute drive from my station, it was reassuring to do it in just over thirty. The Chemist commanded our top attention, no doubt about that. If we were being watched then my rapid response time would no doubt be pleasing. It would indicate just how seriously we were taking the games that The Chemist was setting us. According to the profilers I'd worked with over the years, perpetrators of crimes of this nature often like to be close to the investigation. It gives them an increased sense of power and authority. So maybe The Chemist *was* watching.

Heading up the three flights of stairs to where I knew the fax would have been sent, I could hear a buzz that suggested I was by no means the first to arrive at the incident room. Although it was probably just the guys on the night shift, I knew word would have spread quickly throughout the station once the fax had been received. Virtually every police officer in LA was aware of the case, and would naturally take an interest in any developments. For those on the night shift tonight, especially if it was a relatively quiet night, the arrival of the fax would herald the major talking point of the shift, no doubt about that. I took the steps three at a time and I could have done them with my eyes closed. I was getting used to this by now.

As I arrived at the incident room, I looked around. There were ten or eleven members of the PD gathered round a board. None of whom seemingly had a home to have gone to. It was nearly ten to fucking four in the morning. Someone had pinned the fax on the board, which would be the starting point of the investigation. During the previous two investigations, although I hated to admit it, we didn't have much else on the board by the time girls had died.

'Hey man', the familiar voice of my partner greeted me.

I've had a few partners during my years in Los Angeles, none of them such a force to be reckoned with as my current partner, friend, drinking buddy and all round bad-ass Charlie Holland. I'd called him immediately after The Chemist had hung up on me. He was without a doubt, the one guy you want on your side when the brown stuff hits the fan. As solid as they come, he'd saved my life on more than one occasion, and I'd been in the position to repay the favour a couple of times. I'd known him for years – we first met at training academy back in eighty-four when we were both twenty-one. We'd hit it off almost immediately, both being ultra competitive and ultra dedicated from the offset. It still pains me to this day that I graduated in second place, just behind Charlie. If truth be told, I couldn't have come second to a better man. After graduation, our paths took a separate course. I stayed in LA, Charlie moved to Minnesota and later Colorado, cementing a solid reputation in both states, before finally moving back to LA, and rejoining the LAPD five years ago. We'd been partnered up pretty quickly. I'd certainly covered similar ground to Charlie, albeit in one state, not two. My captain, Captain Neil Williams, had been keen to hook us up – his 'Patton and Holland, you better make

Riggs and Murtaugh look like fucking pussies A-Team', to give you his direct quote. He must have been a fan of Lethal Weapon I guess. Those nicknames had stuck, if for no other reason that Charlie was coloured and I was white and we had kicked almost as much ass as our movie counterparts over the years. Charlie, a hulking figure and with a nose that had been broken on more than one occasion, looked more like a boxer than a detective. This was a card that we had played throughout our partnership; he was one intimidating son-of-a-bitch when he needed to be. He was also one of the most gentle, giving and unselfish people I'd ever met.

'Here we go again, huh?' I shook my head, giving Charlie the familiar greeting of a handshake and quick back slap. We were in for a hell of a day, we both knew that. It was good to see Charlie looked as rough as I felt. He'd been at the pool hall last night too; we'd only parted company a few hours ago.

We made our way to the board, exchanging nods and words with those officers we knew. There was very little small talk. Given the situation we found ourselves in, you would be hard pushed to call them pleasantries.

Looking at the sheet of paper that had been pinned up we saw twelve rows of symbols, each row containing twenty characters. No surprises there, exactly the same MO as the previous two. But different symbols this time – not that I'd been able to make any sense of the previous two. I shook my head again. This bastard didn't want to make things easy for us.

I couldn't help but think of the Zodiac Killer who had terrorised Vallejo and San Francisco, amongst others, in the late sixties, due to the startling similarities to the point of contact. That had been our first and obvious frame of reference when we had received the first one. But there were no instructions for us to publish them, like the Zodiac had given. Oh no, these were just for us.

The tech guys were already on their way. I'd always had reservations about what these guys contributed to law enforcement, but in truth I'd never needed them before. They had also been nowhere near cracking the code by the time the two previous games were over, doing little to reassure me they were as good as they thought they were.

Over the next twenty minutes we could do nothing but stare cluelessly at the sheet of symbols, desperately trying to make any sense of them we could, as more and more people began to arrive in what had now become the most important room in the station.

I'd already called the top tech guy, who was almost half way to the station when I got through to him. Captain Williams had done me that favour at least. The tech guy on call was Dave Ferguson, known all around the PD as 'Fergs'. My computer knowledge extends just about to turning it on and off, typing up reports and kicking the damn thing when it crashes. Fergs, on the other hand, could probably launch shuttles from his if he put his mind to it. In other words, he could do pretty much anything he wanted with them. Including cracking this fucking code.

Automatically checking the clock on the wall, I knew we had a couple of hours until our next point of contact. At exactly 6a.m. we would get the antidote delivered directly to the front desk by a courier, and if I were a betting man, which I am when I know the odds are in my favour, I'd stake a month's wages on it being a different courier firm to the previous two. I wasn't betting today though, I couldn't even begin to guess the odds on this one. Someone had the foresight to brew some coffee, and I helped myself to two large cups. Strong, black and no sugar. I passed one to Charlie who accepted it gratefully. We knew we had a long day ahead and that we would need to be razor sharp if we had any chance of catching The Chemist. Any chance at all.

I could hear people murmuring 'number three' under their breath. One is an isolated incident. Two is extremely worrying. We all knew what three could mean. I was deep in conversation with Charlie, getting our battle plan together, when he uttered the words everyone was thinking, but no-one else was daring to say.

'Patton, if this one dies we got ourselves a balls-to-the-wall, bona-fide serial killer'. Once again, I couldn't help thinking of the Zodiac. One overriding fact kept pounding my head harder and louder than anything else, and this time it was nothing at all to do with the alcohol I'd consumed last night. They never caught that fucker, did they?

3

'So if you were some freelance motherfucker for hire at the time of the Rebellion, you'd work for the Imperial Empire rather than the Allies? Is that what you're saying?'

The lobby of the Kavannagh, a relatively small coffee house, on the outskirts of Eagle Rock, was deserted. Hardly surprising, it was a shade after half five and they weren't due to open for about half an hour. It was your typical coffee house which did just about enough business for the owner to employ several employees to help ease the growing strain that the hours she was working were placing on her; often in excess of seventy hours a week. This included Graham, her college drop-out nephew and his equally hapless friend, Tel.

Graham Keast, known to his friends as Keasty since around the fourth grade, and Tel Pennington, the two lucky employees deemed worthy enough to get up at an ungodly hour five times a week and open the place up, sat back, both puffing at the type of cigarettes you would find difficult to buy from your typical newsstand vendor. They were given about an hour and a half to prepare the place for the day but had long ago figured out how to do it in half the time. If truth be told it wasn't what either of them thought they'd be doing with their lives but having received the ultimatum from his parents of 'Either get a job, or get out', Keasty had turned to his aunt, who had given him the job out of family loyalty as much as anything else. A couple of months later, with the business doing a respectable trade, he'd gotten his friend a job there, which made the fact that he had to come to work all the more bearable. And, just like now, there were plenty of opportunities to put their feet up and do nothing except smoke weed and shoot the breeze.

'Too right', Tel replied to his friend's question. 'What you gotta remember is that these are *freelance* guys, ok? They don't commit to one side or the other. They go where the money is good, whoever pays the most. You're not telling me that your average Stormtrooper gives a shit about galaxy domination or whacking a fucking Jedi? I'll bet the Emperor paid top dollar. And besides, Darth Vader has got to look better on a CV as a previous employer than Admiral fucking Aakbar!'

Keasty chuckled. He had to admit Tel had a point there.

'Anyway', Tel carried on regardless, 'this is a mute point, I don't hold with any film that advocates incest and paedophilia'.

'What the hell are you on about now?' Keasty shook his head, 'We are talking about one of, if not *the*, greatest films of all time. How on earth do you arrive at that shit?'

Tel smiled. He had obviously, in his own clearly twisted way, thought this through. 'Ok then, here me out', he instructed. 'Luke Skywalker spends most of the first film trying to fuck his own sister! There's your incest right there. And the paedophilia? Obi Wan Kenobi is first seen wandering round the dessert picking up young farm boys! He didn't need ketamine to help him there did he? Not with the sand people going round knocking them out for him. Easy goddamn pickings! You've got to admit, you'd be seriously fucking worried if you woke up in some old man's cave, not knowing how you got there, with a sore head, and the old guy's asking you to play with his lightsaber'. By now Tel was laughing, 'Am I right, or am I right?'

Keasty had to concede, put like that it certainly made sense. 'You're sick is what you are, never mind right. Only you would take a family film classic and turn in into something that deranged'.

A momentary pause in the banter was pierced with a thud; the sound of the mail dropping through the front door. Keasty got up to go and check it, hoping that it would include one of their several unauthorised subscriptions that would have upset his aunt if ever she opened them; the type of magazine you really didn't want to leave lying around for your parents to find either. Hey, you had to have something to pass the time! Although it picked up as the morning wore on, usually it would just be him and Tel working till around eight o' clock. His aunt usually came in around that time and worked through till they shut, with a couple more staff coming in later, including a sexy little waitress whose number both Keasty and Tel had been trying to get for the past couple of months.

Thumbing through the mail, Keasty was disappointed to find only run of the mill stuff and not one of the various 'subscription' publications they had delivered to the Kavannagh on their behalf on a regular basis. Bill. Bill. Circular.

Stopping on the fourth piece of mail, Keasty's brow furrowed. 'Hey Tel', he shouted 'Who the fuck is Patton?'

4

Usually I love it when I'm right, but when the white FedEx van pulled into sight at the stroke of six, a feeling of depressing familiarity overcame me. The Chemist hadn't used FedEx before and I knew that despite wasting a couple of hours of our time grilling the driver, going through the motions, it would yield us precisely zero information that we could use to nail The Chemist. Nothing whatsoever.

The antidote for the previous two games had been delivered in a brown package which had contained a syringe. The syringe itself had been clean, no fingerprints, no DNA, no fortuitous solitary hair that would given us some clue as to The Chemist's identity. The Chemist was being extremely methodical, careful and precise. These weren't characteristics that were usually conducive to catching an adversary. Likewise, the packaging was clean and common enough that it could have been bought in any one of around nine hundred outlets in Los Angeles alone.

The last thing the driver, who it turned out was making his first delivery of the morning, was expecting when he pulled up to the front entrance of the station was four armed-to-the-teeth SWATS in his face, but nevertheless, that's what he got. I have rarely seen anyone look so shell-shocked but hey, if I was a courier going about my daily business and four mean looking bastards armed with Berettas pulled me up during a routine job, I'd have probably looked exactly the same.

The package was hustled into the forensics department with an urgent haste. I knew we'd have to run the same tests as before which would take a bit of time but until Fergs had cracked that code there wasn't much else we could do. We could only hope that this time, The Chemist had slipped up and had inadvertently given us something we could use. I wasn't holding out much hope.

About fifty minutes passed with a tedium I was getting used to; the feeling of being able to do absolutely nothing. We used the time to go over a few old cases; we were still in the process of compiling a list of people who we thought *could* be The Chemist. Given my considerable success in Los Angeles over the years, it was a long list and for all intents and purposes, we might as well have been making a list of all the people I'd pissed off over the last decade in the LAPD, which given that I'd arrested some of the most notorious criminals in the state, many of which were with Charlie's help, was turning into a formidable list.

A couple of other officers took the courier for the usual interrogation but it was clear from the off that the driver was only doing his job and nothing more. Just like the previous two, he couldn't give us any description of the person who'd given them the package, or anything else we could use. He'd driven from San Diego; the others had been from San Jose and Benicia. All from California, but to try to cover all courier services in such a vast area would be borderline insanity in terms of the scale of operation required, and even closer to impossibility to be in the right place at the right time. Of course, we would now contact the specific courier to try and get something concrete but it seemed like The Chemist was using them in such a way that when questioned, no-one in the courier firms could remember the order being placed or have any record of it being done so.

Charlie and I were just about to check in with Fergs for a progress update with the code when we were blindsided by an excited Rebecca Newstead. Rebecca had been on the forensics team in the PD for around six years. She was a model professional and took great pride in her work. She had also rushed through a few bits and pieces for me over the years, which had gotten me some results sooner than I would have otherwise done.

'Patton', she almost seemed breathless. 'We might have something – we've got the antidote of course – as usual no trace of evidence, no DNA, no nothing on the antidote itself; not even a *suggestion* of any latents, but we do have something else'.

We followed her down the corridor to where the package was been subjected to the most intense scrutiny by another two members of the forensic department, who I did not know.

'Look at this', Rebecca gestured towards a scanner. 'We've scanned every inch of the jiffy bag at a resolution of 208-1995, that is to say, the highest resolution specification we can possibly do right here and now', she added, sensing quite rightly that the technical specifications meant nothing to Charlie or I. 'We split the lining of the bag and well, you would never see it with the naked eye, but we found this on the inside lining'.

I took her place at the scanner and read three words, one of which made no sense to me. 'Patton – Holland – Kavannagh'.

5

Stella Edwards was trying to open her eyes, which was a struggle to say the least. She felt like she had the worst hangover she had ever had, multiplied by a thousand. Not that at the tender age of seventeen she'd had too many hangovers, but her mom did let her drink in moderation. She had overdone it a few times with her friends though! Pain was shooting through her body, from her head all the way down her back and she had a dull, numb feeling in her left arm and leg.

Slowly, still unable to open her eyes, she thought she remembered someone stepping out of the shadows as she turned the key to her front door. She remembered dropping her school bag and raising her arms to try and fight off her assailant. But that was all she remembered.

She tried to call out but heard nothing. Her mouth was open, she knew that, and in her head she could hear herself calling out, yet she made no sound.

Where was she? She certainly wasn't stretched out on the comfortable leather sofa in front of the TV with a takeaway, sneaking couple of glasses of her mother's Beaujolais while she was at work, and then idly munching her way through a healthy supply of chocolates while she watched that new reality program that had just started a couple of nights ago, but had already gotten her hooked – which she thought had been her plans for last night.

It took a further ten minutes for her to find the energy to open her eyes, only to find nothing but darkness. As she tried in vain to form any sort of reference, any sort of outline of her surroundings, her right hand brushed against a small cylindrical object.

Fumbling around in the dark, it took her and undeterminable amount of time to figure out that it was a flashlight and even longer to turn it on.

With what little energy she could muster, she lifted the flashlight to try and get a bearing of her surroundings. She slowly circled it around her and the realisation of just how much trouble she was in slowly but clearly dawned on her. She dropped her illuminator, cascading her back into darkness.

She was in a box no more than six feet by three feet with nothing but darkness surrounding her from every angle. There was a ventilation pole going up – rather like a snorkel, but other than that, and the flashlight, absolutely nothing. Who had done this to her? Why was she here?

As Stella closed her eyes again, the pain still shooting through her body, she let out a silent scream which would have terrified anyone, if only it could have been heard.

6

LAST WEEK

For one of Los Angeles hottest young journalists, life was spiralling out of control at an alarming rate. Hailing originally from Manchester, England, Paul Britland-Jones had relocated to LA after flying through his Journalism degree at Oxford with first class honours. Sure he'd had offers from the most prestigious of English publications but he'd never really been interested. For him, the ultimate goal was here in America – the land of the Pulitzer – The City of Angels, where success came with many, many more fringe benefits. Now at the age of 38, having spent ten years at the LA Times breaking stories sometimes days, not hours, ahead of his rivals, he had honed his journalistic instinct to a fine art. To this end, he'd had to make some unsavoury acquaintances in order to stay one step ahead of the game. It was not uncommon for him to talk to members of the Los Angeles criminal fraternity more often than his colleagues or editor at the LA Times.

Success, however, had come at a price. He owed money for favours long since cashed in, popped more Prozac than Tony Soprano and usually started his day with a neat double vodka. He hardly looked like the successful journalist that he was. At just over five foot five, heavy bags permanently under his eyes and stubble that would range from anywhere between a day to a week he would often compensate for this by indulging himself in ego-enhancing excess. Drink, drugs, hookers; you name it, he had dabbled in it over the past decade or so. Finding he owed substantially more than he was making, primarily due to the crippling interest rates that members of the underworld applied to 'favours', he was now, having seemingly little choice left, turning his journalistic hand to blackmail. Nothing one would class on a major scale so far, but he had a feeling that was about to change.

It was a shade after four a.m. on a dark November morning. He stood in the shadows of the run-down, some derelict, buildings of Figueroa Street in Downtown Los Angeles, with a hat pulled down low, collar upturned and fingerless gloves to try and stem the cold; his trusty Kodak Rangefinder 2000 hung around his neck ready for action. It was quiet at this time of night, which suited him just fine. He suspected it suited his target even more. Not that the police turned a blind eye to this neighbourhood, but they had bigger, more pressing, concerns. He was confident that he could go about tonight's activities without the fear of being discovered by a member of the state's law enforcement. Many of his rivals would just love to break a story about him being questioned by the police. He had members of the LAPD who tipped him off with nuggets of information so he was pretty sure some of his rival journalists would have similar unofficial informants only too willing to pass on his misfortune to them if he should find himself suddenly detained by the LAPD.

A sudden gust of brisk wind made Britland-Jones shudder, and he glanced around him, almost nervously. He was sure when he'd first arrived in LA, that this had been an up-market, prosperous neighbourhood, but now, with crime in this part of town rife, and constantly rising, it was now home to mostly crack heads, squatters and prostitutes – not a place where he was accustomed to hang out in the early hours of the morning, but a place where he was hoping to acquire some blackmail-worthy photographs of a certain someone.

Another half hour passed, with only occasional activity. A homeless person, difficult to tell whether they were male or female, shuffled off the street into a squat. A couple of teenagers sped by, trying a couple of doors on the only parked car on the street, presumably after a quick steal. Then, just as he was contemplating returning to his nice warm bed for a couple of hours, a door opened on one of the houses across the street. His eyes lit up as he brought the Kodak to his eyes – this is what he'd come for:

Click.
Yeah, that was a good one!
Click.
Oh, yes, you can really tell who that is can't you?
Click.
I hope you had a good time up there. It will cost you more than you think!
Click.
One more? Just to be on the safe side?
Click.

As he lowered the camera, despite the cold, a wry smile came over Britland-Jones' face. Knowing there was no-one around that could hear him, he couldn't resist gloating over the images he had just captured.

'Thank you very much Senator Conway', he was almost laughing now. 'We will speak very soon. Very soon indeed'.

7

It took us no time at all to compile a list of who or what Kavannagh could be, or what Kavannagh might mean. In fact, just doing a quick sweep of the LAPD databases brought back only one possibility – a small coffee house in Eagle Rock. Something I suspected was no accident on the part of The Chemist. It seemed that The Chemist was just as careful with the locations of the games as with leaving no trace of evidence.

It was also no surprise that The Chemist now seemed to be including Charlie in the game. Charlie had remained by my side during the games for the first two girls, Keeley Porter and Jennifer Hughes, and he was as determined as I was that we wouldn't be adding a third dead girl to that list. The Chemist had no doubt been keeping tabs on our lack of progress during the first two games and it therefore made complete sense that The Chemist would know about Charlie. This was the first time Charlie had been mentioned in any aspect of a game though, an accolade which gave him no concern.

'Bring it on', he growled. 'Let The Chemist play my fucking game and see who wins'.

Neither of us had any idea what lay in store at the Kavannagh, I only knew that whatever it was, it was only the first of many steps. Fergs was having a tough time at his end, after more than two hours working on the code he was nowhere, despite having another four 'techies' who had joined him over the course of the morning. He had even had the PD bring in a recently paroled Richard Bradshaw to 'voluntarily assist' them as a gesture of his commitment to his reformed ways. Bradshaw, I was told, had just served eleven years for major computer fraud which involved breaking the security codes of LA's Federal Reserve and transferring around forty million dollars into various accounts around the world. Now Fergs had mentioned it, I seemed to remember reading about it somewhere a long time ago.

It didn't take us long to get to Eagle Rock but we knew that we were now racing against time. By six a.m. tomorrow morning, one way or another, it would be game over.

Pulling up outside the Kavannagh at around ten to eight, from a preliminary scan of the outside it seemed like business as usual. Several customers could be seen sitting inside and people were coming and going like they usually would on any ordinary day, seemingly oblivious to anything outside their own little worlds.

Nevertheless, I wasn't taking any chances. Guns drawn at the ready, we ditched Charlie's Subaru Impreza WRX, which had made such good time from our station to Eagle Rock, in a side alley. We did a quick sweep of the parameter of the Kavannagh, then burst through the front doors, badge in one hand identifying myself to the two guys behind the counter.

The look of initial shock of us bursting in gave way to a nod; almost a gesture of recognition, once I'd identified myself as Patton.

'Yeah man', Graham – well it said that on his badge – nodded. 'This came for you in the post this morning –

couple hours ago. 'We wondered who the fuck you were'.

Keasty reached to the side of the counter and brought out an envelope. 'We opened it – we didn't know what it was', he continued. 'It's all there though, even the key'.

As I reached for the envelope, I heard the couple of black and whites that had been dispatched as out backup, arrive outside. They had left at the same time as us but the way Charlie drives no-one was catching him. If he wasn't a police officer, let's just say that Formula One could have been his chosen profession.

'OK guys', I gestured to the pair, 'who was here when it was delivered, just you two?'

'Yeah, just us', Tel confirmed.

'You both handle this?' I waved the envelope.

'Yeah we did'. I just hoped they hadn't completely covered the thing in prints.

'OK, we're gonna need statements and prints off you both. You're gonna need to close. You want to tell your customers? You got two minutes'. Charlie was already itching to get things in motion and to have a look in that envelope.

Keasty and Tel began announcing their apologies to the customers, most of whom had taken an interest in what was building as soon as Patton and Holland had burst in. Those who hadn't initially been interested certainly began to be when the black and whites pulled up, sirens screaming, disrupting the tranquillity of their early morning coffee; looking up from their various chairs and the couple of black leather sofas that aligned the far wall of the coffee house. 'I'm sorry', Tel said to a nearby customer who had just over half a cup of latte left, 'but I'm going to have to ask you to leave – we have to shut. I'm not sure what's happening but the LAPD have asked us to close'.

Taking a final swig of latte, leaving the cup just under

half full, the customer stood up, picking up a newspaper and coat obligingly from the clean black leather on one of the sofas.

'No problem', The Chemist replied, gesturing to Patton and Holland. 'Looks like you've got your hands full'.

In an irony not lost on The Chemist, a member of the LAPD, one of the black and whites, actually held the door of the Kavannagh open for them to leave and in so doing, The Chemist couldn't help but smile. Patton and Holland were right on schedule.

8

LAST WEEK

Despite only having had a couple of hours sleep the previous night Senator Conrad Conway was in a good mood, he loved this time of year as it affirmed just how powerful an individual he had become. He was in the lift of the Aon Centre, the second tallest building in Los Angeles, ascending towards to sixty-first floor which, as always, took a good few minutes. From there he would walk casually to the end of the corridor, swipe a card and use his right thumbprint to gain access to the stairwell leading to a room on the sixty-second floor. To his knowledge, you could count on two hands the number of people who could access that room at this present time. The reason for that was simple; the exclusive room on the sixty-second floor was the designated place for the bi-annual meetings of the Animi – a group of individuals who could influence the major events and decisions in Los Angeles for their own personal gain, desired outcome or political ambitions. He had been told by the member that proposed him, that they were called the Animi after the ancient concept of Animism that refers to souls as ghosts and that's exactly what they were as far as Los Angeles was concerned – ghosts. No-one, other than its members, had any idea whatsoever of the events that they had controlled over the years or the magnitude of change their actions had resulted in.

As the lift ascended, he afforded himself a glance at his reflection in the mirrored panels and he broke out in a wide smile, revealing the perfect white teeth he had flashed so many times during his political career. His permanent tan suggested he took far more holidays than he actually did and made his thinning blonde hair seem even blonder His stocky build meant that he cut a daunting figure when arguing his point in the political arena.

Reaching the sixty-first floor, which was, as usual, deserted, he walked to the end of the corridor to an unmarked door with a card reader. Swiping his gold card, he made his way to another door with fingerprint detection. Once his thumbprint was recognised, he entered a ten digit code he had committed to memory many months ago. Opening the final door, he then eagerly marched up the stairs to the meeting room and despite being a couple of minutes early, he saw he was the last to arrive.

Looking round the room, he gave the customary nods and greetings to his fellow Animi – City Attorney Jameson Burr – the individual who had proposed him almost two years ago. Mayor Cyprian Hague – the very public face of the anonymous Animi, now in his second term as Mayor, Justice Of The Peace Thomas Brittles, Joint Chief of Staff Lee R. Brindle, Animi Chairman – District Attorney Paul McCrane and finally, owner of one of the biggest television networks in the United States – Robert Farrington.

Powerful though he was, Conway knew he was among esteemed company and always acted accordingly. These meetings, although always seemingly informal, had, at times, altered the course of LA's history; through mutual consent of decisions the Mayor would publicly take, sentences that would be passed on certain individuals, influence within the White House and, when circumstances dictated, the removal of troublesome individuals from the public eye – all reported with whatever slant they needed by the Farrington Network.

It went without saying, that whatever was discussed within these walls was never repeated. There were certainly no minutes taken, and it was with the up-most care that each member ensured there was no record of them ever having being there.

It was Chairman Paul McCrane who spoke first. 'Gentlemen, once again here we are. I'd like to thank everybody for taking time out of their hectic schedules to find the time to attend, but as I'm sure you all agree, we have one or two pressing matters to attend to this time around'. There were various grumbles of agreement from the members around the room.

'Not least of which, the activities of who the media', he turned half-nodding to Farrington, 'has dubbed *The Chemist*. Jameson, would you care to update us?'

Jameson Burr cleared his throat and stood up. 'Well we've all seen the news, haven't we? It seems we might have a problem. As we discussed just over six months ago, Paul and I drew up a list of candidates of individuals that could, well, operate on our behalf. Individuals that would have no hesitation in assisting us with a problem in an upcoming trial. We settled on one person who we thought was right for the job. The person that the media, as Paul quite rightly pointed out, has since dubbed *The Chemist*'.

'So where did you dig this person up from?' Thomas Brittles was keen to know more, 'It's not like you can randomly walk up to someone in the street for this line of work is it?'

'Indeed not', Jameson continued 'and it's funny you should say that Thomas. This person was convicted of a particularly nasty triple homicide seven years ago, you denied their appeal personally'. A look of surprise dawned on his face, as if he were fitting the last piece of a jigsaw into a particularly difficult puzzle.

'You mean to say that *that* individual is free, roaming the streets of LA as we speak', Brittles was almost incredulous.

'That is exactly what I mean to say', Jameson nodded in a sombre tone. 'We had this individual covertly released from San Quentin six months ago, although you can be assured that there is no paper trail – as far as the system is concerned, this person has not, and never will be, a recorded inmate of San Quentin. The governor is a very close personal friend of ours. In fact, we have, at some considerable cost to ourselves, practically erased this person from existence. As far as we can tell, there is no record on any system, anywhere. This person was supposed to be at our service, to carry out several actions at our discretion, after which, we would have returned this person to San Quentin for life. Solitary confinement would have been the order of the day. However, as we now know, things didn't quite go according to plan'.

'We should have used one of our existing contractors', Conway chastised, shaking his head. 'It's not as if we don't have several people we can reach out to for favours is it?'

'Well that was an option that came up, Conrad', Burr responded. 'But as we know, this isn't one action, it's four; and four actions means that the manhunt for the perpetrator would be massively increased once the obvious link between the actions is established; and with that, the risk that the perpetrator could be linked with us increases also'.

'Remind me again why we thought it pertinent to go down this avenue', Brindle wanted to know. He had been absent from the last meeting of the Animi six months ago when this plan was implemented, having to remain within easy reach of the president as the campaign trail intensified throughout the country. His attendance today had only been confirmed last night. Even though he had been sure he would be able to attend, his schedule was often subject to external factors beyond his control. He had, of course, been apprised of the contents of the last meeting but was keen to go over the reasons for their current course of action one more time.

'Four witnesses in the upcoming Peroza trial could not be persuaded to retract their statements', Burr said. 'Surprising I know; we don't usually have too much trouble in this area. They are due to testify in two weeks. We have stalled this process as long as we can, they should have testified almost six weeks ago. As we know, their testimonies will no doubt result in the conviction of Manuel Peroza who we used last year to convert five million of the Animi's laundered capital into untraceable real estate in Los Feliz'.

'Why go after the witnesses?' Brittles asked, 'Why not just go after Peroza? Seems to me if there is no Peroza, there is no problem'.

'Manuel Peroza is the cousin of one of our most influential backers and they have called in their marker', Burr stated. 'His elimination was not, and is not, an option. I can say without any reservation at all that we do not want to make an enemy out of this particular backer. That of course, left us the only choice of ensuring that the witnesses at the trial do not testify. And that in turn left us with the problem that we are dealing with today. Four witnesses disappearing at the same time are a problem – and one that would not come without its own substantial investigation. We needed to ensure that we knew exactly where whoever was carrying out these actions was going to be once the actions were completed. We can't run the risk of employing anyone to carry out these actions then being picked up somewhere down the line on an unrelated charge and having us as leverage to plead out a lesser charge. Our plan was for Caldwell, The Chemist's real name by the way, to be released, eliminate the four witnesses, then be returned to San Quentin, no questions asked'.

McCrane took the floor. 'Caldwell was placed in a safe house with two guards who thought they were safeguarding a witness to a mafia hit. To cut a long story short, both of the guards were killed – nastily I might add – and Caldwell escaped then completely disappeared; we looked of course but Caldwell became invisible. We, well both Jameson and I, assumed that Caldwell fled the state, maybe even the country. We tried our usual sources, pulled in several favours but nothing. And we didn't hear anything until now.'

'What about the usual means of tracking?' Farrington wanted to know. 'I assume that we took the usual precautions?'

'Tracking?' Conway interjected. 'What do you mean tracking?'

'We have only had cause to use this process twice before', Farrington stated. 'Before your time here actually, Senator. On both occasions we took the precaution of injecting a tracking device into the toe of our subjects so we could keep track of them and know exactly where they were if a situation like this ever arose'.

'Of course we did', McCrane stated indignantly, as if he would fail to implement such an important procedure! 'The day after the guards were killed, I received this, mailed directly to my office, absolutely goddamn untraceable'. McCrane reached into his briefcase and pulled out a box. Setting it on the table, he gestured to Jameson Burr to open it.

'It's been in a storage facility all this time', McCrane added, and as Burr opened the box, there was an audible sharp intake of breath around the room.

'Jesus Christ', Cyprian Hague was the first to speak, 'Caldwell cut off the fucking toe you injected the tracker into'.

'There is one other thing,' McCrane continued. 'And this is *not* a matter of public record'. He reached once more into the briefcase and pulled out a single colour photograph. 'This was taken at the safe house, when we first discovered Caldwell had killed the two guards. On the kitchen wall of all places. Written in one of the guard's blood', McCrane shook his head. 'Poor bastard', he added.

Animi. When the time is right, I will come for you all.

'So how do we know that Caldwell is The Chemist?' Brittles asked the question on everybody's lips. Burr nodded, he'd been expecting that question.

'I received an e-mail yesterday, from an internet café in Vancouver of all places. It goes without saying we have had the CCTV checked and no sign of Caldwell. And the email account is the café's generic outbox account. Absolutely nothing to help us there'.

'This email', Conway wanted to know. 'What did it say?'

'Very simply', Burr informed, 'it said *Animi, The Chemist says the time is now*'.

There was a pause of around twenty seconds or so as they digested the news; the members of the Animi were visibly shaken.

McCrane thought it was time to summarise. 'Caldwell has had seven years to think of God knows what whilst incarcerated in SQ, six months of freedom to put a plan into place, and now seems to want to play some kind of sick game, which includes us. All I know is this; we've got some fucking psychopath running round LA playing this deranged game, which, my good men, like it or not, we now seem to be a part of. Caldwell obviously has bad intentions in mind as far as we are concerned. If the police don't catch Caldwell, well then our next meeting could very well have a somewhat depleted attendance. If Caldwell's caught, well we are quite high-profile individuals if I do say so myself; I would not doubt that the bastard would trade us in, in a heartbeat, as part of some kind of deal if it were on the table. Finding Caldwell before Caldwell finds us is our only option'.

The Senator, and likewise his fellow Animi, bar Burr and McCrane, could not believe this. Six fucking months! And to top that off, now they all find they are on The Chemist's shitlist. Sensing a growing animosity, concern and general panic around the room, McCrane did what he could to ease the tension. 'Gentlemen, simply put, now we have a problem, we will deal with it', he said with his customary authority, as he began passing round copies of the file he had compiled with all the information they had on Caldwell to the rest of the room.

As 'Plan B' was drawn up over the course of the next couple of hours, Conway couldn't shake the feeling that this wasn't going to have a happy ending.

Before I could re-open the envelope we'd just picked up from the Kavannagh, my cell rang. Flipping it open to my ear, I hoped this was good news. 'Patton', I answered, passing the envelope to Charlie, though I was desperate to see its contents. I could see two of the black and whites, having evacuated The Kavannagh, questioning and fingerprinting the two employees. Although we needed their fingerprints to eliminate them from the envelope, I suspected they would be of no further use; clearly they were pawns in the game The Chemist had devised for us. Their fingerprints would probably be all over the envelope, but even if they hadn't handled it at all, I knew that The Chemist wouldn't have been so careless as to leave any other fingerprints for us.

'Patton, its Dave Ferguson', the voice was excitable. 'We've had a breakthrough, well to be more specific, Bradshaw has come through for us. He brought in his own software, which I'm ashamed to say puts ours ....'

'Get to it man', I interrupted. 'We don't have the time'.

'Yeah, OK', Fergs sounded a little more in control. 'Well we think most of it is just random garbage, translating as more random garbage for each algorithm you apply to it. But we had Bradshaw run his code-breaking software on it, and after a couple of hours, well, we think we have an address.'

The couple of seconds silence on my end must have relayed how stunned I was. 'Patton? You there?'

'Yeah I'm here …. Give me the address!' Something didn't sit quite right with me. Were we supposed to break part of the code so soon? We'd had guys working round the clock trying to break the previous two but with no success. Or was Bradshaw really that good?

'Well the address we've got from the code is 22 Sutherland Boulevard. It's about ten minutes from the Kavannagh'.

'Got it Fergs', I thought I knew where Sutherland Boulevard was. 'Keep going on the rest of that code, there may be something else'.

I turned to Charlie, who was holding another sheet of paper in his hands. Shaking his head, he passed it to me. It only took a second for me to read over, but seemingly longer for it to sink in.

'The game has only just begun', printed in large bold type. Then underneath; *'I have only just begun'*.

'There was also this …'Charlie handed me a small aluminium key. 'Maybe a deposit box or a locker or something, there's no engraving on the key but there is a number, three sixteen. Could be for anything really'. He paused for a couple of seconds. 'We're getting played here man, you know that, right?'

He was right, of course, but what choice did we have? We had no leads, no idea who was doing this and all we could do, was to 'play the game' and hope that whoever The Chemist was, slipped up and somehow gave us something we could use. One thing I did know, when we had our break, we were taking no prisoners.

'Yeah I know that', I nodded, 'but I'll tell you this Charlie boy – we're gonna get this bastard one way or another'.

I just had no idea how.

10

After leaving Patton and Holland at the Kavannagh, especially after that nice policeman had held the door open, The Chemist almost felt happy. Now, cruising at a steady 70mph down the Ventura freeway, The Chemist was audibly laughing.

Well, what was not to be happy about? The skies might have been overcast, but it was dry, bright and surprisingly warm for this time of year. The open freeway stretched out invitingly, and on any other morning The Chemist might have taken full advantage of new-found freedom by driving from city to city committing unspeakable acts. The calming strains of the Red Hot Chilli Peppers' 'Scar Tissue' played in the background. Most importantly, The Game was on track. The Chemist didn't know whether or not any of the code had been broken but that was not important. They *should* be able to break the code. After all, the previous two were unbreakable, simply due to the fact that there was no code to break. They were test runs, practice runs for Patton, and now Holland, but also practice runs for The Chemist as well. Response times had been checked. Procedural ambiguities ironed out. The Chemist also had to check that Patton was still worthy of attention, despite what he had done, which he was. Holland had been a surprise. Patton was always going to have had a partner, a confidant, a policeman friend he would call upon during a particularly nasty investigation, but Holland was surprisingly assured. At around six two, and, at The Chemist's best guess, around two-twenty, two thirty pounds, and with a deceptively quick speed about him, Holland could prove to be a formidable adversary if and when the time came. It was obvious by the way they conducted themselves that Patton and Holland had been friends, not just partners, for a long time and The Chemist still couldn't decide whether this was a good or a bad thing.

Seeing an approaching exit and checking the time, The Chemist raised a quizzical eyebrow.

'I wonder …do I have the time?' The Chemist said out loud. 'Of course I do'. It was probably worth checking again, regardless, given the events that were planned later on today.

Taking a sharp right off Ventura, The Chemist gunned the Cadillac XLR towards Echo Park, where the pupils of Belmont High school would be arriving within the next thirty minutes. Yes, there was plenty of time.

Even though The Chemist was driving at just under the speed limit all the way, not wanting to attract any unnecessary attention, at just before quarter to nine the silver Cadillac pulled up adjacent to the main entrance of Belmont High which was, as always, a hive of activity just before the nine a.m. roll call. There were plenty of cars and people milling around, and for anyone who wished to remain anonymous in a crowd this was definitely an added bonus. To the casual passer by, hell, even to any police who might just happen to drive past, The Chemist looked for all the world like a parent who might have just dropped a child off for school. Nothing at all to arouse any kind of suspicion. Just they way The Chemist liked it.

Several people walked past the car over the next couple of minutes but not one turned to look at The Chemist inside the car. If they had, they would have assumed that the person in the car was daydreaming idly into the distance but in fact, The Chemist was keenly scanning the high school entrance. Today being a Thursday, she should be here any time now, probably with her two best friends as usual, ready to learn some more about English, then Biology, then, after a break, American History where if the teacher's timetable was adhered to as strictly as The Chemist's timetable usually was, she would be continuing her discovery of the American Civil War 1861-65, specifically Lincoln's Emancipation Proclamation.

Ah, there she was, looking as pretty as she usually did, flanked by her two best friends, who's names The Chemist neither knew, nor cared to know. They were insignificant, unimportant; not part of *The Game*. Lucky for them.

She looked so happy too, and why wouldn't she be? Seventeen was such a fantastic age; several admirers taking turns to try and gain the affections of one of the most popular girls in their year, every Friday and Saturday night booked up, her diary full of offers from the star quarterback to the high school's wrestling team captain. Well that would be changing in the non-too distant future. The Chemist was smiling again, as the three friends went through the school gates, up the twelve stone steps leading to the main doors and finally through the entrance, until they disappeared from view. All the time The Chemist was focussed intently on the middle girl.

As the school doors swung shut, The Chemist started laughing again. 'Hello again number four, look at you – the apple of your father's eye! He should be so proud of you, and rightly so!

'Or should I say, hello again, *Katie Patton*'.

11

As we drove to Sutherland Boulevard, the ten minutes or so it took us to get there seemed like an eternity. We took the time to review what we knew, which at this point, didn't fill the ten minute drive.

Keeley Porter and Jennifer Hughes were nineteen and twenty-two respectively, so the same age-range. There was no evidence of anything sexual – no traces of semen in or on the bodies, no bruising around the vagina or anus. At least that in itself could be significant, we just didn't know yet. What that told us was that there were other motives for the abductions and killings. There were no traces of DNA on the bodies, which had been left fully clothed, or on the clothes themselves. Both girls had been from good families, good backgrounds and both had bright futures ahead of them. The strength of the Clozapone dosage had made both girls so unrecognisable that they had only been initially identified through ID they were both carrying and then later confirmed with the state's dental records. Neither girls' parents had been able to visually identify them once the bodies had been recovered; the Clozapone had done too much damage. One of the M.E.s told us that he had rarely seen such rapid decomposition of someone's vital organs in such a short space of time. There was nothing to suggest any other violence on the part of The Chemist; no battery or assault of any kind. That at least told us that there had not been any signs of a struggle during their capture and that maybe both knew their assailant or felt comfortable enough in their captor's company not to try to run. Or maybe they were both simply taken by surprise and they didn't have time to struggle. Chloroform maybe? At this stage it really was guesswork. They had both been found in different locations; Keeley in the boot of an abandoned car at a scrap yard and Jennifer in the empty water tank of a disused warehouse on the other side of town. We'd only found both when we got a second fax to the station after each 'Game' had concluded. We got these twelve hours after the game time elapsed. That is to say six p.m. the day after initial contact. We'd had the lab run some tests looking at how fast certain amounts of Clozapone reacted with different organs and tissue. Our best, educated, guess was that, having aligned samples taken from both girls with the research they had conducted, that the first twenty-four hours would be painful but no irreparable damage suffered. That occurred from about twenty-four hours through to thirty-four. Of course each girl would have a different immune system, different medical history and different defences so we couldn't say for sure, but at least what we knew gave us the belief that if we found these girls within the game time, they would suffer no permanent physical damage. I was pretty sure though that the mental damage suffered by any survivor would be somewhat longer lasting.

Without the faxes though, the bodies of the two girls would still have been where The Chemist left them now. We hadn't even been close to finding them. I was beginning to think these games were un-winnable, that it was just some sick fucker trying to get infamous quickly. I hated to admit it, but The Chemist was succeeding on that count. After Jennifer's body had been found we were keen to stop the similarities between the two leaking to the press. We made no mention of Clozapone during any questions fired at us by the media but someone had been unable to stop themselves from leaking the pertinent information. Whether this was accidental or someone purposefully providing information for their own gain was yet to be determined, but once the media found out about the similarities, hysteria had broken out. A third would not only fuel that panic but would also send the message to the public that the LAPD were powerless to stop this from happening. And that pissed me off big time.

When we weren't busy playing *The Game* we had our other PD requirements to attend to but we spent all the time we could, including most evenings and several sleepless nights trying to figure out who could be behind this horrific spate of murders. A few possibilities had come up; but one by one we had eliminated them all for various reasons.

The mechanics and structure of the games told us we were dealing with one seriously intelligent and motivated individual, but I guess you didn't need to be Sherlock fucking Holmes to work that one out.

We drove the last couple of minutes in a grim silence, each wondering what lay in store for us at this address. I was pretty sure it wouldn't be 'number three'; we were far too early into *The Game* for that. I could only take solace in the fact that at least we *had* broken part of the code and that we had therefore made more progress in this one than in the previous two. I just had a feeling that we were making exactly the amount of progress that The Chemist wanted us to make. Just as this thought sent an unnerving shiver down my spine, we pulled into Sutherland Boulevard.

12

LAST WEEK

At just before nine, the piercing sound of the alarm clock interrupted a particularly deep, and some would say – well at least he would say, deserved sleep. He had a rare day off; no meetings scheduled, no media requirements, no magazine interviews. Actually, scratch that. He did have a meeting with a couple of the guys down at the Chester Washington golf course at noon, where he hoped to avenge the narrow defeat of last month's eighteen holes and with any luck, make back the four thousand dollars that defeat had cost him. Not that he particularly needed the money, he just fucking hated losing.

Eyes still half closed, sticking the alarm clock on snooze, Conrad Conway rolled over, arm outstretched, expecting to feel his wife lying beside him, but felt nothing. Where was she? He half remembered her saying something about going out when they went to bed last night but he hadn't been paying too much attention. He suspected that it might involve shopping of some sort, something his wife had become very, very good at, using up a sizable chunk of his ample annual earnings on regular basis. As long as it wasn't even more shoes he could live with that. Nevertheless, he made a mental note to double check his next credit card statement; there would probably be several additions on there.

Deciding to forgo the snooze, he got up, and putting on his robe he headed down to the kitchen. Ah, at least she had put the coffee on before she had gone out, that was good. Pouring himself a large cup, he wandered to his front door to collect the paper. This was how a day should start; cup of coffee, a read of the sports page …. Not that he didn't love his job and all the power, money and fame that came with it but he did occasionally miss having his own time to relax. That was certainly a rare commodity nowadays!

Picking up the paper, something caught his eye that afforded a second glance. A white envelope hung through his letterbox. Knowing it was too early for his lazy postman – he very rarely received his post before eleven, Conrad idly wondered what it could be. It was marked just 'Conway', no other postal markings and no stamp

Taking a large gulp of coffee, he strolled back to the kitchen. Eyeing the back of the sports page, he was pleased to see that his good friend Manny Ramirez had hit two home runs during the LA Dodgers' decisive victory over the Arizona Diamondbacks last night, taking his season total to fourteen, and a staggering .396 average. He had missed the game last night as he'd had to attend a charity function and didn't get in until just after midnight. He'd have to give Manny a call later on and congratulate him.

Sitting down at the breakfast table which was cluttered with the usual condiments and mess, an eye still half on the sports page, he tore open the envelope and pulled out the contents.

What the fuck was this? Conrad was open mouthed as he thumbed through five photographs of him leaving his secret place in Figueroa Street with a young prostitute in clear view. There was also a letter:

'Good morning Senator, I trust you're having an enjoyable morning? Or were? As you will see from the photographs, I understand you have been keeping pretty busy in the early hours of the morning. What would your wife say? What would the papers say? .... Should we find out? I think not. Well, not yet anyway. My silence has a price. $50,000, 11pm, three days time. I will contact you with more details soon, you just get the money! Keep up the good work! The Bully.'

Conrad re-read the letter a couple of times before slamming it down on the table, almost knocking over his coffee in the process. The Bully? The fucking Bully? Who the fuck was that? Well if he wanted to play, let's play.

Never averse to operating beneath the law when needed, Conway poured himself a second cup of coffee and sat motionless in his designer kitchen, which he didn't much care for; his wife had insisted that they get one installed despite, in his opinion, there being nothing at all wrong with the one they already had. Still, it made his life more peaceful; his wife had been pre-occupied with colours, cabinets and tiles for weeks. As usual though, he had picked up the bill.

His mind was racing at a thousand miles an hour as he silently began to plan how to catch this prick, and what he would do with him once he was caught. After half an hour or so, the rest of the sports pages remaining unread, he headed back upstairs for a shower. He had the fragments of a plan now, one he was sure would work but he'd need to make a couple of calls later. Despite this, he knew that his first day off for over three weeks, and his last for another two, was already ruined. He just hoped his back nine didn't suffer as a result.

13

James Tetley knew one thing for sure; there was no way he was going to do any more time in prison again. He'd just served three years for armed robbery and what a hellacious three years they'd been. He knew how to look after himself, and had had to do so numerous times throughout his time there. His two hundred and fifty pound frame of solid muscle meant that although he was by no means the biggest or meanest cat in the yard, the majority of fellow inmates kept a suitable distance, and very rarely fucked with him.

There had been one or two notable exceptions. A couple of members of the Aryan Brotherhood hadn't taken too kindly to his refusal to join The Brand, and had spent the best part of six months taunting, beating on, and eventually, trying to shank him. He had been prepared for that though, and had formed a secret alliance with a couple of inmates who had taken care of business for him, on the understanding that when he was paroled, ten thousand dollars would be transferred to two accounts of their choosing. These guys were well connected, and well respected. Non-payment was not an option. Always one to think on his feet, Tetley had agreed to those conditions and would worry about the money at a later date. Now was that time.

Having no particular place to go, he'd made the relatively short journey from Marin County to Los Angeles and had hooked up once again with his old buddy Jimmy Burke. They had taken several scores over the years and worked well together. Well, apart from the time he had been caught, resulting in his three year stretch, obviously. Burke had been with him on that one as well but had evaded capture and Tetley was never going to give his old friend up as an accomplice and had served his time in silence to the authorities, despite the numerous attempts to prize the information out of him.

He had spent a couple of weeks now, here in LA, celebrating his newly-paroled freedom with Jimmy, as well as several buddies he hadn't seen in, well three years or so. He'd gotten word a couple of days ago, that the two inmates he'd agreed to pay for that favour were eager to see deposits made, and Tetley knew he had less than a week to make good on his word.

All of which, had led him here, not only with Jimmy Burke but also a driver, Phillip Moseley who he didn't know but who came with Jimmy's strong recommendation, and that was good enough for him. They were parked discretely outside the Pacific Union Bank, which had been open for business for around an hour. It wasn't the busiest bank in LA, but that was perfect. As long as they took thirty thousand dollars, the even split would be enough for him to pay off Billy Graziadai and Evan Seinfeld, the two inmates to whom he owed the money. He turned to Jimmy. 'We're in, we're out right? No fucking about. We grab thirty to forty grand and split. We don't have the time to get greedy, right? Three minutes max.'

'Just like old times my man, just like old times', Jimmy grinned revealing his uneven teeth, stained yellow from years of nicotine abuse. He'd loved taking scores like this with Tetley and had been genuinely gutted when Tetley had been arrested but never in doubt that his accomplice wouldn't shop him to the police.

'Hey, Moseley', Jimmy instructed, 'Keep it running'. Seizing the opportunity of a deserted sidewalk, they pulled down their balaclavas, and cradling their Mossberg 500 pump action shotguns that Jimmy had managed to acquire, debunked from their getaway car and made haste into the unsuspecting Pacific Union Bank, whose unsuspecting staff were about to have their quiet, mundane working day turned upside down.

14

Driving slowly down Sutherland Boulevard, it appeared to be like any other typical suburban residential area. Well maintained houses and gardens; just your typical house for your typical family. Toys and bikes lay on several front lawns where children had presumably being playing last night, which indicated that this was a seemingly safe neighbourhood, where parents would happily let their children play, comfortable that their surroundings offered no threat. It didn't seem quite like an environment where you would find a potential serial killer to me. A couple of sprinklers watered some of the lawns we drove past and there were a couple of neighbours painting a fence, chatting and laughing as they did so. There were hundreds of areas just like this all across the state. So what was so different about this one?

We pulled up about a hundred or so yards from number twenty-two, not wanting to alert anyone to our presence. For a couple of moments the car was silent as we both pondered what lay ahead. Then my cell rang again.

'Patton, its Captain Williams', he sounded pretty annoyed. Then again, like the rest of us, he was perturbed by the futility of our current situation. 'Well no surprises, number three makes it official. Quantico has dispatched an agent to assist us in our investigation'. He was right, this came as no surprise to me; the FBI were always going to have made their presence felt if this went the way it had gone. 'They're sending an Agent Baler', he continued. 'When he gets here, I'll have him hook up with you in the field. By all accounts this guy is pretty shit hot, maybe he could help us figure this out'. That the FBI deemed it necessary to send us someone didn't dent my professional pride. Any help, any different angle we could get on this, would be welcomed. All that mattered was stopping The Chemist, and quickly. It didn't matter how.

'I hear you Captain', I replied. 'We've just pulled into Sutherland now, no sign of anything out of the ordinary as yet'.

'Be careful boys', Williams for a moment sounded almost fatherly. That was a new one. 'Proceed with extreme caution', he paused momentarily, checking something. 'Backup is one minute out, three cars'.

'Make sure their sirens are off', I cautioned. 'If we weren't meant to break the code this early, I don't want anyone announcing our arrival to the whole neighbourhood. Tell them we're going in with a standard four by two formation'

'Understood Patton,' Williams acknowledged. 'Stay in touch'.

Charlie was nodding, signifying I didn't need to repeat any of the conversation I just had to keep him up to speed. 'Good call with the sirens man', he growled, 'this bastard could be going down right here and now', he didn't sound convinced. 'I do have one question though. If we're not supposed to be here now, then all well and good; we'll surprise the fuck out of whoever is in there'. He paused, almost as if he didn't want to ask. 'But what if we *are* supposed to be here now? What if we're exactly where this freak wants us?'

I stayed silent. That was a question for which I had no answer.

15

LAST WEEK

Paul Britland-Jones watched undetected as Conrad Conway loaded his expensive golf clubs into the boot of his Aston Martin DB9 coupe, a car which cost more that he had made in the last tax year. Conway, face like thunder, looked annoyed and somewhat distant. He took that as a good sign, the Senator must have received his special delivery this morning. He was far enough away from Conway's house that he would not be noticed, but close enough to see that from the Senator's reaction, his letter had been read.

As far as the LA Times was concerned, he was tracking down a lead for his next story and not checking on the progress of his first really high profile blackmail attempt.

He wondered for a minute whether he should break the story about the Senator's extra-curricular activities instead of blackmailing him. He wouldn't get fifty grand out of it but he was sure he would be pretty well compensated for it as it would be a major story for the gossip loving citizens of Los Angeles to get their teeth into. The city often times thrived on scandal. But on reflection he really did need that money. Sporting a wicked grin, he contemplated breaking the story after he had received his fifty grand anyway. That would top it up to nearer seventy, and would definitely be enough to get him out of the shit. Yes, he might just do that.

He planned to have the Senator drop off the money on Pier D at Long Beach, just under the Gerald Desmond Bridge then have one of his contacts collect the money on his behalf for a small surcharge. He had made many contacts over the years who would come to him with little bits of information, knowing he often paid a good price. These were usually unsavoury characters; often drink dependant, often drug dependant and often surviving by lurching from one minor criminal activity to the next. Although he looked upon many of these individuals with contempt, recently it had been striking him just how similar he was becoming to them.

He would change that though, as soon as he had paid off Bobby Hambel with the fifty grand he owed him, he'd be in the clear. He thought after that, maybe checking in with the AA would be an idea, and he was pretty sure that weaning himself of the Prozac would be easy enough. He had dabbled sporadically with class A varieties, a little heroin here and there, a little cocaine on occasion, but that was strictly recreational, and he certainly didn't feel the urge to dabble every day, like he currently did with the Prozac. Nevertheless, over the last couple of years, he'd spent an extraordinary amount on fast living and it had begun to take its toll.

He'd had a wake up call a couple of months ago when he came to in his rented Porsche 911 having wrapped it around a lamppost at three a.m. one morning, hooker passed out in the passenger seat, and six grams of crack cocaine sprinkled on the dashboard. Catching a lucky break in that there seemed to be no-one around, and extremely keen to avoid the minimum five year sentence he'd receive should he have be arrested, he'd paid the hooker off with what little cash he'd had on him and managed to stagger home, grab a shower and three hours sleep. Reporting the car as stolen at nine a.m. that morning, despite not having an alibi, there was nothing to tie him to the scene of the totalled Porsche. Although he'd presumably crashed his car, he'd sustained no visible injuries, although his ribs hurt like hell, and the hooker was hardly likely to be a forthcoming witness, for obvious reasons. He thought the police had their suspicions but it was a case of what they could prove, not what they thought they knew. Of course his fingerprints, DNA and everything else had been all over the car, it was his car so they were bound to be. He was just fortunate that a couple of days ago, when meeting a couple of his petty criminal contacts down on San Pedro Bay, one of them, Carlos Trujillo had begged to sit in the drivers seat to see what it was like, much to Britland-Jones' amusement. Seeing no harm in it, and because Trujillo had come up with the required goods that evening, he'd agreed, making sure he took the keys out of the ignition, just in case. It was as close as that poor bastard was ever going to get to a Porsche, he knew that much. And thank the Lord he'd agreed; as a result of that, there was DNA the police could not match on the driver's seat and steering wheel, and that was enough to exonerate him from any wrong-doing in the eyes of the law. Somehow, throughout his years of criminality, Trujillo had evaded the LAPD and their penitentiary system, hence the unidentified DNA.

Once that had been put to bed, he remembered staring into a mirror after getting out of the shower; wiping the steamed up mirror down with a towel, and thinking that he looked a lot older than his thirty-eight years. He looked nearer forty-five, maybe forty-six. That, combined with his distinctly too-close-for-comfort brush with the law convinced him that a change was in order. There was just a matter of paying off Bobby Hambel first, to ensure he kept his kneecaps attached to his legs.

Watching as Conway pulled out of his driveway, down the road and out of sight, he reached into his pocket and pulled out a second envelope, one that contained the instructions for the money drop in three days time.

Less than a minute later he was heading back to his office at the LA Times. He supposed he better at least *try* and get a little work done today.

16

To say that things were not going according to plan would be the understatement of the year, and James Tetley was beginning to worry.

It had started off well enough, but around the one minute mark it became clear that Jimmy was here for more money than they had agreed in the car. They had burst through the doors of the Pacific with Jimmy firing off a round into the ceiling to show they meant business.

'Nobody fucking move', he commanded, 'We will kill you all if we have to'. Tetley knew this was an empty threat of course. Over the many jobs they had pulled together over the years they had beaten people, sure, sometimes maybe even a little excessively at times when they felt a point had to be made, or when you got some prick with ideas above his station looking like he might turn into John Rambo at any moment unless he was taken out swiftly, but they had always stopped short of actually shooting anybody. And Tetley didn't particularly want to start today.

Taking his position by the door, as he always did, he let Jimmy control the cash collection. Looking at his watch, they were twenty seconds in.

For Jeannie Sharples, a slightly overweight clerk in her

late forties, whose ambition was never going to stretch beyond her current position and who had been complaining as recently as yesterday afternoon to her fellow window clerks that she was tired of the doing the same thing day in, day out, her reaction of using her right foot to trigger the silent alarm as she raised her hands on the command of this tall thug with a nasty looking gun to hand, was automatic. She hadn't even realised she had done it, until she was drawing her foot away from the trigger. Eventually realising what she had done, she felt a hot flush come over her face, and she just hoped the masked gunman put this down to the shock of the hold-up rather than any incriminating action on her part.

'Start bagging it up, bitch', Jimmy really sounded the part. 'And fucking hurry up about it too. All of it, come on!'

As the seconds ticked away, it soon dawned on Tetley that Jimmy was not sticking to the terms agreed a couple of minutes before, in the car.

'Hey man, forty thousand tops, that's all we need', Tetley hoped he sounded calmer than he actually felt. Burke half turned towards him, still watching Jeannie and two other clerks fumbling behind the glass counter, bagging up what they could, although they were shaking so much it was a wonder they could bag up anything at all.

'That's not gonna do it man', Burke shouted, 'I need at least eighty. We don't get eighty I'm a dead man'. Tetley didn't have time here and now to get into they 'whys' of Jimmy's situation, all he could do was mouth 'Fuck' under his breath and continue to man the doors. For a split second, he wondered if he should bail, but the thought of Graziadai and Seinfeld not receiving their money kept him rooted to the spot.

None of the six or seven customers in the bank were going to give them any trouble and the one security guard in the place had voluntarily surrendered his piece the moment they had stormed in. Tetley didn't blame him for that, they guy must have been in his late fifty's and was never going to be any sort of match for himself and Jimmy. Hardly worth risking losing your pension over, never mind your life.

Three and a half minutes and counting. Tetley was beginning to get nervous. 'Hey come on, we've got enough, we gotta get out of here', he was almost pleading. He was sure he'd just heard a siren. Burke, however, remained steadfast. 'One more minute, man, just one more minute'.

Shaking his head, Tetley glanced outside just in time to see two police cars screech round the corner. The sight of their getaway car hastily speeding off rendered him momentarily speechless. He watched helplessly as one of the cars sped past the bank after Moseley. Well that was something at least, if they were going down for this then he hoped they would at least also catch that sinking-ship deserting motherfucker.

Before he could get his words out to warn Jimmy, the cops were seemingly out of the second car and swarming towards him at the door. Tetley raised his Mossberg to his shoulder to take aim, but it was too late. The earth-shattering sound of splintering glass was followed by a sharp, piercing pain, as a bullet from one of the ascending officers lodged itself in Tetley's upper thigh. The force of the bullet cascaded him backwards a good four or five feet, and dropping his shotgun, Tetley crumpled in a heap grimacing in agony.

If the sound of the sirens hadn't alerted Jimmy Burke to their impending problem, the sound of bullets, shattered glass and his friend's agonising cries certainly did. Spinning round, eyes raging, staring in disbelief as three armed officers filed in, shouting various instructions at him, he did the only thing that made any sense to him at the time.

He opened fire.

Considering he'd had no formal training with weapons, and that the only target practice he'd ever really had was on bottles and the like as a teenager, he did remarkably well. His first shot caught Officer Reed squarely in the chest. Although Reed was wearing the state issued bullet proof vest, the force of the blast was enough to wind him, taking him momentarily out of action. Officer Hart took Burke's second shot straight through the neck, piercing the trachea and shattering the top of the spinal chord on exit, killing him instantly. As Burke was about to get a third shot off two bullets from Officer Coen hit him in the shoulder and stomach. Coen's third and fourth were both head shots, and Jimmy Burke was dead before he'd even begun falling to the floor.

James Tetley watched as one of his best friends waged his one-man war against his LAPD counterparts, then passed out from the pain of his leg wound just as what was left of Jimmy Burke's body crashed to the ground.

17

Even though we were anxious to get in there, Charlie and I duly waited for the back up to arrive, which it did with a commendable amount of silence, as instructed. Unless, as a resident of the Boulevard, you were standing at one of your front windows looking out directly onto the road or happened to be at the front of your house doing one-or two odd jobs like a couple of the residents were, you would never have known about the significantly increased police presence.

Signalling that we would take the front, I silently directed three teams of two officers round the sides and back of the detached number twenty-two. Once at the front door, we gave it about thirty seconds for the rest of the team to get in position. I nodded to Charlie, who took the door off its hinges with one powerful kick.

Seconds later, I heard a crash, which signified that my team was also coming in from the rear. So far, so good. No surprises. Nothing out of the ordinary. A quick sweep of the ground floor rooms uncovered nothing further. It just appeared to be your typical suburban house. The kitchen was clean, but with several dirty plates and bowls piled high in the sink and the leftovers from a meal lay on the breakfast table. The living room looked comfortable and well used; cushions and magazines strewn across the sofa, a dining room that looked more for show than for any practical purpose. *But we were here for a reason, weren't we?* Whilst Charlie and I had taken the downstairs, two of the backup team had taken upstairs.

'Hey Patton', I heard one of them shout, the sense of urgency in his voice undeniable. 'Get up here! Master bedroom'

Taking the stairs three at a time, my mind was racing. Was this what we were here for? I'm not quite sure *what* I was expecting but I was surprised, even bewildered at what we found.

Looking very tired and extremely frightened was a woman, sitting up in bed, hugging her knees tight to her chest and pulling the duvet cover right up to her chin. The room was spacious and daylight penetrated the room from a slit in the drawn curtains.

Whilst the rest of the backup re-scouted the house under Charlie's supervision, it took me around five minutes of questioning to ascertain some basic facts. Once over the initial shock of having four strangers burst into her bedroom, she was extremely forthcoming and a couple of quick checks via the PD confirmed her story.

Her name was Laura Edwards and she worked as a full time nurse at one of LA's busiest hospitals, The Cedars Inter-Community Hospital in Inglewood. She was on overnighters this week, meaning that she started work at ten at night and worked through to eight in the morning after shift handover at half past seven. Looking around the room, I could see her nurses uniform slung over the back of a chair, and her bloodshot eyes spoke volumes; turned out she had been in bed for just over half an hour before we burst in.

'Do you have *any* idea why your address would be in a code, given to us?' I asked. I had been vague with the details, certainly no mention of The Chemist, or the fact that we were chasing a potential serial killer.

'I don't, I really don't', she seemed genuine to me. 'I'm sorry I can't be of more help to you Detective Patton'.

Charlie returned and a quick shake of his head confirmed that there was nothing relevant after a preliminary search. I declined to tell Laura at this stage that several officers would remain here all day anyway, and that she was unlikely to be going back to sleep.

I sighed, looking around the room, more out of exasperation and frustration than anything else. I had no clue how to proceed from here, but there must be a reason we were here, that's assuming Ferguson was right about the code. What was it we were missing?

Out of the corner of the eye, something did catch my attention, and on first glance I dismissed it but then a thought crossed my mind. I said nothing but calmly traversed the room to a dressing table, processing my initial thought. Oh God, if I was right this was well and truly fucked up.

Taking several moments to clarify my train of thought, and play out the consequences of my next move in my head, I knew I had no option but to ask. The more I thought about it, the more I thought I was right.

'Laura', my voice was quiet and unassuming, 'who is that in the photo with you?' I gestured to a glossy 4x6, set in a tasteful black frame. The only picture that adorned the dressing table, in fact. I asked the question, but deep down I already knew part of the answer.

'Oh that?' Laura smiled, 'Me and my daughter Stella', she was obviously a very proud parent. 'It was taken last year on holiday on her eighteenth birthday. It's lovely don't you think?'

A quick glance at Charlie confirmed that I didn't need to spell out what I was thinking for him.

'And where is Stella now, Laura?' I hated to ask. If I was right her whole world would come crashing down in a few minutes.

'Oh, she'll be in college by now. She's a good girl, really dedicated. She never misses a day. She's had excellent grades all year too'.

'Does she go to a local college?' I continued to gently probe for information, wanting to prolong what I suspected was the inevitable for just a few seconds more.

'Yes, she goes to the Los Angeles Community College', she was still smiling. 'It's a really great program they have there, you know'.

Charlie slipped out of the room, and I knew that he going to verify whether Stella was actually in college or not. It almost felt like we were going through the motions though. I already had a gut feeling that we had just identified the girl we were currently trying to save from The Chemist, right when we were supposed to.

I too excused myself from the bedroom, I had to know if I was right on this call, and if I was, I was still unsure exactly how to proceed.

Charlie was on his cell, and from the roll of his eyes, I could tell he was on hold. 'Should know in a couple minutes, man. I've had a black and white in the neighbourhood pull a code 10-20'.

The couple of minutes of dead-time, whilst we verified whether or not Stella Edwards was at her college, gave me the opportunity to play out the positives and negatives of what I should tell her mother.

Sensing I was in two minds, Charlie helped me sway the right way, as he often did. 'Hey man, if it was me, I'd want to know'.

'Yeah I know', I nodded. 'How do you...'

Charlie raised a finger, cutting me off. He was no longer

on hold.

'You sure?' his expression remained grim, 'I mean, you have checked and double checked, right?'

'She's not there', he said, shaking his head, 'and hasn't been there all morning. She never made the roll call'.

'Goddamn it!' I couldn't help myself, despite fully expecting that confirmation.

'What we gonna do man?'

I just shrugged my shoulders. 'We're going to tell Laura that we think her daughter has been kidnapped by The Chemist, and that she has less than twenty hours to live'. I realised that that approach might have seemed clinical and heartless, but I reckoned that was the best way to get Laura Edwards to focus and help us with her part of The Game. I hoped to God she came through, for us and for Stella.

18

LAST WEEK

Without exception, every member of the Animi left the Aon centre with a decidedly more uneasy feeling in the pits of their stomachs than when they had arrived, going onto their next appointments with a newly acquired sense of consternation.

As was the case when these meetings came to a head, they all left at different times and from different, pre-arranged, exits in order to remain anonymous and so that no ties between them were ever established.

Lee Brindle left first, as he always did; the demands of his particular job, and the fact that he was not based in Los Angeles, meant that not only were the meetings mainly prioritised around his usually nightmarish schedule, but that his time either side of them was particularly precious.

Conway was next, closely followed by Cyprian Hague, who was rushing to a press conference that he had already delayed once, and couldn't afford to again; something about promising extra funding for several schools and hospitals across LA. Well, anything to get him that record-breaking extra term. If he made it to his next term, that was. After today's meeting he was by no means certain that he would.

Farrington and Brittles left within five minutes of each

other, albeit from opposite sides of the building, and from different floors.

If anyone had been watching any of the members leave, they would have noticed a distinct increase in the number of times they looked over their shoulders, and a slight increase in pace.

As Brittles left the room, Burr stood up and walked to one of several half empty decanters on a table and idly poured two scotches. 'Well Paul, do you think they bought it?'

Paul McCrane took a moment to reflect on the events and conversations of the last couple of hours and brought his hand up to his goatee, stroking it thoughtfully as he spoke. 'I'm pretty sure they did', he mused, taking a large swig out of the glass in front of him. 'I was pretty convincing, well we both were'.

'The email was a particularly nice touch, I thought', Burr flattered.

'Ah yes', McCrane agreed, 'Well if there is one thing I can do, it's think on my feet when I have to'. He picked up the decanter for a refill.

'We have made the right decision Paul, I'm sure of that'. McCrane was sure as well, or at least he thought he was. Still, it was affirming to hear that from another.

'Yes, I agree with you there. Conway's actions have been inexcusable and you were right with your initial feelings. His actions cannot be condoned', McCrane was clarifying what they were doing almost as much for himself as for Burr. Even though this decision had been made for some time, it was still a massive decision on their part. 'This way, when Conway meets his untimely death, no-one here will ask questions; they will just assume that Caldwell got him first. They will be more terrified, if anything, and we can work that to our advantage. We can be their saviours. Something for which they will forever be in our debt.

'Also, what is so perfect, is that we can make it look as though it *was* The Chemist,' Burr took the reigns. 'If we tie him up and inject him with Clozapone the media will obviously pick up on the similarities and assume that The Chemist is making some kind of high-profile *'No-one is safe'* statement. Our hands are clean'.

What McCrane and Burr had told the rest of the Animi was true, up to a point. They *had* released Caldwell from San Quentin and then Caldwell *had* killed the guards and escaped.

The photograph taken on the kitchen wall of the safe house however, with the words written in blood? An easy fabrication for a seasoned pro like McCrane. The email from Vancouver? Simply didn't exist, although if he really wanted one, he could have had one within the hour, backdated for appearance purposes.

What he hadn't told the rest of the Animi, even his close friend Jameson Burr, was that he had received a phone call from Caldwell the day after the LAPD had discovered the body of the first girl, Keeley Porter. It was a phone call that he hadn't been expecting but had nevertheless remained calm and composed during the thirty second or so interaction. Caldwell had actually thanked him; the words 'If not for you, the girl would still be alive' had actually chilled McCrane to the bone. Even his moral code, tenuous at best, hadn't been impervious to that jibe by Caldwell. It was only once he'd read and watched the news reports that evening that he had realised that the individual that he had released from San Quentin was in fact the latest killer to be terrorising Los Angeles. It was a rare feeling of regret that he'd felt once again, when the body of Jennifer Hughes had been found stuffed callously into a rusty, decomposing water tank in an abandoned warehouse. Whilst part of him wanted Caldwell to remain at large, for so long as

Caldwell evaded the authorities there was no chance of the police linking The Chemist to the Animi, as the body count continued to rise he actually felt an increasing sense of responsibility for what was happening. He knew if he revealed Caldwell's actual contact to the rest of the Animi he risked showing his remorse and moreover the remorse could be interpreted as a weakness, which would never do. Nevertheless, whilst The Chemist's vendetta against the Animi was complete fiction, a cover story for something he and Burr were about to do, he remained uneasy at Caldwell's freedom.

'Our hands are clean', McCrane repeated, his face displaying none of his misgivings to his associate. 'That, my friend, has got to be one of the sweetest sayings in the English Language'.

Burr took a sip of scotch and nodded appreciatively. 'I want to thank you Paul for your help in this matter. I don't know what I'd have done without your help'.

'It's what old friends do for each other', McCrane acknowledged, although in truth, his help was on a far greater scale than one might expect, even from a lifelong friend.

Three weeks ago, Burr had turned up on his doorstep around eleven o' clock one evening completely unannounced, enraged and from the overpowering smell of his breath, slightly drunk. McCrane had ushered him inside, alert to the fact that this contravened the usual Animi procedure of communication and was strictly forbidden. Even for lifelong friends such as Jameson and himself. Had it been anyone else, he would not have even answered his door.

Once inside, he tried to placate his friend's fraught demeanour. 'Jameson', he asked. 'What's happened? What's wrong?'

It took a few minutes to get any kind of answer out of him, Burr preferring to pour himself another drink rather than respond to the question. 'Fucking bitch', he finally managed. 'I'm going to kill the bastard, that's what I'm going to do'.

'What do you mean?' McCrane coaxed, although he suspected that even those few words Burr had spoken had given him the general answer.

'She's having an affair, that's what I mean', Burr spat. 'She left her cell at home this morning when she went to work. I'd had my suspicions for a couple of weeks so I checked her voicemail'.

'And I take it you found something?'

'There was a message on there from two days ago', Burr looked genuinely hurt and McCrane looked on sympathetically. 'Let me just say it confirmed my suspicions … graphically'.

'And there's no way you could be mistaken? Taken it out of context perhaps?' McCrane asked. Burr looked up, fighting back tears.

'If you had heard it …' He tailed off, going scarlet with rage as he recalled the message he had heard himself that afternoon. After a minute, he regained some of his composure. 'There's more', he told McCrane. 'The message I heard this afternoon was from Conrad Conway'.

McCrane sat down, digesting what he'd just been told. It was no secret amongst the Animi that Conway wasn't exactly faithful to his wife, but to sleep with another member's wife? That had crossed a line, absolutely no doubt about it. It was something that could not be tolerated under any circumstances. 'What do you want me to do?' he asked his friend. Burr drained his glass, considering his response.

'I want you to help me kill him', he answered.

Having known Jameson Burr for more than three decades, that was the answer that McCrane had been expecting. His friend was not one to let anyone who crossed him, either in business or pleasure, go unpunished. Conway had crossed Burr in the worst possible way. 'I'm sure we can come up with something', he responded, his mind already weighing up one or two options. 'Give me a couple of days to think about it, let me see what I can work out'.

19

Breaking the news to Stella's mother was no easier than I had expected. I'd done it myself, my tone as compassionate as I could be, but my words must have seemed cold and stark. I was sure we weren't here just to learn Stella's identity. There must be something else; the next step, the next part of the game. As our initial search had uncovered nothing but the photograph, I suspected that the mother held the key. And the sooner she realised that, the more chance her daughter had of coming out of this alive.

I did all I could to assure Laura Edwards that there was every reason to believe we could get her daughter back safely. She clung to the slim possibility that we were mistaken. It was true that at the moment we had no hard fact, merely speculation, but the code had brought us here, her daughter fitted the profile and was presently unaccounted for. What were the chances we were wrong?

I completely understood her need to cling to that, and if that's what got her through this, if that's what made her more receptive to our questioning, so be it.

We relocated to the living room, having given Laura just enough time to pull on a robe. Our questions over the next half an hour or so were nurturing, coaxing as much information as we could out of Laura. The PD had an on-call psychologist who had arrived on-scene after around twenty minutes, and was in danger of undoing all our groundwork by taking a completely different tack. We didn't have the time to backtrack.

From what we could gather, Stella just seemed like your typical average girl. Just like the other two. No reason on earth why they should be singled out for special treatment by The Chemist. Her mother and father had separated a couple of years ago, but Stella had not let this detract from maintaining an excellent academic record that didn't waiver once during that difficult time. She was a popular girl, lots of friends and a good social life, yet her mother said she had never overstepped the mark in that respect. She had been a good girl.

We quickly built up a picture of a happy girl with her whole life ahead of her. This would be yet another tragic loss if we didn't win the game and get her back.

Just as the psychologist was about to backtrack yet again, with a seemingly irrelevant line of questioning, Charlie asked the question that perhaps, in retrospect, I should have asked at the beginning.

'Laura?' he asked, remembering the engraving on the key we'd been given by The Chemist. 'Do the numbers three-sixteen mean anything to you?'

Her brow furrowed as she tried to answer his question. 'No, no I don't think so', she was searching through the possibilities in her mind. Then, just maybe, a glimmer of hope. 'Oh wait, I think, yes I'm sure, well her email address'.

'What about it?' Charlie asked.

'I'm pretty sure three-sixteen is part of it', she realised. 'In fact, I'm certain'.

There it was – the next piece of the puzzle, the next part of the game. 'Laura,' I asked, 'where is Stella's computer?'

20

Upon relaying this discovery to Captain Williams, he decided to send Dave Ferguson directly down to the Edwards house. This was a good call; we didn't want to overlook anything. They hadn't had any more success with the code, and they had Bradshaw there now anyway, and he seemed to be the code expert. 'If there's anything on that computer, I'll find it', he assured us. Still, he had only just left the PD, and we were eager to uncover what we could.

'Leave this to me, man', Charlie advised, 'I might not know how to break a code, but I can boot the fucking thing up and we can look at her email, no problem'.

I was all for that. 'Let's just hope she doesn't have a password'.

Three minutes later, it was moment of truth time. We held our breath as Stella's laptop went through the final stages of booting up, both of us let out an audible sigh of relief as it went through to Windows with no password prompt. One break there, at least. A couple of clicks later and we had signed on to her email.

'Well, her mother was right Patton', Charlie confirmed. 'There it is man, right there, look, s-edwards316@hotmail.com, that's gotta be it.'

'Well there must be something', I was searching the screen. 'Hell, try her inbox'.

Charlie made the necessary clicks and took us her inbox. There was just one email in there. The header read 'Good morning Detectives'.

'Fuck me ...' Charlie couldn't hide his surprise. I had to agree, although I was aware that this brought us a step further into the game, it also established that we were right about Stella. Her mother would have to know. I might leave that one to the psychologist, after all.

'Well, do we open it or not?' I asked. I really wanted to know what that e-mail said.

'I don't know, man', Charlie was doubtful. 'How long before Fergs gets here?'

'About fifteen minutes', I reckoned.

'Thing is, man, the thing might be booby trapped'. Seeing my blank face, he needed to clarify. 'It might have a virus that wipes the email off the computer as soon as you read it. Permanently. It might have information we need to read more than once. If we open it, we might not get it back'.

'Game over', I nodded. It was agreed that we wait for Ferguson. Despite time being of the essence, I knew Charlie was right. We couldn't afford to potentially destroy a vital piece of evidence. Stella couldn't afford us to either.

By the time Ferguson got there, we'd already relayed the information to him and he had concurred. After assessing the laptop for several seconds, he started plugging in wires, routers and boxes before he'd even said hello. It seemed he was just as keen to play a part in this.

'You wanna tell us what you're doing there, techno-boy?' Charlie had a way of cutting straight to the point, 'and in language we can actually understand, man'.

'If the email has a virus linked to it, then this box right here, will copy the email in real-time, as we open it. If it suddenly disappears, then we have a copy'.

'Won't that copy have the virus too though', maybe Charlie knew more about computers than he let on. Ferguson almost looked like he was happy he'd asked the question.

'No no', he looked assured. 'This box right here, one of my 'not quite off-the-shelf' magic boxes, will filter out and kill off any virus'. Ferguson looked particularly proud. 'So then we have a clean copy of the email that we can read, or re-open as many times as we need to'. Well, at least we understood what he was talking about, which was a first.

'How long will it take you to set up?' Charlie wanted to know. We both did.

'Done'. Well I hadn't expected him to be that quick setting up. I was suitably impressed. 'Go ahead and open it', he gestured to the laptop.

The three of us gathered round the computer, and you could have heard a pin drop in the room. The sense of anticipation was palpable, even from Fergs. I clicked on the e-mail, steeling myself for what it might contain.

21

The Chemist had left Katie Patton for now to go about her business in maybe the last day of her perfect little world. She was where the game would really begin. She was the main event.

It didn't really matter where the next part of the game was set, as long as it was within half an hour or so of Sutherland Boulevard. With this in mind, The Chemist chose to drive through Angelino Heights and up to Silver Lake and after twenty minutes pulled up alongside a diner on Sunset Junction. This was one of the previously scouted locations that could be used once, anytime The Chemist wished. Yes, Sunset Junction would be perfect.

If Patton and Holland were still on schedule, they should have figured out the identity of Stella Edwards and hopefully, any time soon, they would open their email.

Pulling a pager out of the glove compartment, The Chemist visually confirmed that no email had been read. A page would be sent automatically by the computer when the email had been opened. A thin smile broke across The Chemist's face, remembering the little surprise that had been left at that particular address. The LAPD wouldn't see that one coming that was for sure. And for certain, it would throw them into chaos and turmoil. It would make no sense to them, but then again, the rules weren't theirs to make, were they?

Knowing that even when the email had been opened, there would be around an hour or so before Patton and Holland made it to Sunset Junction, The Chemist relaxed a little. Maybe a coffee would help? After all, half a cup of latte had been cast aside in a hurry when the Kavannagh had been evacuated earlier this morning.

Deciding that nothing could be done to advance the game any further, The Chemist parked brazenly in front of the diner. Well why not? No-one had any clue where to look for The Chemist just yet and it was doubtful if anyone ever would.

Once inside, a large white coffee purchased and window seat occupied, The Chemist basked in the glow of the mid-morning Californian sunshine. Suddenly, with the customary lack of warning, the familiar feeling of a sharp pain of a migraine invaded the serenity. It was like someone was prodding with a hot needle. The Chemist, through closed eyes and gritted teeth, didn't wish to draw any unnecessary attention and fought through the pain, suffering in silence.

These migraines came and went fairly quickly; sometimes thirty seconds or so, sometimes a couple of minutes, but very rarely any longer than that. During this time, The Chemist often had flashbacks to various points of the past. The Chemist had at first tried to control the flashbacks, but soon found that this was impossible. The only solace was that they didn't last very long.

As The Chemist had been active in Los Angeles for over fifteen years there were many memories for the subconscious to unearth, many of them horrific. As well as Los Angeles, The Chemist had occasionally strayed into

Sacramento and San Bernardino County, just for a change, but Los Angeles was home.

The Chemist was sure that if any criminal profiler ever had the misfortune to conduct an analysis, and if The Chemist truthfully admitted to the many, many atrocities committed over the last decade and a half, then every single one of them would point to the same thing; the one thing that had been a catalyst to the acceleration from teenager to monster.

And it was that one thing that The Chemist was reliving during this particularly piercing migraine.

Caldwell had returned from school one afternoon, with younger brother Andrew, to find their mother cowering in the kitchen, sobbing, holding the side of her face, which had turned black and blue.

In retrospect, it probably wasn't unusual for their alcoholic, abusive father to beat on their mother. He handed out beatings often enough but never to Andrew. At least that had been something to be thankful for. Being the eldest, Caldwell's cards had always been marked from the start. Andrew, two years behind, had been lucky.

Caldwell had fought the temptation then to end the abuse once and for all, but cowardice had prevailed and the beatings had continued for another few months.

Finally summoning up the courage, Caldwell had waited in the shadows of the dark landing of the house one Friday night, knowing that Dad would return in the early hours of the morning and slowly stagger up the stairs before finally crashing into bed in a drunken stupor.

Right on time, at one o' clock, he had returned, and sure enough, muttering obscenities under his breath, slowly began the ascent. There was a definite feeling of adrenaline pumping around the veins, as the grip around the baseball bat, ironically an eleventh birthday present from Dad, tightened.

Even though for last few hours, Caldwell had thought about nothing else, doubt somehow managed to creep in and Dad staggered past. Just as he was about to turn the bedroom handle, Caldwell slowly rose from the darkness and landed an almighty blow to the top of Dad's head. Strong blow though it was, it didn't knock him out. He turned around obviously shocked and in a mood to kill. His eyes were enraged and had widened when he saw who had struck baseball bat over his skull and grabbed his assailant by the throat.

A brief struggle ensued, and hearing the commotion, Mother opened the door and was horrified to see what was unfolding. She had rushed to them, trying in vain to break them apart, and in so doing, caught a flailing arm from one of them squarely under her chin, the force of which propelled her sideways and over the banister rail. Both of them had momentarily put aside their altercation, looking on helplessly as she had fallen fifteen feet to her death; her neck snapping back immediately on impact, her body crumpled, motionless, in a lifeless heap at the bottom of the stairs.

Dad had turned back, open mouthed, but with a look on his face that said 'What on earth have you done?' just in time for the baseball bat to land surreptitiously across the bridge of his nose. Reeling from the impact, it had taken surprisingly little effort to push him in the same direction as Mother.

Even at that relatively young age, instinct had taken over, and the individual who would later become known as The Chemist had simply packed up a few things and left. Before doing so, Caldwell had opened another bedroom door, where Andrew was sleeping peacefully. He had remained oblivious to the events that had unfolded on the landing. Scrawling the word 'Sorry', on a scrap of paper, Caldwell placed it next to Andrew and kissed him goodbye. As what had just occurred fully sank in, tears began rolling down Caldwell's cheek; not for the loss of father, abusive bastard; not for the loss of mother, she must have known about the beatings all along. But for the loss of Andrew.

22

As soon as we opened the email, the screen went black. After a pause of around twenty seconds, during which time all of us were standing around the laptop transfixed to the screen, the Schoolhouse Rocks 'Three Is A Magic Number' faded in. The Chemist must have been laughing at us. Stella was number three wasn't she?

The cartoon video I remember seeing as a child began to play, in sync with the music. I glanced at Charlie who looked as puzzled as me. Was this all it was?

The video and song played out, and I was pretty sure there was going to be more. The Chemist would no doubt have enjoyed watching us stand around helplessly as the little joke played to its conclusion.

The screen went black again and the words 'Catch me if you can' scrolled down from the top. The Chemist was certainly pushing all the right buttons; we were growing more and more agitated.

'This fucker knows how good they are, man', Charlie observed. 'Here we are again, jumping through hoops just because somebody says 'jump'. Give me five minutes alone with this prick'. It was five minutes I knew we'd all like.

All of a sudden, Dave Ferguson, who had up to that

point been watching the unfolding events in silence, made a loud exclamation, 'What the hell?'

'What's up Fergs?' I questioned, 'What is it?'

'That light right there', he pointed to one of the several boxes he had plugged in. The LED was bright red.

'What about it, man?' Charlie continued for me.

'It's just come on, that's what about it'.

'And what does that mean?' we both wanted to know.

'It means that a signal has been sent to a remote device, could be a phone, could be a pager, a signal to say that the email has been opened', Fergs explained it as best he could, in lay-mans terms.

'So someone knows we have just opened and read the email?' Charlie clarified.

'Exactly', Fergs confirmed.

Well it made sense that The Chemist had to somehow track the game. That however, was ingenious. I was about to run a couple of ideas past Charlie when Fergs piped up again. 'Holy shit!' he muttered. I followed the trail of his pointing finger, back to the box. Another red LED had come on.

'What? What does that mean?' I demanded.

'It means that the computer has just received a return signal from the remote device. That's not good'.

Before I could ask what 'not good' meant, a deafening explosion came from downstairs. The force of the blast broke every window in the room and sent the three of us cascading into walls, furniture and each other. Shaking off the blast, we sat speechless and stunned. The three of us were unscathed but we obviously hadn't been in the direct line of the blast.

I reconciled my senses to where I thought the blast had come from, and even though my sense of direction was somewhat muted, I was pretty sure it had come from the living room. That's where we had been questioning Laura Edwards.

I didn't need to ask Fergs what 'not good' meant anymore.

23

As the pain of the migraine subsided, The Chemist's eyes opened just as a feeling of being watched was becoming apparent. The waitress who had served the coffee was hovering expectantly.

'Are you, are you ok?' she asked. 'You looked like you were in pain for a while there'. The Chemist sensed she was asking merely out of kindness, and was no threat. She was probably hoping for a bigger tip. If only she knew who she was speaking to! Nevertheless, it wouldn't do to draw any further attention by being impolite. 'I'm fine, thank you', The Chemist managed to look grateful for the waitresses concern. The waitress hovered for a moment, maybe hoping to strike up a conversation. That was a definite no-no. Mercifully, at that moment, the pager sounded and The Chemist turned back to the waitress. 'Migraine that's all. I'm sorry', The Chemist almost sounded apologetic. 'I have to get this'.

'Oh, that's ok honey,' the waitress replied, the groundwork for a bigger tip completed. 'You have a nice day now, y'hear?' The Chemist just nodded and turned to the pager. Ah, there it was. The pain having fully subsided now, The Chemist was jubilant. Patton and Holland would just have finished looking at the email. Quickly pressing six buttons, sending a return signal, The Chemist folded the pager away, back into the coat pocket, and downed the remainder of the coffee. There was no rush. There was still plenty of time. As usual, the LAPD were a couple of steps behind.

Leaving the correct money for the coffee, no more, no less, on the table next to the empty cup, The Chemist casually walked out of the diner. Scuttling across to the table, the waitress was dismayed to see that there was no tip. How rude. After she had been so nice and concerned and all. Shaking her head she picked up the cup and saucer and slammed them onto the counter, angrily putting the money into the till. She was unaware that The Chemist had just left her the biggest tip possible. She was still alive.

24

For a moment we just looked at each other as the sense of what might just have occurred gradually sunk in. Fergs looked completely shell-shocked; field work was not his speciality.

'Stay here Fergs', I commanded. 'Get what you can off that computer. Can you trace where the signal came from?' Getting no answer, I had to repeat myself. 'Fergs, can you trace that goddamn signal?'

'Yeah, I think so,' he finally managed, still sounding stunned.

'Then get on with it. We don't have much time'.

As soon as we left the bedroom, it became apparent that the house had suffered considerable structural damage on the ground floor. Doors had become detached from their hinges, a couple of the walls had been blown right through and some of the lower stairs had crumbled, leaving our descent down somewhat perilous. The eerie silence that becomes an area where a bomb has exploded, once the debris settles, was only interrupted with cries and moans for help. I was right; it had come from the living room.

With Charlie close behind me, we made our way carefully down what was left of the stairs, another two almost giving way under our considerable combined weight.

Nothing quite prepared me for what we walked into. Going onto the scene of an accident is always tough, but then again, this hadn't been an accident had it?

Guns drawn purely out of instinct, we combed the remnants of the living room, almost unable to come to terms with what we were seeing.

Laura Edwards was dead. It seemed she must have been sitting near where the bomb had exploded; both her legs had been blown completely off her abdomen. The psychologist was dead also; I could see from where I was standing that he had been horrifically burned all over. Officer Cowap, a good guy, lay face down and a quick check of his vitals confirmed he had also died. One officer I knew only by sight had also died; he'd been blown through the downstairs window. Whether the blast itself or the sheet glass from the bay window had killed him, I couldn't tell, but he was covered in blood.

Two officers had been in the hallway when the bomb had exploded and had been trapped under falling debris. One had a particularly nasty cut to his left leg, the flesh had been cut to the bone and you could visibly see muscle, tissue and sinew. He probably didn't feel like it, but he had been very, very lucky.

Charlie made the 911 call, while I helped stabilise the surviving officers. Then I called Captain Williams who was as dumbfounded as we were. 'Patton', he sounded grave, 'what the hell is going on here?'

In the few moments I'd had to think, I found it hard to imagine that Charlie and I had been primary targets for the bomb. We hadn't played enough yet, had we? Nevertheless, it was an unnerving statement of further intent on the part of The Chemist. A statement that told us to expect the unexpected, that anything could happen at any time and that The Chemist was far cleverer than we were. At the moment, how could I disagree?

'Patton, hey, Patton', I heard Ferguson shout from upstairs, and I sensed a little excitement back in his voice.

'Yeah Fergs, what's up?' I yelled back.

'I think I've traced the signal. It came from Sunset Junction'.

I rounded Charlie up and we left Sutherland Boulevard in the hands of the arriving EMTs and a secondary LAPD team. We didn't have much, but once again, it was all we had to go on.

25

LAST WEEK

The day after Burr and McCrane told him of their impending problem with The Chemist, the uneasy feeling in the pit of Cyprian Hague's stomach remained unabated. He was worried, of course. Well who wouldn't be? But it all seemed a little bit, well, strange. Not that he'd had any reason thus far to distrust his fellow Animi; they had accomplished many great things in Los Angeles, his home town. He had very much played an integral role in what they had done over the last five years and knew that the public perception of him would be extremely different if they knew what went on behind closed doors and some of the decisions he'd helped to make. But no, the public loved him. His image, right from the start, was built on wholesome family values; that had actually been his first campaign slogan. After the scandal and corruption of his predecessor, that was just what the public had craved. So that's what he had given them. Or at least that's what they thought he had given them. The Animi had worked so effectively since its inception. They almost seemed unstoppable now. Invincible even. Even so, something about the information ushered upon them by Burr and McCrane didn't sit quite right with him. He had wondered if they had their own agenda, maybe working an angle for their own undisclosed purposes. He'd dismissed that as nonsense paranoia; his over-active imagination running riot. Still, despite this, the thought had returned and had returned several times over the last twenty-four hours. So much so, that he now sat in his luxurious office at Getty House with the phone in his hand and finger hovering, wondering whether or not to make a call. There was no denying that McCrane, chairman of the Animi, was the figure head of the group with Burr most definitely his second in command. What were they hiding? He suspected there was something that they weren't telling the rest of the group but he couldn't quite put his finger on it.

Eventually deciding that being sure, and watching his own back, was the right way to go, he made the call to an old friend Nick Tanner, who also just happened to be Chief Analyst of the LAPD Video and Imagery department. Hague wanted to check that what McCrane and Burr had told the rest of the Animi was indeed accurate. He knew that any crime scene photos and videos would pass through Tanner's department, even the covert operations, such as guarding a witness to a mafia hit; the story purported by McCrane at the meeting.

It took only a couple of minutes to get hold of Tanner. His old friend had been happy to hear from him, and it had taken a further couple of minutes of small-talk and pleasantries before Hague could cut to the chase.

'Listen Nick, I need a favour. There's something I think you can help me with'.

'Well if I can help, I will Cyprian, you know that', Tanner had replied, ready as always to assist the Mayor where he could.

'About six months ago, two guards were killed safeguarding a mafia witness. Ring any bells?' There was a pause on the other end of the line, Tanner taking his time to think. He must deal with hundreds of photos and videos on a weekly basis.

'Yeah it does actually, nasty. Why Cyprian? What are you after?'

'Do you think you could get a copy of all the crime scene reports and photos for me? Needs to be below the radar, Nick.'

'Well obviously, I'm not supposed to...' Tanner momentarily pondered, weighing up the pros and cons of his decision, 'but I suppose I could. Call it a favour banked, if you will?'

'That's great Nick', Hague had hoped he would agree. 'I need it a soon as you can, when can you get it together?'

'Give me an hour. You want it couriered?'

Hague was taking no chances. 'I'll collect it myself Nick, see you at five'.

He hung up the phone, undecided as to whether or not he wanted to find out if Burr and McCrane were telling the truth. Either way, he suspected he was going to have massive problems somewhere down the line.

26

As soon as he regained consciousness, James Tetley knew he was in trouble. He opened his eyes slowly, and surveyed his surroundings, groggily. He remembered Jimmy stalling for more time at the bank, and he also remembered the firefight between Jimmy and the cops. He also, very vividly, remembered Jimmy's body collapsing in front of him, or at least, what had been left of him. That was a sight that Tetley knew would haunt his dreams to the grave. He gagged, and momentarily fought to stop himself throwing up his breakfast all over the hospital bed.

Trying to raise his right hand to his mouth, just in case, he found that he couldn't but heard a slight rattle as he tried to do so. Looking down, he realised that the bastards had handcuffed him to the bed. As if he was going anywhere on one leg.

Despite the intravenous painkillers slowly dripping into his system from his left hand, he had a sense of where he was and knew that pretty soon, well just as soon as these drugs had taken effect probably, he would be transported to a local station where he would be held until he was convicted of parole violation. That meant he was straight back to prison, more than likely back to San Quentin.

If that was the case, not only would he be back in prison, he would also have Graziadai and Seinfeld pissed that they hadn't gotten their promised bounty. He would have to hastily promise that an associate would be taking care of that for them imminently, a promise that he in all likelihood couldn't keep. Then they would probably kill him. Best case scenario, they would seriously hurt him.

He'd once seen them sever an inmate's arm, just below the elbow. They had been on laundry detail; him, Seinfeld, Graziadai and several other inmates, including the unfortunate Mendes. Seinfeld and Graziadai must have had the guards in their back pockets, because they must have heard Mendes' bloodcurdling screams. Seinfeld had somehow prised the laundry goods delivery lift open. The lift had been on the next floor, which had been only slightly above their floor; no more than two feet. There had been an exit on the opposite side above them. Graziadai held the guy to the floor, a foot on his upper arm; the arm hovering ominously over the open lift pit. They had then sent the lift cascading down to their floor, severing Mendes' arm from his body. The resulting screams had given Tetley several sleepless nights over the following few weeks. And all this over something as trivial as Seinfeld thought Mendes had been serving him smaller portions than anyone else the last couple of lunchtimes. Now Mendes wouldn't be serving anybody. Not with his right arm at least. Mendes had somehow survived, in spite of the massive blood loss that had occurred, and had gone through extensive rehab in following four months or so. Almost as soon as he was back, Mendes had been subjected to daily ridicule from Graziadai and Seinfeld but never once ratted them out to any of the prison staff. Well not to any of the ones that weren't on the take, anyway. He must have thought that life with one arm was at least better than no life at all.

So it gave Tetley no comfort to imagine he could expect a minimum of the same level of treatment from these guys. All the IV in the world wasn't going to make that thought any less painful.

Fucking Jimmy. If they had stuck to the agreed time, they would have been well clear. Moseley could probably have covered ten to twelve blocks before the police had shown up, he'd have his ten thousand dollars, everyone would be happy. Instead, he was laying here with a fucked up leg, facing the unnerving prospect of prison certainly, and death a distinct possibility.

Sensing his situation was futile, he lapsed into a vague level of concentration on the room's television, his eyes half open. Farrington News blared onto the screen, complete with the annoying jingle he had heard so many times before. During the restricted 'television time' at San Quentin, Farrington News was an inmates' favourite for no other reason than the anchorwoman was something of a stunner. A definite nine out of ten. You very rarely heard the actual news when she came on, the catcalls, shouting and whistling were often deafening. He could hear it now though; the top story was something about The Chemist who might or might not have struck again. Having nothing better to do, Tetley gave the screen as much attention as he could muster, actually savouring the sight while he still could.

About a minute into the broadcast something she said caught his attention. What had she said then? Maybe he had imagined it? Glancing at the IV drip, it was nearly empty so he guessed that it would be taking effect by now. But wait, there it was again.

Instinctively, he tried to sit upright, forgetting about the handcuff around his right wrist and the IV drip in his left hand, causing a sharp pain as the metal cuff scraped the skin off the top of his hand, and he had almost knocked the drip stand over.

Had she said *Clozapone*?

That rang a bell from somewhere. Where the fuck had he heard that before? He had definitely heard it from somewhere.

It took a couple of minutes, Tetley fighting to remember, battling against the saline that was carousing through his system. Nevertheless, it eventually came to him. He was sure he'd talked to a particular inmate during his time at San Quentin, and he was sure they had talked about Clozapone and its effects that day, amongst many other things. He hadn't seen that inmate in the six months between that conversation and his parole.

Was that inmate The Chemist? If Tetley was right, that might be just the sort of information that would broker him a deal. Worming his left hand free from the drip, he began to urgently press the call button.

27

Pulling onto Sunset Junction, the sun glared down, sending a shimmering heat across the car windscreen. Much to his chagrin, Fergs was along for the ride. We needed him to pinpoint the source of the return signal. He hadn't wanted to come. I suspect he was still reeling from the detonation at Sutherland Boulevard, but I wasn't taking no for answer.

We slowed to a crawl as Fergs concentrated intently on one of his little box of tricks that was far too technical for the likes of Charlie and I to fully understand. He'd managed to isolate the co-ordinates of the return signal; Stella's laptop had not been damaged by the blast. He'd transferred them to a portable tracker and that was that. We had a fix on the signal, easy as you like. The fact that the device that had sent the signal had not moved during the entire ride to Sunset Junction from the Edwards' house made me familiarly apprehensive.

'Hey Patton, we're almost there ... slow down Holland', Fergs looked up, scanning Sunset Junction.

'Pull over Charlie, we'll take it on foot from here', I instructed.

'I think I've got a fix', Fergs voice was hushed. 'Couple

of hundred yards up, turn left and you got a phone box another two hundred yards, past a diner. That's it'.

For the third time today, I un-holstered my pistol. 'Be careful, man' Charlie advised.

'You too'. We'd already seen far too much carnage today. Neither of us wanted to see any more. With one obvious exception.

I radioed in our position, then we left Fergs in the car and jogged at full pace to the corner. We had the phone box in our sights and paused to check out our surroundings before covering the final stretch to the phone box itself.

'Looks clear to me', Charlie was scanning the phone box and beyond, I had taken the ground leading to the phone box.

'What about over there?' I pointed to a couple of people hanging around outside the diner.

'Looks like a couple of muso bums to me', Charlie said. 'Par for the course on Sunset Junction, man'. He was probably right. Sunset Junction was a hive for musical activity and its roots had spawned several bands on the alternative scene in the eighties and nineties. I seem to remember reading somewhere that a couple of members of Faith No More, who had been big before they split up several years ago, started off here.

'What do you think, man, should we take it?' Charlie wanted to move.

'Yeah, let's do it. Looks clear', I agreed, 'Let's move!' We had backup on the way but I didn't think we had time to wait for them as we had only just given our position. A few minutes might make all the difference to Stella.

It took only thirty seconds to reach the phone box, and in truth we had no reason to suspect it was safe; for all we knew there could have been another bomb hooked up to the damn thing.

Charlie remained on the phone's parameter, circling, looking for any possible threat. I looked inside; there must be something there for us.

Sure enough, I was right. A pager was taped behind the phone; no doubt the same pager that had activated the bomb earlier this morning.

'Careful Patton, careful', Charlie advised from the outside. I didn't say anything, I just nodded. Charlie opened the door, though there was no way that the phone box would hold us both.

'Just looks like a normal pager to me', I said, 'but we'll get Fergs to check it out. Maybe there's something on it?' I passed the pager to Charlie who after a quick check, came back with the same verdict.

'Let's see if Ferguson can work some more of his magic', he shrugged. 'You sure there's nothing else?'

'Well we'll dust the box for prints when forensics get here, but there's nothing else left here', I informed him. 'Goddamn it', I slammed my fist into the side of the phone box, venting my frustration. What time we on? How long we got left?'

'It's just gone eleven,' Charlie checked. 'Just under nineteen hours left', he quickly calculated.

Just as he said that, the phone began to ring.

28

LAST WEEK

Cyprian Hague sat in his spacious black BMW, parked back in the driveway of Getty House. He sat for a moment in silence, his brow furrowed deeply, looking in wonder at the unopened file he had picked up from Nick Tanner just over half an hour ago. He had wanted to remain inconspicuous; so thought that heading straight back was the safer decision, rather than risk being seen outside the LAPD, even though he had taken the a seldom used back entrance, conveniently located right next to the Video and Imagery department. Nick Tanner had come through for him, just as promised. He didn't know if that was purely out of friendship, but he suspected not. Somewhere down the line, he would be repaying the favour, no doubt. It never hurt to have the Mayor of Los Angeles owe you one, did it?

Taking a deep breath, and quickly glancing out of the car windows, despite being in the relative safety of his own grounds, he sliced open the envelope.

It took several moments to wade through its contents. There were several photos of the guards' untimely demise and Hague visibly shuddered as he viewed them; it looked very nasty indeed. One of the guards had been lying in a pool of blood so large, that the actual scale of the photograph had to be indicated on the back, and that was frightening. It looked like Caldwell was a particularly violent and deranged individual. That made Hague look around once more, aware of his ever-increasing paranoia he shook his head. Still, something was not right; he desperately tried to think back to the meeting and what Burr and McCrane had told them.

All of a sudden, it hit him. So much so, that he actually asked the question out loud. 'Animi. When the time is right, I will come for you all. The writing in blood on the wall. Of course. Where is *that*?'

Another quick flick through the contents of the file confirmed that despite the graphic and unsettling nature of the pictures, there was not one of writing on any wall, in blood or otherwise. There should be though; everything else was here. Why wouldn't that be in here?

Pulling out his cell, he hit redial and connected straight back through to Nick Tanner. 'Hey Nick, its Cyprian'.

'Cyprian, hi', Tanner replied. 'I wasn't expecting to hear from you again so soon. Is everything ok?'

'Thanks once again for the favour Nick, you really pulled one out of the bag for me there. Listen, are you sure that was everything? I mean, there's no way you could have missed something out?'

'Absolutely not', Tanner sounded almost offended, as if his professional integrity was being called into question. 'Everything I have here, you have a copy of there. Everything'. Well if Tanner was sure, that was good enough for him. Tanner was one of the most methodical and thorough people he had ever known or worked with.

'Ok, no problem, Nick. Just checking. Thanks again'.

'Ok Cyprian, see you soon', Tanner replied, then hung up.

It didn't make sense. The photos should be there. There would be no reason for them not to be.

He sat, stroking his chin with his thumb, carefully considering the possibilities. None made any sense.

It was one of the many strict, unwritten rules of the Animi that contact between its members should be kept to a minimum to avoid any ties between them ever being established. Their paths would cross naturally in their day to day business, of course, some more than others, but other than in the natural line of duty, communication between them all was very much discouraged. Nevertheless, Hague was somewhat puzzled and thought that this could certainly be classed as an exception. He picked up the cell once more, dialling a number. It rang twelve times times.

'Hello', a voice said.

Contact, although discouraged, had at times been necessary in times of severe emergency; times where an urgent phone call was needed to relay information between them, particularly if one or more were in transit. Each member of the Animi had taken the name of an Oscar winning actor as a pseudonym so that they could speak anonymously, avoiding their real names. You never knew when someone might be listening, who really shouldn't be. He had picked Robert De Niro.

'Mr. Brando, hello', Hague replied. 'It's Robert De Niro'.

'Mr De Niro, this is highly irregular. I trust this is important?'

'It is. At least I think it is, I'm not sure', Hague responded.

'Go on'.

'Cast your mind back to our last meeting. Our friend who escaped, yes?'

'Yes'

'And how they escaped, yes?'

'Yes'.

'I have copies of all the photographic evidence relating to the escape'.

'And?'

'There's no writing on the wall in blood. None at all.'

'But the guards were killed?'

Yes they were'.

There was a silence on the phone for a minute which suggested Mr. Brando was compiling the information he'd just received, and what it could mean.

'Well then Mr. De Niro, we could have a problem', Brando contemplated. 'I suggest we meet. Shall we say usual place, usual time, tomorrow?'

'I think that would be a prudent move on our part Mr Brando', Hague replied, then terminated the call.

He didn't feel any better than he had done before he'd called his compatriot, but at least it was someone to bounce ideas off. Maybe figure out why there had been no photos on file of the message from The Chemist on the kitchen wall of the safe house. And maybe figure out why McCrane and Burr had told them there was one.

29

For several seconds both of us were transfixed by the ringing telephone and it was Charlie who spoke first. 'That *must* be for us, man. It *has* to be!' he said. I concurred.

I pointed to my eyes with two fingers then to outside, signalling to Charlie that he should keep watch; be extra vigilant. If this was The Chemist, then we were probably being watched. Anything could happen. I took a deep breath, composing myself, and then another. Eventually, I picked up the telephone, bringing the receiver cautiously to my ear. 'This is Patton', I said, straining to pick up any background noise, any clue to The Chemist's location.

It was the voice I'd heard three times before. An eerie, almost electronic sounding voice, obviously disguised with some kind of digital effect. Did that mean I would recognise the voice if I heard it undisguised? That had been a question that had been rattling around the inside of my head for several weeks.

'Good morning, Detective Patton,' the voice said, 'and also good morning to Detective Holland'. I would fill Charlie in after the call, for now he was where he needed to be.

'Well you've got our attention', I replied. Although The

Chemist had called us, I had to drag out this conversation. I could see Charlie already on his cell outside the phone box, hastily trying to authorise a trace on the call.

'I'm sure I have', the voice sounded cold, all the more so for its mechanical tone. 'But I have not even *started* yet. I'm glad I have this opportunity to speak to you, I was afraid we wouldn't get to talk. I wasn't sure if you would make it this far, but you haven't disappointed me'.

'Glad to hear it', I could think of nothing else to say.

'And poor Stella', The Chemist continued, 'Time is just ticking away, isn't it?'

'Tell me where she is'. I knew it was futile at best. Still, I had to try. 'Where's Stella?'

'Well you will find out one way or another, eventually, won't you?' The Chemist taunted, 'I'm aware you are probably trying to trace this call, so I'll be brief. I just wanted to say, 'hello' really, now we've been chasing each other around for a few weeks, and that I do hope you are enjoying our little games together. But don't forget Detective Patton; fourth time's a charm!'

I took that to mean The Chemist was confident that Stella would die, and a fourth game would eventually begin. My stomach turned at the prospect.

'But for now', The Chemist paused seemingly for effect, 'Let's just say that the next step is in your car, along with a little surprise for you'.

The line went dead. Then it slowly dawned on me. We had left Ferguson in the car.

30

I rushed past Charlie, leaving the receiver hanging, knowing full well he would have my back a split second later.

'Hey man, what's the score?' Charlie's voice came from just over my right shoulder. I was sprinting now, beginning to breathe hard. 'What's going on?'

'The Chemist told us to check the car', I panted. I took Charlie's silence as an indication that he understood the implications of that last sentence.

Reaching the corner, I used the side of the diner to swing round to prevent my momentum carrying me past. I had a visual on the car but couldn't tell from here if there was anything wrong. I could see that there was no-one around the car; no-one in sight in fact. Shit. Our backup hadn't arrived yet. Where the hell was it?

Charlie overtook me on the home straight and I knew even before I reached our car that the news wasn't good. Charlie stood, bent over; his hands on his knees, trying to get his breath back, shaking his head.

I pulled alongside him, just as out of breath as he was, probably even more so. I didn't see the envelope with my name on it at first. It was hard to focus on anything other than Dave Ferguson, who sat upright in the back seat, his head slumped forward; the pool of dark blood still growing around him on the car interior and dripping onto the floor.

His throat had been sliced almost from ear to ear, dicing his larynx in two. From the projected blood spatter all over the car's ceiling, windshield and front seats, it looked like an artery had also been nicked causing a high-pressured jet of blood to spurt from his neck with every one of his final heart beats. It looked nasty and I only prayed, if God had any mercy, that Ferguson had never seen it coming.

'Motherfucker', was all Charlie could muster, and that pretty much summed it up.

Turning away, cursing the fact that we had left Fergs alone and that our backup hadn't arrived in time, I sensed his murder had been opportune, not a planned part of *The Game*. The next letter eventually caught my eye. Tucked inside a window wiper, like some cheap flier advertising an even cheaper product; there it was.

Just waiting to be opened.

Charlie's cell went off, and it was Captain Williams, who took the news of Ferguson's death hard and went ballistic that the backup units hadn't arrived but he didn't blame us for not waiting. He knew we were against the clock. Nevertheless, he remained focussed and re-composed himself giving us news that up until now, I hadn't dared hope would come.

'There's an ex-con, a guy called James Tetley, he tried to take down the Pacific this morning', he sounded angry now, the reality of losing Ferguson hitting home. 'Took one in the leg, and is laid up at LA County. He claims, and I can't stress that enough guys, he *claims* he knows who The Chemist is. How likely that is, I don't know, but this guy has got a quite bit of previous. He's been around so who knows?'

We're going to need another car here Captain' I said, not wanting to look back on the Subaru for one second.

How long before you can get us a ride?'

'And don't send us no piece of shit either', Charlie chimed in. It always amazed me how he could keep his sense of humour at the grimmest of times, and I envied him that.

'Take one of the backup units', he growled. 'When they fucking arrive'.

'Copy that, Captain', I confirmed as I heard sirens in the distance approaching. 'They're here now'.

As much as I disliked just leaving Fergs there for all to see, we had no choice. The backup units would have to take care of the crime scene until CSI arrived. Less than two minutes later we were speeding towards Hollywood Boulevard, the latest envelope unopened in my pocket

31

As I scanned through the information we had on James Tetley, which had been delivered to my PDA, I wasn't sure if this was a waste of our time or not. That we had a possible lead on the identity of The Chemist was completely unexpected, and I remained highly sceptical. After all, The Chemist had been meticulous so far, leaving absolutely no trace and no evidence. It seemed highly unlikely that somebody would be able to provide us with an identity. From the profile we had built up, it was clear that The Chemist was a loner, an outcast, but highly motivated. Still, The Chemist had to have a massive ego to be playing these games in the first place. Was it out of the realms of possibility that The Chemist had bragged to someone, gloating over our lack of progress?

More to the point, could we believe this guy, Tetley? Was he just offering up some fictitious information to try and strike some kind of deal? I suspected he wasn't overly keen to return to prison, and I've been in the position before where ex-cons who re-offend will say and do just about anything to try and preserve their freedom. If this was a dead end we wouldn't just be wasting our time, we'd be wasting Stella's.

'Hey man,' Charlie saw I was despondent. 'This could be it. This could be just the break we need'.

I nodded. The thought briefly crossed my mind that this was still part of The Chemist's game. Was it a planned part of *The Game*, becoming even braver, even more taunting? I soon cast that aside, there was no way the botched bank robbery at the Pacific this morning could have been planned and executed with the outcome that had prevailed. This had to be something that The Chemist didn't know about.

It didn't take us long to reach the hospital. After mulling over the prospect in hand, I was actually cautiously optimistic now. Perhaps Charlie was right. Maybe this was the break we were looking for.

We arrived at ward 5A a couple of minutes later and it was James Tetley who spoke first. 'I think I know who you're looking for', he sounded pretty convincing. 'But let me say right off the bat, I give you The Chemist, you give me a deal. I want this bank thing gone and I want witness protection. And even if you don't get The Chemist, I want relocating. I won't be safe if The Chemist is out there. If it becomes public knowledge I gave you The Chemist I'm a dead man, I'll tell you that.'

I'd heard it all before. It was pretty much your standard demands from someone who is looking at a long time back behind bars.

'I'm sure we can work something out', I replied 'but we don't have much time. If you have something for us, then give it to us and give it to us now. We will have to work out the details of any deal later'.

'Not good enough', Tetley retorted. 'I want the deal first. No deal, no Chemist'.

'Your choice', I said to him. I'd never been one to give into the demands of a grass and I wasn't about to start now. Invariably what they had to lose was more than you had to gain. 'You got one more chance before we walk out of here. Who is The Chemist?'

Tetley remained silent. I gave him ten seconds or so. 'Goodbye James. Enjoy prison'.

We turned and walked towards the exit. Charlie was already out of the door and I was almost there, not looking back. Sensing his only chance of a reprieve was almost gone, Tetley's hand was forced. 'Wait, wait!' he called out. 'The Chemist, I think it's Caldwell'.

Hearing the name, I momentarily froze but then spun around, looking Tetley directly in the eyes. 'Caldwell?' I repeated. 'You said you think The Chemist is Caldwell?' I looked on in disbelief.

'Yeah I do', Tetley nodded. 'We were in San Quentin at the same time. Tell me one thing Detective. Is Clozapone unique to this case? Are there any past case histories where injecting Clozapone has been a factor? A calling card maybe?'

I paused, not sure whether to divulge that information. Well, what harm could it do? 'It is unique', I replied. 'First time, first case I've ever worked where it's been used'.

For James Tetley, this was all the confirmation he needed. 'Well then Detective. I'm pretty sure the person you're after *is* Caldwell. Sarah Caldwell'.

I pulled two seats closer to the hospital bed. 'Tell me everything you know about Sarah Caldwell', I instructed. 'Be quick but leave nothing out. I'll get you your deal'.

If I'd been wondering why The Chemist was targeting me, that question may have just been answered.

32

Although it had been some eight years ago, I remember it like it was yesterday. I remember lots of things like they were yesterday. Don't get me wrong, I love what I do. I like to think I've made a difference during my career in the LAPD. I've made some wrong calls here and there, of course I have, but I can hold my head high and stand proud of what I've contributed. There are very few individuals in the LAPD, either active or retired, that could hold a candle to my arrest and conviction rate. For the most part, I've done things the right way; I've never planted evidence, only used excessive force when absolutely necessary and I could swear on the Bible that I've never put away an innocent man.

I've sailed close to the wind on occasion, but the job sometimes needs you to. I've made some bad decisions, some errors of judgement and I whole-heartedly regret every one. There are some members of the LAPD who shrug their bad moves off easily, putting them down as inevitable. Many police officers liken their wrong calls to that of an ER doctor: Sooner or later you are bound to get slapped with a malpractice suit simply because the law of average dictates the more patients you see, the more pressure you are under, the more opportunity you have for things to go wrong. Our situation was similar; the more bad guys you arrest, the more chances you have to screw up. It was as simple as that. Just under eight years ago, I'd made one of those errors of judgement.

It had been a routine bust. We had got the tip off from a reliable source; one of mine in fact, so we had every confidence there would be the whole fifty keys of cocaine at the address we were given in Crenshaw, which would have been just enough for a base offence level 36 bust – a damn fine result. It was there, no doubt about that, and that was a shit load of cocaine. The only problem was that when we turned up to make the bust, at a shade after seven o' clock one morning, the dealer we expecting to arrest was in the middle of selling it to three more scumbags, who were heavily armed with P90 submachine guns, and had thought nothing of opening fire on us immediately, as soon as we rammed the door down.

The team had fortunately only sustained a couple of minor injuries; two officers took a flesh wound each and thankfully our numbers were intact. As you would expect from highly trained individuals, we had more success. The dealer and one of the buyers were gunned down in return fire. Two of the buyers fled the scene through the back of the house, killing the police officer coming in from the rear. I led the chase but couldn't get a clean shot off on either of the buyers.

Only a hundred yards or so behind them, I watched them run across Chesterfield Square towards a parked two-door Sedan. Just as I was radioing the movements and location of the suspects, one of them got clipped in the side by a passing Volvo, taking him down hard. I shouted to one of the officers coming up behind me to take the fallen buyer, I was carrying on in pursuit of the other one.

Just as he made it to the Sedan, speeding off immediately with tyres squealing, a squad car rounded the corner, pausing only momentarily to pick me up.

The chase lasted around eight minutes, winding through the King Estates and up to Windsor Hills. For the last three minutes of the pursuit, as we sped up the narrow winding road that led to the top parts of Windsor Hills, it was clear that this guy wasn't pulling over. In retrospect, I shouldn't have done what I did but sometimes your thinking gets clouded and the adrenaline sometimes masks the right decision.

Without really thinking where we were, I edged out of the window, just enough to give me a clear aim at the Sedan. I'm an extremely good shot when the opportunity presents itself, even if I do say so myself, and I'd only needed one shot to take out the rear passenger side tyre.

The effect had been immediate; the Sedan lost control and went into a tailspin. We had to slam on the breaks just to avoid a collision. What I remember most about that day is the look of sheer panic on the Sedan driver's face as our eyes met for a split second when the Sedan was in the middle of its second complete revolution. I knew then I'd made the wrong decision and I knew then where the Sedan was heading.

All I could do was watch in disbelief as the Sedan careered sideways, spinning out of control and smashed through the roadside barrier, dropping almost two hundred feet and exploding viciously upon impact. I swear I could almost feel the heat from the explosion all the way up, where we had come to a complete standstill.

The driver of the Sedan on that cold December's morning turned out to be a pretty insignificant dealer in the grand scheme of the LA underworld drug culture, but word on the street had been that this guy had been talking about grand plans and had loftier ambitions than his current status afforded. He was one to watch maybe, could have been a mover and a shaker in the years to come; and who knows, maybe he would have been.

The incident had been pretty well publicised after the event. Although the LAPD backed me fully and there was never any suggestion, by the PD or by the media, of any wrongdoing on my part, I knew deep down that I'd made the wrong decision. One of those 'bad' calls.

I remember going home that night to find a reporter from the LA Times, I think it had been Paul Britland-Jones, on my doorstep. Exhausted though I was, I took the time to answer his several questions. I'd always enjoyed a good relationship with the media, and the resulting positive coverage I would receive after this incident was a testament to that.

He asked me if I had anything I'd like to say regarding the death that morning of Andrew Caldwell.

33

Turns out, James Tetley could be right. Aware we needed to get back to 'The Game' soon, to avoid The Chemist getting suspicious, I'd given him ten minutes. During that time he told us that he had served time at San Quentin. Two years into his sentence, he'd been stationed on mail delivery detail. As far as work stations went, this was a pretty good one. The governor and guards of San Quentin, much like any other prison, would assign inmates duties to carry out within the prison. These duties came with certain privileges, which could, and often would be taken away from an inmate if violent or disparaging behaviour was discovered and proven to have been committed. Quite often proving that an inmate had attacked, or in some cases killed, another inmate was entirely different from knowing they had. The prison naturally segregated themselves into groups; The Aryan Brotherhood, with whom Tetley had the trouble, The Italians, The Muslims, The Irish, The Latinos, The Bikers.... Fitting into none of these, Tetley kept himself to himself as much as possible, trying to have no conflict with any group, figuring this was the best way to try and keep himself alive during his sentence. It hadn't worked out that way of course, as his current situation could attest to;

the trouble with the Aryans had ultimately led him back to hospital and given him the urgency to strike the deal. He had seemed quite desperate not to go back. He said that making it out of San Quentin alive once was lucky. Twice would be nearly impossible.

There had been another segregation of prisoners. One enforced by the governor out of obvious necessity, rather than by the inmates themselves out of any natural 'common ground' instincts. The Women. They were confined to their own wing, adjoining the main three blocks. As San Quentin only housed around fifteen female inmates at any one time, this wing was more secluded and had much less of an authority presence; quite often only one guard.

As part of his weekly mail delivery rounds, he would go into this wing, just as he would all the others, and it was during these rounds that he had initially made contact with Sarah Caldwell.

She had been in the last cell on the wing; even more secluded than the rest of the women. Just like every other male inmate, and indeed probably some of the female inmates, it hadn't taken long for Jimmy to start to crave female attention and company. Three years had been a *hell* of a long time! As far as the female inmates went, Sarah had been by far the most attractive, although given the competition around her, that wasn't much of an accolade and not that the environment was conducive to anything other than talking in any case. She had long black hair that she would tie back in a ponytail, clear blue eyes and a smile that definitely brightened his day on the rare occasions she flashed it. She had a medium build but not even the prison issued uniform could hide the fact that she had a killer body. Boy, would he love to see that.

He'd started off by making small talk initially. Just a greeting here, a smile there. Gradually over the course of seven months or so, the exchanges had grown to full-blown conversations and often they would talk for an hour or more, depending on whether or not the guard was being a prick.

There was one guard, Dave Barnes, who would let them talk as freely as they liked and for as long as they wanted. It helped that Tetley would sometimes bring a smuggled bottle of vodka for the guard, stashed in the mail cart. Quite often, after Tetley and Caldwell had finished talking, a good portion of that bottle would have been consumed by Barnes.

On one occasion, Barnes shared the bottle with them, and they had spent a very enjoyable hour getting fairly drunk. Barnes had left them to it, and it was during the resulting conversation that Tetley had asked her a question. 'So if you were to ever get out', he said, giggling under his intoxication, 'what would be the first thing you'd do?'

'I'd play a game', Sarah giggled back. 'I'd play a great game'.

'What game would that be then?' he'd enquired. 'Twister? Monopoly?'

'Oh a very different kind of game, James. One where I injected my victim with Clozapone and try and get the police to find her', she giggled again. 'But I can't tell you any more than that'. Bringing her index finger to her lips, she smiled. 'Shhhh!' she whispered. 'Keep that to yourself', she laughed. 'I need to have payback!'

Barnes had returned at that moment, saying that time was up. He had to go back to his block. 'Just make sure you don't look drunk', he warned, 'and don't mention my name, or I will fuck you up, you understand?'

Tetley nodded. 'No problem, boss'. Then, turning to Caldwell; 'Bye Sarah'.

That had been the last time he saw her. When he had come the following week, her cell had been empty. He'd asked

Barnes where she had gone, but he'd simply shrugged, saying he had no idea and, more to the point, couldn't care less. He'd asked a couple more of the guards too but had pretty much the same response. It had been a mystery to him too, up until he'd seen the news report in hospital.

As much as he'd valued his friendship with Sarah at the time, it wasn't as much as he valued his freedom now.

Charlie and I listened intently as Tetley gave us his story. It sounded plausible enough, and I radioed Captain Williams to get a hold of San Quentin records and this guard Dave Barnes to see if we could confirm it.

True, aside from the identity, Tetley had no more details but if he was correct, this would be a massive break for us. It would certainly give us an edge we didn't have before. It might just save Stella.

Telling Tetley that if he was right, we'd do what we could to keep him out of prison, we left the hospital room and stepped out into the corridor. I took that opportunity to fill Charlie in about Andrew Caldwell. Upon hearing the chain of events up on Windsor Hills, he let out a hard breath. 'Well we have motive for involving you, man, that's what we have', he said. 'And if Tetley is right, that makes sense. Did you ever see Sarah Caldwell after Andrew's death?'

'I'm not sure', I replied. 'I went to his funeral. Felt like I should, like I owed him that. There were only a couple of other people there; couple of his friends I think. I did see a woman standing under a tree, near the burial but just far enough away that she wouldn't be approached. Maybe that was her', I shrugged.

'Could be man, yeah', Charlie agreed. He waited expectantly.

'That's all I got Charlie boy, there's nothing else', I said.

'I was just thinking it might be a good time to open that next envelope'

Caught up in the revelation that Sarah Caldwell may be The Chemist, I'd almost forgotten about that. Reaching into my pocket, I pulled it out, and began to tear it open.

34

LAST WEEK

Cyprian Hague pulled into the main car park of the Walt Disney Concert Hall on South Grand Avenue. Darkness had set in a couple of hours ago and car park E was deserted. It was the perfect place to meet; it would either be deserted, like now, or full of concert goers and therefore easy to blend in. He remembered seeing a particularly pleasing performance of the Los Angeles Philharmonic Orchestra a few weeks ago at this very venue. He was here for an entirely different purpose tonight.

It was a shade before ten and he'd been here for about fifteen minutes or so. He knew he'd be early but that was a force of habit with him now. He'd rather be early and drive around the circumference of the building, just checking that there was nothing suspicious, no-one there who maybe shouldn't be. Especially now, given his increasing paranoia over the last few days.

He'd met with various members of the Animi here over the last couple of years, maybe only four or five times in total. Each member had their own designated car park to avoid several cars being seen together; raising questions, arousing suspicion. His was car park E. There was a seating area set just off the main entrance which was where any meeting always took place. Leaving his car, he hurried to the rendezvous point, hands in his pockets and pulling his scarf up to his mouth; it was freezing, but this meeting was necessary.

Arriving at the seating area, he couldn't see anyone waiting for him. Preferring to stand, shuffling his feet to keep warm, he checked his watch.

'Good evening Cyprian,' Mr Brando stepped out of the shadows.

'Good evening Conrad', he reciprocated. 'Thanks for meeting'.

'I've been thinking about our conversation yesterday', Conrad said. 'Are you positive that there were no photographs of the writing on the kitchen wall?'

'Absolutely', Cyprian replied, 'I thought the same. I had my source double check and believe me; if there was writing on the wall, there would have been a photograph of it, and it would have been with the rest. My source would definitely have had that photograph. It wasn't there'.

'Your source', Conway enquired, 'Reliable? One hundred percent?'

'He's never let me down before Conrad, and he's also an old friend. He's got no reason to lie to me. I can't understand why the photograph wouldn't be there'.

'Well as far as I can see, there are two reasons', Conrad mused. 'Either your source is wrong; there is a photograph showing The Chemist's message to us, or there never was a message, and McCrane and Burr have somehow manufactured one, and for some reason want us running scared'.

Hague nodded in agreement. 'Well that's what I thought as well Conrad, and knowing my source like I do, I can only conclude it's the latter'.

'But why?' Conrad questioned. 'Why would they need to do that? It doesn't make any sense.'

'I've been thinking about that too', Hague said, 'And that one has got me. I've got no idea why they would do that'.

'So what are we saying? That there is no Chemist?' Conrad wanted to know.

'Well there must be a Chemist', Hague reasoned. 'The news is full of that shit. I'm just not sure how much of what Burr and McCrane told us is true'.

'So you think that we're safe then?' Conrad continued. 'That The Chemist isn't going to take revenge on the Animi?' He seemed relieved. 'Because I don't mind telling you, I've been looking over my shoulder the last couple of days'.

'Well if Burr and McCrane were lying about the photo then maybe there never was a message from The Chemist to us. If The Chemist isn't planning on taking revenge on us then that only leaves one possibility'.

'And what's that', Conrad said somewhat nervously; it looked as if he already knew.

'That McCrane and Burr have an ulterior motive for wanting us afraid.

'Well what could that possibly be', Conrad exploded. 'And why not tell the rest of us?' he asked, although his affair with Burr's wife was beginning to sound alarm bells in his mind. He wasn't about to disclose that to Hague though. If Burr knew about the affair, then he had a very good reason to plot some sort of revenge. Maybe he'd found out and enlisted McCrane's help?

'Again, I've been thinking about that too', Hague advised. 'I can only think that they have a reason for keeping us in the dark and that can't be good'.

Shaking his head, trying desperately to put together all the pieces of the puzzle, something suddenly clicked with Conrad Conway. He turned again to Cyprian Hague.

'Not knowing what we suspect we now know; suppose we still thought there was a message from The Chemist and suppose one of us was to meet with, shall we say, an untimely accident. After the meeting we just had, what would be your first reaction?'

Hague pondered this question momentarily. 'That The Chemist had carried out the threat. Or at least started to'.

'Exactly', Conrad enthused, sure he was on the right track. 'Everyone would assume that, no questions asked'.

So what your suggesting is that Burr and McCrane are about to take one of us out, for some reason?' Hague was almost incredulous. Still, he had to admit, it seemed the only plausible explanation.

'Right again', confirmed Conrad. 'Question is, who, and why?' Again, he declined to make Hague fully aware of the facts. Perhaps in hindsight the affair hadn't been such a good idea. No amount of fun was worth paying for with your life!

'I've got no fucking idea. Listen, do we bring the others into this?'

'Let's not just yet', Conrad paused. 'Listen I have an idea, let me put out a couple of feelers, see what I can come up with. Stay in touch though, you think of anything, let me know!'

Both Conrad Conway and Cyprian Hague left the Walt Disney Concert Hall even more worried than when they arrived.

Hague would drive straight home, checking his wing mirrors every couple of seconds as he drove nervously through the night. Conway wasn't heading home just yet. It was half past ten, and very shortly he had to meet one blackmailing son-of-a-bitch that liked to call himself 'The Bully'.

35

Even as I was opening the envelope, I couldn't believe we had the potential identity of The Chemist. I just hoped that the Captain would dig up the guard from San Quentin, and that Tetley's story could be verified, one way or the other.

I also knew that if we confirmed that it could be Sarah Caldwell, Charlie and I would turn over every stone in the state until we found her. I was reeling from the events that had unfolded so far today. Giving Charlie a quick sideways glance as I pulled out a sheet of paper, I could tell he was in the same frame of mind.

'What does it say, man?' Charlie demanded, 'What's the next step?' I double checked what was on the sheet of paper; it didn't say much.

'WLA 14th 1500 – be on it – getting closer', I replied, 'That's all it says Charlie boy. Just that'.

'What the hell does that mean?' Charlie was getting more and more agitated. I took several moments to digest the latest message, possibilities tumbling around my mind.

'The 1500 has got to be a time, can we agree on that?' I questioned. 'What else could it be?'

'Yeah man, sounds good to me', Charlie looked at his watch. 'That gives us a couple of hours. We need to figure out the rest, let's call it in'.

'It also gives us a couple of hours to look into Sarah Caldwell is what it gives us', I stated. 'We need to move fast with this. We have to appear to be following her rules. We can't let her suspect we may know who she is'.

I called in all the information we had gathered, both from James Tetley and from the latest instructions in the game. Captain Williams immediately said he would put together a secondary unit, specifically to unearth what they could about Sarah Caldwell. Running parallel to that unit, he assigned the tech guys to the message from The Chemist. He was confident that the message would pose no problem and he agreed that the 1500 sounded like a time. Maybe the rest related to some kind of timetable? If there was somewhere we had to be at three o'clock, we would fucking well be there. He rounded it off by telling us that Agent Balfer from the FBI had an ETA of ninety minutes and that we might as well head back to the station and bring him up to speed if he arrived before the next part of the game began.. 'Rest assured guys,' he concluded, 'wherever you need to be come three o' clock, you will be there'.

We were about half way to the station when he rang me again. 'We think we got a result on the message. There are a couple of things it could be, but we think the most likely scenario is that it refers to the LRT and that you have to get on it at the stop on 14th Street, West Los Angeles, at three o clock obviously'.

I could have kicked myself for not figuring that out. The Light Rail Transit in LA is a massive network. I seem to recall reading a while ago that it was the third busiest in the country taking in excess of something like three hundred thousand commuters a day. Crazy figures.

'As to why?' he added, 'We've got no idea. That's your department guys. Any ideas?'

'Well if it is Sarah Caldwell, then I think I know why she is targeting me Captain. As to the purpose of the game, I honestly have no idea', I said, disheartened as to the lack of information we really had. I only hoped we would turn up something soon that we could use.

'Goes without saying, we're having SWAT on 14th. We'll have them there for two. If she's there, we'll nail her boys. Fill me in on Caldwell when you arrive Patton'.

'We'll see you soon, Captain', I hung up.

For the rest of the drive we mulled over why The Chemist would chose that location for the next part of the game. Was it just picked at random, or would it serve a higher purpose?

Ever since we'd spoken to Tetley, there had been a voice inside my head that was getting louder and louder. It kept repeating one thing: 'You killed her brother'.

Something told me that if The Chemist was indeed Sarah Caldwell, then she wasn't anywhere near through with me.

Not by a long shot.

36

LAST WEEK

Now that he was standing under the Gerald Desmond Bridge waiting for Senator Conrad Conway, Paul Britland-Jones wasn't sure if this had been a good idea or not. It had seemed like a good idea several weeks ago when the idea had first come to him. After seeing the Senator on the news and wondering if a potential blackmail had been there it hadn't taken too much effort on the part of himself to dig up background information on Conway. From there, he'd spent three or four weeks surveying and tailing him whenever he had the spare time; mainly at night but he had done a couple of days too. He had a feeling that the night time was where the Senator would undo himself, and he'd been right on that score. He'd seen Conway with drug dealers, prostitutes, members of the criminal fraternity; he had built up quite a substantial file on one of the most respected individuals in Los Angeles. He'd also seen the Senator arrive and leave the Aon Centre a couple of times, but had no idea why he'd been there.

After Conway had received The Bully's first letter, along with the compromising photographs of the Senator on Figueroa Street, he'd telephoned him the following day to verify his instructions. The resulting conversation didn't really go according to plan.

It had been Britland-Jones' intention to have Conway drop the money then have one of his contacts pick up the money. When Britland-Jones was satisfied that the money was there, he would have the photographs delivered by courier to the Conway residence. Conway had angrily said that that was unacceptable and the only way he would do this was if they were to meet face to face, then he had hung up saying that no matter what The Bully had on him, he could exercise damage limitation through the press and media via one of his close friends at the Farrington Network.

Realising that the Senator was not going to compromise on this, he had phoned back, agreeing to his terms. Not that he was intimidated, but he realised this was a one-shot deal, that Conway would indeed have powerful friends and allies; and that he was playing a dangerous game. Perhaps more dangerous than he had first thought. Nevertheless, Bobby Hambel would become an equally dangerous prospect if he didn't receive his pay-off.

The meeting place of Gerald Desmond Bridge remained however, and true to his word, Britland-Jones had come alone. He had taken the liberty of placing the file he had on Conrad Conway in a safety deposit box and leaving instructions with a fellow journalist; and in fact fellow countryman; Jacob Hunt that if he didn't receive a phone call by nine o' clock the following morning to go to his house and retrieve the key that would open it. It was by no means a guarantee of his safety, but it was the best he could do.

This stretch of Long Beach was deserted at this time of night, which was the reason Britland-Jones had picked it. It also had excellent visibility for anyone approaching from either side, and just to be on the safe side, he had arrived here three hours ago, at eight p.m. Taking a considerable amount of time to check he wasn't being watched, he now stood in the shadows of the bridge and was satisfied he was alone. All he had to do now was wait and see if the Senator showed up.

At five past the agreed meeting time, Britland-Jones' alert ears pricked up. He heard the low purr of an expensive car approaching. He squinted in the dark to see if he could determine who was arriving. Sure enough, even in the darkness, he recognised the Senator's Aston Martin. Out of instinct, he placed one hand on his Browning 9mm; a pistol he had procured from a contact several months ago when he'd realised he was operating more and more outside the law.

The Senator walked up to the bridge. Britland-Jones could see he wasn't carrying anything. He better have brought the money! He pulled up a flashlight and flashed it once, signifying the agreed meeting place. Conway could have spent hours wandering around the lower constructs of the bridge not knowing where The Bully was standing.

As Conway climbed the final couple of steps towards Britland-Jones, they made eye contact for the very first time.

'The money', Britland-Jones quizzed, 'have you brought it?' Conway stayed silent for a moment; then replied.

'There's been a change of plan my friend. You won't be getting the fifty grand off me'. Britland-Jones reached down towards his firearm. This had not been the news he was expecting.

'I'd like it if you kept your hands where I could see them', Conrad sounded calm, 'I appreciate that the photos you have of me are worth something to you, and obviously, I would like all negatives and anything else you may have on me'. Conway had long ago realised that if The Bully had these photos, he would probably have a lot more on him.

'Go on', said The Bully, curtly.

'I will give you something though, but it isn't fifty grand. You won't be getting that, not off me anyway. I'm going to give you something worth a lot more, but in return I expect any and all information on me to be in my hands by noon tomorrow'.

'And what are you going to give me?' Britland-Jones was curious. This was an unexpected turn of events but one he still may profit from.

'What I'm going to give you', Conway grinned, commending himself on his own genius, 'is Paul McCrane and Jameson Burr'.

37

By the time we got back to the station, the team charged with unearthing anything and everything on Sarah Caldwell had already been assembled. As time was critical, Captain Williams had gathered every spare officer and detective he could reach, with the promise of more on the way. There were twelve people frantically scrambling at files and on phones; hell, even Williams' secretary was in on the act. I'll say one thing for the Captain, when he said 'jump', most people jumped. Whilst the frenzied activity looked promising, the news wasn't good.

Over the next thirty minutes, every search performed, every phone call made, every lead chased up gave us nothing on Sarah Caldwell.

We sipped the department's trademark shitty coffee as we filled in Captain Williams about our conversation with Tetley, and with my ties to the Caldwell family. I remember reading at the time of Andrew's funeral that he had a sister, Sarah, but there was no mention of any other family. Not that I could recall, anyway. Captain Williams listened with his usual seriousness, his brow furrowed deep in thought. He'd been my Captain for nearly six years and had no aspirations to move any further up the ladder. Maybe he thought he got enough grief in his current position and that maybe that would increase exponentially should he have been promoted. At fifty-six, with his considerable experience and ability, he was certainly more than qualified and it was common knowledge that he had declined a promotion a year ago. His years off the streets had seen him put on more than a little weight but his height compensated for this to a degree. Nevertheless, he often wore an expression that suggested his wife constantly nagged him to lose a little weight, something that his mild addiction to Twinkies wasn't going to help.

There was a knock on the door. Permission to enter granted, Detective Shawn Axon strode in, a look of bafflement on his face. 'I don't know what to say', he addressed the room in general. 'We're an hour in, and by now, you would have expected at least one or two flags to have shown up. But we've hit nothing. It's almost like she doesn't exist. No record of DNA on file, no record of passport being issued, no record of a driving licence, no social security, never voted; nothing.'

'You're sure this Andrew Caldwell guy you ran off the road had a sister?' Charlie mused. 'I mean, it was a long time ago, man. You sure?' Before I could answer, Williams' phone rang, and we sat in silence whilst he had a short conversation, scribbling notes on a pad. The desperate look on his face had given way somewhat, to a look of hope.

'We might have something', he informed us. 'There are no records at San Quentin of there ever having been a Sarah Caldwell there, but we have tracked down Dave Barnes. He was fired from San Quentin couple months ago; drunk on the job. Turns out he lost his home shortly after that and moved back to LA, now lives with his sister in Westwood, just off Rancho Park'.

'We got time to go get this guy?' I demanded. In less

than an hour and a half we had to be at 14th in West LA. Or at least we thought we did.

'Don't see any reason why not', Williams commanded. 'Rancho Park is fifteen minutes away from 14th, as long as you're there on time, why the fuck not?'

'And the SWAT team?' Charlie wanted to know.

'Will be en-route in less than half an hour. They've been through all the schematics, they know where they need to be. They'll be covert, of course. The media are already sniffing round this one and we don't want them causing any more hysteria than they already have'. Williams had long ago realised that he held most of the media, and certainly most of the press, in utter contempt. 'Get hold of Barnes', he said, tearing the address off his notepad. 'See if he can confirm if Caldwell ever had the pleasure of SQ. We want proof. Also, get a description. If she's at 14th at three when you guys get there, we'll see her'.

If lady luck was beginning to shine on us, and I prayed she was, then I asked two more things of her right now; That Dave Barnes was in when we got to Westwood, and, with it being early afternoon, that he was sober.

38

Arriving at Westwood, we were cautiously optimistic. I had to have faith that we had made a breakthrough here. We just needed Barnes to confirm that Caldwell had been a prisoner at San Quentin, which would give us more than we had ever had previously.

Although the majority of Westwood is a pleasant, kempt area, a section of it leaves a lot to be desired to say the least. One block had become run down and ramshackle, and is just as much home to drug dealers and prostitutes as it is to the law-abiding section of its community.

Approaching the address we had been given for Barnes' sister, I shook my head at how down-at-heel this area had actually become.

'Careful man', Charlie advised. 'Watch your back man, you never know'. If there was one thing today had taught us, it was to expect the unexpected. We found Barnes' address in the far corner of the shitty part of Westwood. No surprise there; I'd guessed as much. Striding purposefully towards the front door, I let Charlie take the lead.

After several moments, a grossly overweight woman, who I suspect was nearly fifty but looked closer to sixty, answered the door. 'What the fuck you want?' she demanded, revealing a hideously toothless expression. 'Who the fuck are you?'

The greeting put our backs up immediately. I never expect politeness as a given, but a little common courtesy doesn't go amiss. We both flashed our badges to identify ourselves. 'Is Dave Barnes at this address?' Charlie questioned as we barged past her into a dank and dark front room. 'We need to speak to him urgently'

'He's in bed is where he's at', at least she looked like being a little more co-operative now she knew we were PD.

'Go get him', he said ominously.

We waited patiently for Barnes to compose himself which took a few minutes. Still, when he appeared, he looked a mess; Stained white vest, jogging pants and nursing what looked like the hangover from hell. Five or six days of greyish stubble and tangled, matted hair aged him almost as much as his sister and he walked slowly, yet with little purpose. The stench of stale whisky hung in the air, which I figured was pretty much a permanent odour in the house. Christ, even if he confirmed what we wanted him to confirm, could we take his word for it?

'Dave Barnes?' I asked, to which he merely nodded as he sat down. 'I'm Detective Patton, this is Detective Holland', I gestured to Charlie, getting the formalities out of the way. 'We have some questions regarding your time at San Quentin, specifically the time you spent guarding the women's wing'.

'I maybe an alcoholic, Detectives, but even I cannot forget my time at San Quentin', he acknowledged. 'No matter how much I drink', he added, almost an afterthought, maybe trying to justify his addiction to us. 'Saw some sights in there, I can tell you'.

Although I could see what I was saying was taking a few seconds to sink in, he seemed cohesive enough, despite his appearance.

'Do you remember an inmate called Sarah Caldwell?' I cut straight to the chase. 'She would have been there around the time you lost your job?'

His response was immediate. 'Yeah, I remember her', he nodded. 'She was in there for a triple homicide or something'.

'You sure she was there?' Charlie asked.

'Sure I'm sure', Barnes answered. 'She was there the entire nine or ten months I was posted on her wing. Pretty easy gig, I'll tell you that. About a week before I got fired, she disappeared though. No idea where she went, but she sure as shit wasn't at San Quentin anymore'.

'How do we know your telling us the truth?' Although we were hearing what we needed to hear, I couldn't help but remain sceptical. 'You need to convince us'.

'Wait there Detectives', he seemed cautious. Barnes shuffled off to another room.

Just as I was about to lose patience with him and drag him back into the front room, he reappeared, holding a large box. 'Be in here somewhere', he mumbled. Looking up at us as he rifled through the contents, he told us that the box contained all his personal effects from the day he was fired, and he hadn't opened it since the day he left San Quentin for the final time.

'Ah I knew I still had it here somewhere.' he informed us, 'I was supposed to have submitted this during my final week there. I realised I'd got it when I was packing my shit up was hardly going to submit it after they'd fired me. The bastards.' He gestured to me to take the piece of paper he had found.

What I had in my hand was as close to confirmation that Sarah Caldwell was indeed a former inmate of San Quentin as we were going to get. It was an official list of all prisoners of Wing D, about ten months ago. On the list was prisoner number 188571; Sarah Caldwell.

Giving the sheet of paper to Charlie, I turned back to Dave Barnes. 'Listen', I said. 'We need a description of her, right now. Can you remember what she looks like?'

Barnes smiled, and pouring a drink with one shaky hand, he reached back into the box with the other. 'I can do better than that', he croaked. 'I've also got her photograph'.

I took it off him immediately and studied it intently. Without a doubt I could see the resemblance to Andrew Caldwell. She was actually kind of pretty, but her eyes were stone cold dead. I wondered for a moment what had made her that way, if there was something that triggered it; that started her along the path she had chosen for herself.

I noticed Barnes seemed a little distracted, as if he were trying to place a name or a face. I followed his line of vision to a small television that had been playing with no sound since we had arrived. 'Is there anything else you can tell us?' I quizzed.

Eventually, having searched his somewhat diluted memory bank for what seemed like an eternity, he gave us his reply. 'It may be nothing', he almost whispered, 'but the week before I was sacked, the *day* before Sarah Caldwell disappeared from San Quentin, I was called up to see Governor Tassiker.'

'Your point being?' Charlie barked.

'I saw him shake hands with a man leaving his office, just as I arrived. I hadn't seen him before but I definitely heard the man thank Tassiker for a favour. He even said something alone the lines of 'one less to worry about', or something.

I didn't have a clue what Barnes was on about, and even less of an idea if it was relevant or not, but decided to humour him. After all, we'd gotten more out of Barnes than we could have hoped for. 'And who was this guy who met Governor Tassiker then?'

'I don't know', Barnes shook his head and pointed at the television. 'But I'm certain that's him'.

I turned to look at the TV again, which was showing a news report on a man in a sharp suit and who had a charismatic smile that he flashed at the cameras three times in almost as many seconds. It was someone who was instantly recognisable, one of LA's most prominent individuals. It was District Attorney, Paul McCrane.

39

After we left Barnes, I couldn't shake the feeling that the last thing he had told us was vitally important. We now knew a couple of things; that Sarah Caldwell had indeed been an inmate at San Quentin, and that somehow she had been released and all trace of her having been there had been erased. That, to me, seemed like a major operation and not something that could just happen overnight. Someone must have wanted Caldwell out of there for some reason and that someone must have yielded considerable power. Like a District Attorney perhaps?

Upon hearing we had the confirmation from Barnes, the Captain pondered his next move. He was backing us to the hilt. He was sending Shawn Axon down to San Quentin to speak with Governor Tassiker. 'Axon's good,' he reassured us. 'It's gonna take him a while to get down there, but he'll be heading to the airport shortly. If there's anything to uncover down there, he'll find it'.

'Tassiker must have known', I agreed. 'It's here in black and white, Caldwell was definitely there'. I also ran the theory past him that Paul McCrane had been seen with Tassiker a day before Caldwell had disappeared.

'Could be co-incidental', he mused. 'Still, we have to

tread carefully here Patton'. McCrane's reputation preceded him; he was not someone to mess with. 'Are we saying that we think McCrane had something to do with freeing Caldwell?' he asked, 'Just so we're clear?'

'Listen Captain', I answered. 'The paper we have from Barnes is hard evidence. It's fact. That some alcoholic pisshead thinks he saw someone meeting with Tassiker several months ago; well that's an entirely different proposition', I continued. 'We're going to need a lot more than that, a lot more. Having said that, it can't hurt to look into it, can it? It's the best we've got!'

'If you're right, and I say *if* with extreme caution', Williams retorted, 'then we could start to piss on some big boys' bonfires here Patton', Williams cautioned. 'You ready for that?'

'Listen Captain', I affirmed. 'All that matters to me at the moment is stopping The Chemist. Stopping Sarah Caldwell'. I knew I spoke for Charlie too.

'OK then. Listen, I'll co-ordinate with Axon on this end with regard to Tassiker. You never know, he *might* confirm McCrane was there, although I suspect that even if he was, Tassiker won't give us that information that easily. You guys better get yourself to 14th. Swats are in position. I've circulated your description of Caldwell. Something tells me she'll have changed her appearance if she plans on being there though', he noted. I agreed with him there.

With Charlie driving, we made it to 14th with time to spare. It's hard to describe the feeling of not knowing whether or not you are being watched. We had no way of knowing for sure, but it was a feeling that crept up on me again as we ditched the car and headed for the crowded station on 14th in West Los Angeles.

40

LAST WEEK

Paul Britland-Jones' recent feeling of events spiralling out of control was one that he woke with the morning after his meeting with Conrad Conway, not that he'd had much sleep anyway. He'd awoken from a fitful dream that he forgot as soon as he opened his eyes at just after six o' clock, and spent the rest of the morning deliberating as to whether or not he should keep his midday appointment with the Senator.

Conway had made it quite clear the previous night that he did not give in to blackmail, and had made it even clearer that if his dalliances with prostitutes, or indeed anything remotely derogatory, was made public, then that was the last news story he would ever break. Britland-Jones had believed him. He'd been naïve to expect anything less. Still, desperate times called for desperate measures, and the journalistic instinct within him couldn't help but be intrigued with what Conway suggested. The Senator had then made him a curious offer. Once McCrane and Burr were disgraced and out of the picture, he would pay Britland-Jones the fifty grand he wanted. 'Call it an incentive for doing what I need you to do', he commanded. Arranging to meet in an underground car park in La Cienega, just outside of Ladera

Heights, the Senator had left last night's meeting with a busy night in prospect.

For his part, Conway had endured an equally restless night. Leaving The Bully, he'd mused how fortunate the unsuspecting journalist had been. If the events of that evening had not unfolded the way they had, if Hague had not aroused suspicion regarding Burr and McCrane, if Conway himself hadn't quickly manipulated Britland-Jones' pathetic blackmail attempt to his own ends; then someone this morning would have been reporting that the body of a young Englishman had been found floating face down in the water at Long Beach pier. Nothing would have been traced back to Conway himself. When pressed, he could always find an alibi for a certain place or a certain time; that had never been a problem. And if The Bully's threat that if any harm should come to him, someone else would leak the story? To hell with that! He'd just claim it was a vicious smear campaign by one of his rivals and that any evidence they had was circumstantial. His smooth tongue would steer round any sordid details and that would be that. It was a major hassle that he was keen to avoid, but if that had been the only option left open to him then he would have dealt with it regardless.

Conway had not driven straight home but to a row of small lockups in Korea town. It was the perfect place, maybe one of the only places in LA where he could go about any business unrecognised. The residents of Korea town didn't give a shit who he was and that suited him just fine.

Many years ago, just as he was starting to climb the political ladder, his mentor, Burton Wheeler, a sixty-four year old ex-politician in LA who had championed him from the beginning, had given him a sage piece of advice.

'Conrad', he'd warned. 'If I can offer you one thing, I offer you this'. Conway, young and eager to learn, had leaned closer, wanting to glean anything he could learn from this old man. 'Find somewhere secret. Somewhere that no-one knows about. Somewhere that only you know is there. Keep records, and by records I mean dirt, on everybody you work with; friends, enemies, even family if you have to. You never know when a friend will become an enemy and vice versa. You never know when something insignificant, something trivial, will become important. Important enough to save your career, maybe even important enough to save your life'.

Wheeler had passed away suddenly, a mere four days later. Deeply upset at the time, Conway had attended his cremation with his words of warning still echoing in his ears.

41

Charlie and I stood on 14th awaiting the arrival of the train thought we were required to board. We'd had no confirmation from The Chemist that we were on the right track with this, that wasn't her style though was it? For all I knew, we had completely misread the last instruction and were not even close to where we needed to be. I hoped for everyone's sake that we were right.

It was just building up to rush hour; it wouldn't be quite there for another hour or so, but it was late enough in the day for the station to be fairly crowded; people leaving work early, students with free periods at the end of their day and just general commuters, free for the day going about their various activities. Between us, we cased each individual, just in case Sarah Caldwell was here, watching us. I didn't think she was, but I couldn't say for sure. The photo that Barnes had given us was about as recent as we could hope for, but I was certain that she would have drastically altered her appearance by now. I did recognise one or two undercover officers that Williams had also placed at the scene; one dressed as a respectable business man in a suit complete with financial paper and briefcase, one as an everyday shopper, laden with bags which I knew would be dropped in an instant should anything happen here that required backup.

I looked up and surveyed the several tall buildings that overlooked the station. Although invisible to the naked eye, even with twenty-twenty vision, I knew the SWAT team was in place watching the station, covering our backs. It should have been reassuring but it gave me little comfort. In truth, I thought the chances of Caldwell being here were slim to none.

We had a couple of minutes before the train was due, which gave us a chance to contemplate what lay in store. 'How long do you think we're supposed to be on this train?' Charlie mused. 'We must get another instruction from somewhere?' The question hung in the air whilst I mulled over the possibilities. He was right, I mean, there had to be something on the train to give us our next move. How else were we supposed to progress?

The train arrived, on time, pulling slowly into the station. As agreed, we stood back until the last minute, watching passengers board and disembark at the platform, watching for anything out of the ordinary. The two undercover officers followed our lead; the business man pausing to look at his cell, the shopper seemingly struggling with her bags. Seeing nothing that caught our eye, we boarded with a few seconds to spare at the rear entrance, our plan being to methodically scout the train over the course of a few minutes. The two undercover officers would strategically station themselves near the front and middle doors, watching as passengers boarded during subsequent stops.

For the next half an hour or so, we remained vigilant as the train travelled from 14th down to through Lincoln and 4th, then took us along the coastline past Santa Monica Fairway and Victoria. We had walked the length of the train and doubled back to our original position, seeing nothing that warranted further attention; no-one suspicious and nothing that might have communicated our next move.

'We're just getting jerked around here man', was Charlie's summary and I was beginning to think he was right. Either that or we had completely fucked up on The Chemist's previous message, which I was also beginning to contemplate. We had less than fifteen hours to find Stella and we were standing here on this train doing seemingly nothing constructive to try and find her in time.

Just as the train left the Maxella stop, just past Venice, the train driver reactivated his intercom.

'Urgent message for Detectives Patton and Holland', came the voice. 'Urgent message for Detectives Patton and Holland: Please rendezvous by the lockers at Fisherman's Village, Marina Del Rey. I repeat, please rendezvous by the lockers at Fisherman's Village, Marina Del Rey'.

That stop was about five minutes away. We hurried up the train, needing to ask the driver a couple of quick questions before the stop. As we made our way, we passed the undercover officers; brief eye contact conveying that they should also get off at our stop. We found the driver who identified himself as Mike Livings. He told us that his head office had just radioed the message to him; that was all he could tell us. It would be easy enough for someone to contact the head office posing as someone from the LAPD, needing to get a message to detectives in the field I suppose, and I thought this the most likely scenario. Nevertheless, Charlie contacted Captain Williams again. We would need verification that this had been the case.

Stopping at Marina Del Rey, it was only a few minutes jog to Fisherman's Village which is a large man-made harbour; one of the largest in the world in fact. Where to begin with the lockers though? We'd agreed jogging up, that the most likely location was the boat rental and trip departure area, which seemed to be the main focal point for a lot of visitors and tourists.

As we ran down the gravel paths of the harbour entrance towards our destination, we could see several yachts and boats sailing around the harbour. A couple of school parties were also close to the harbour edge, kayaking and canoeing. The sound of laughter, splashing and the occasional roar as someone capsized or fell off was almost surreal as we arrived at the entrance. The lighthouse, the top of which had only been visible due to our approach level, now became visible in its entirety and it was a breathtaking sight to behold, however momentarily.

Flashing both our badges, we were granted immediate access, with no questions asked and a girl on one of the ticket windows told us where the lockers were. The two undercover officers followed, albeit at a discreet pace; the shopper had now ditched her bags.

As we got to the public locker area, we stood for a minute to get our breath back. 'I gotta get to the gym more often man', Charlie joked. 'This running thing's over-fucking-rated'. I nodded in agreement as we looked around. Nothing suspect caught my eye as we stood and watched; a few people came and went, putting personal items in lockers as they went on their way down to the harbour; a few people returning from a day's activities, laughing and joking, recounting the day's highs.

'Any ideas, man?' Charlie asked. 'We're here! We're rendezvousing!' I scratched my head; there must be something here, but what? We stood in silence for a good couple of minutes. I'm not sure if we were both thinking, or if we were waiting for something to happen. Suddenly, Charlie broke the silence. 'Hey man', he pointed. 'What about locker 316?'

'We've got a key', we said simultaneously. We'd been

through so much in the last few hours that I'd forgotten we had the key at all. So had Charlie, up until now. Just because 316 had held relevance in Stella's email address, didn't mean to say it was redundant. And that key had to be for something.

'You know what? I think you could be right there', I slapped Charlie on the back.

It only took us a few seconds to locate locker 316. Remembering the bomb that had gone off at Sutherland Boulevard this morning, I felt another shudder go down my spine. I retrieved the key from my pocket and gently slid it into the lock. It fitted. One small turn anti-clockwise and a click of the lock authenticated the key as a match

'Bingo', Charlie whispered, as with some trepidation, we opened locker 316.

42

Just as locker 316 was about to be opened, Sarah Caldwell pulled up again outside Belmont High School, barely six feet from where she had parked this morning. It was almost as if she had never been away. It had certainly been a hectic day! Her piercing blue eyes squinted slightly in the sunlight. Even now, after six months, she wasn't accustomed to seeing so much daylight. A shiver ran down her spine and she smiled, revealing teeth whiter and more even than they had any right to be, given the amount of time she had spent in prison. She was tingling with excitement now; she was here to snatch the grand prize. She was here for Katie Patton. This had always been the time she was going to make her move on Patton's daughter, that was partly why she had engineered the current game the way she had, to ensure that Patton and Holland were very much otherwise engaged at this specific time. She could always keep Katie stashed, securely and terrified, whilst the current game played out to its conclusion, that was not a problem. No problem at all; in fact she would rather enjoy that. Although she had a very detailed, time-specific plan for each game, her quick brain and natural instinct could adapt it at a seconds notice. She had shown that today when Patton and Holland had left that guy in the car on Sunset Junction. That had been too good an opportunity to pass up. Nevertheless, she couldn't take any chances here, and had to make extra-sure that Patton would be far, far away from Belmont High School today. Marina Del Rey was far enough.

Over the years she had come to understand that it is most people's natural instinct to trust a woman much more implicitly than to trust a man, and she had exploited these beliefs for her own gain numerous times, just as she was about to once again.

She knew Katie's route home probably almost as well as Katie herself. She has spent weeks observing, building up Katie's daily and weekly routine, and she knew that Katie would today leave her two friends at the corner of MacArthur Park at the edge of Westlake and head right on over to the library on the end of 6th Street. This was a particularly quiet stretch of the neighbourhood. Perfect for the intentions The Chemist had in mind.

Right on cue, she spotted Katie leaving for the day; chatting and laughing with her two best friends. Sarah Caldwell eased the car into first gear, crawling anonymously into the road, sixty yards or so behind her target. Patton had taken her brother away, it was only right she should take his daughter.

Several minutes later, Katie's friends departed, like she knew they would. The Chemist checked the time; she knew the library was a five minute walk from here.

Taking an alternative route, so she wouldn't be seen by Katie, she sped towards her destination. She would need to be there in less than two minutes, a couple of final touches to prepare.

She made it of course, as she knew she would, with time to spare. The street was also deserted, which would make it all the easier.

She spotted Katie in her rear view mirror and, reaching under the passenger seat, pulled out a map of Los Angeles, winding her window down simultaneously. Looking suitably confused, she studied the map; her peripheral vision confirming Katie was getting closer and closer. Then, just as Katie was a couple of yards behind the car, she shook her head vigorously and let out an audible sigh. It seemed as though her heart stopped beating; would Katie take the bait? No reason why she shouldn't. She imagined she looked like she could pass for the mother of one of Katie's friends, someone who Katie would trust without thinking.

'Excuse me?'

Oh she had! How perfect! That would make things so much simpler. Still, The Chemist pretended not to hear.

'Excuse me?' Katie repeated. 'Are you lost? Can I help you?'

'Oh', Sarah turned her head, looking startled. 'Hey there, honey', she lifted the map up looking exasperated. 'Yeah, I'm lost! Husband wanted to give me directions, but I wouldn't have it!'

Katie smiled. 'Where are you going? Maybe I know it?'

'Well I'm looking for El Pollo Loco, it's a Mexican restaurant. Should have been meeting my husband there twenty minutes ago. My cell's died too, can't even call him to give me the directions now', Caldwell smiled back. 'Much as I'd hate to admit I was lost', she added.

'Oh I do know it', Katie replied, 'It's on North Street!' The look on Sarah's face was convincingly blank.

'I'm afraid I don't really know this part of LA very well dear', she said. 'Could you show me on the map here?'

'Of course I can', Katie nodded, 'No problem'.

As Katie leant in to the car to point out North Street on the map, Caldwell reached for an innocent looking cloth on the passenger seat. Katie hadn't been close enough to smell the pungent chloroform that The Chemist had doused the cloth with not two minutes before.

Perusing the map, Katie could see exactly where North Street was. 'It's right there, just past ....'

Sarah Caldwell dropped the map, and brought her right hand up to keep Katie's head firmly in place, reaching for the cloth with her left. Bringing it up to Katie's mouth and nose, Katie tried to struggle but her assailant was too strong, and the chloroform too overpowering. Her body went limp, and Sarah Caldwell was like lightening. She dragged Katie through the window and manoeuvred her into the passenger seat. Reaching into the glove box, she quickly bound Katie's legs, and tied her hands behind her back, before finally fastening the seatbelt. Now she just looked like a passenger who had fallen asleep. Just perfect!

Glancing around, the street had remained deserted. Katie's entire interaction with The Chemist, from conversation to capture, had lasted less then ninety seconds.

She had done it! She had got Katie Patton. A feeling of immense excitement washed over her like a tidal wave. She couldn't wait for Patton to find out she had his daughter. Despite all the time she had invested in preparing the current game, she wondered for a minute whether or not she should abandon that game, and start this one straight away. She hadn't thought of that before, but the excitement of snatching Katie was all consuming. Maybe she should let Detective Patton decide?

Shifting the car into reverse, The Chemist picked up her cell, complete with voice digitiser, and dialled a number she had memorised long ago.

'Hello, LAPD?' a voice greeted. How may I direct your call?'

'Detective Patton, please'.

'I'm sorry he's unavailable at the moment'.

'Patch me through bitch', The Chemist snapped. 'He'll want to take this call, wherever he is. Tell him that The Chemist wants to speak to him again'.

43

LAST WEEK

Telling his editor that he was chasing a big story, actually partially true this time, Britland-Jones descended to the lowest level of the agreed meeting place; the car park in La Cienega. It was extremely dark; the car par lighting offering only a cursory illumination. It was also early enough in the day for the bottom level to be virtually empty which was probably why the Senator had picked it as a meeting place to begin with. Glancing in the mirror as he parked, he noticed how bloodshot his eyes were and he resolved to get a good nights sleep that evening. Conway had told him just to remain parked in the corner furthest from the entrance and that he would find him.

For twenty minutes, The Bully waited impatiently, swearing that if the Senator failed to turn up, he would forget the arrangement and throw together a quick story about the Senator and his night time activities that would be front page news as quickly as next morning's early edition. Just as he was about to restart the ignition, having grown tired of waiting, a black Bentley pulled out of the shadows and parked in front of him, blocking his exit. As the electric window glided down silently, Britland-Jones saw the Senator's stony face. He noted that at least Conway looked like he'd had a similar amount of sleep to himself which was a small consolation.

'Get in', Conway motioned, 'and bring your things'. By 'things', Britland-Jones knew he meant 'all the dirt you have on me'. He'd been in two minds whether to bring it all, or hold one or two things back, just in case. In truth though, whilst he had a considerable amount of material, he didn't have quite as much as he suspected Conway thought he did, so he brought it all. Besides, if Conway thought he was holding anything back, he could turn nasty. Up close and personal last night, he'd seemed as much of a frightening proposition as Bobby Hambel, to whom he owed the fifty grand in the first place. Gathering the lose sheets of paper and photographs off his seat into a folder, he made his way cautiously to the Bentley and got in on the passenger side.

'Is it all there?' Conway wanted to know.

'It's all there, all I have on you', he replied, hoping now that Conway believed him.

'If it's not, and I find out it's not, the're will be severe repercussions, you do realise that?' Conway's voice was calm; almost unnerving.

'I understand', he replied. 'It's all there. What have you got for me? And why do you want McCrane and Burr out of the picture?'

'The 'why' is none of your concern', laughed the Senator, 'but what I have got for you is enough to cause some serious questions to be asked of the City Attorney and DA. The deal I'm giving you has got a time limit on it, just so you know'.

'What's the deal, and how long have I got?' he questioned.

'I need you to break a story, any story you like, I don't really give a fuck. There's enough there. A story that will lead to the arrest of both Jameson Burr and Paul McCrane.

I also need your word', Conway paused, realising the absurdity of asking a journalist for his word, 'that you will not look to investigate anything that should happen to them subsequent to their arrest'. Conway knew that when they were arrested, even with the increased security their arrests would warrant, he could pay someone to ensure both McCrane and Burr met with an unexpected knife to the throat. In everyday life, as McCrane and Burr went about their business, he wasn't sure he could get someone close enough to them to carry out his wishes; hence this deal with The Bully.

'I need the story to break within seventy-two hours, but not within the next twenty-four. I will call you, at your office, sometime tomorrow afternoon, so be there! I'll either give you the green light, or I'll call the whole thing off'. This news slightly alarmed Britland-Jones.

'If you call the whole thing off, then I've got nothing', he almost stuttered. 'My silence will have a price, Senator'. Conway stared long and hard at the journalist for several seconds, considering his response.

He'd thought about this long and hard; most of last night in fact. He still wasn't sure of McCrane and Burrs' agenda, if they had one at all. He had needed to act, and act fast though, so decided to get the wheels of this plan in motion now. This way, he would have a day to do some further digging of his own, to see what he could come up with. If his digging unearthed something that needed to be taken care of, like his affair with Burr's wife being exposed, then he would have this plan in place. If, however, he decided that no further action was needed on his part, he could simply cancel the whole thing.

'Ten grand', he countered. 'Non-negotiable'. Ten grand? Well maybe Bobby Hambel would take that as a down payment. Ten grand was better than nothing.

'Ten grand it is', accepted Britland-Jones. 'So what have you got for me then?' Conrad reached into the back seat of the Bentley and picked up a thick file.

'This', he announced, 'has details of various illegal activities over the past three years undertaken by McCrane and Burr'. Britland-Jones knew this could be potentially explosive material.

'Like what?' he asked, almost wanting to snatch the folder from the Senators' grasp to see for himself.

'I'm sure you will peruse the file at your leisure', Conway smiled, 'but just to give you a flavour; bribes given out, bribes received; things of that nature and that's just for starters'.

Britland-Jones took the file off him, almost gratefully. 'What now?' he questioned.

'What now?' Conway sneered, 'Is that you get the fuck out of my car'. He still hadn't forgotten that this piece of shit had tried to blackmail him in the first place. Maybe, when the threat of McCrane and Burr had been nullified, he'd have to re-visit The Bully. 'Now!'

The tone of Conway's voice suggested that Britland-Jones shouldn't wait to be asked twice.

Back in his car, he put the light on and had a preliminary flick through the file he'd just been given. His eyes lit up as he read. The Senator had been right, there was certainly plenty there.

Conrad Conway merely re-started the engine of the Bentley and drove out of the car park, never looking back to see what Britland-Jones was doing. He had other meetings to attend to today, but he had an important phone call to make first to one of the private investigators he had on his payroll. He'd awoken Nathan Morris in the early hours of the morning with a job for him. Morris, unable to refuse the Senator's orders due to the fact that Conway knew about his predilection for borderline underage girls but had kept quiet thus far, had asked for nine or ten hours to complete what was asked of him. Conway had replied that nine hours was acceptable and it was now time to ensure that Morris had kept his promise. Given the information he had on Morris, he was sure that Morris would be done by now.

44

On the morning of the underground meeting between Conway and Britland-Jones, Jameson Burr was working from home, catching up on some paperwork. He'd got rather a lot to do before he made his way to court this afternoon, but he would make time to fit in his business with Paul McCrane later in the morning, no doubt about that.

Settling in for a long session, overlooking several prepared prosecutions by his junior staff, his mind occasionally wandered to the timetable of events he and McCrane had drawn up regarding Senator Conway's upcoming murder by 'The Chemist'. They had initially decided on five days from now but he had a strong feeling, hardly an epiphany but a strong feeling nevertheless, that it should happen sooner than agreed. He would sort that out later. For now, he was otherwise engaged; two of these prosecutions were happening this afternoon; he had meant to look at them last night but time had run away from him and his wife had dragged him to some God-awful charity dinner that had been the absolute pits. All the time, he'd thought about Conway and his wife. He was sure that his wife didn't suspect he knew anything. Once Conway had been taken care of he would deal with her alright. He didn't know how yet but she would pay too.

Looking over the imminent cases, he spotted something that warranted a call to the junior who had prepared it; a relatively new junior Becky Gardener who had joined his staff three months ago. She'd made a promising start.

Deciding it was definitely too early for a scotch, he refilled his coffee mug and looked up Becky's cell number. It wasn't a number he'd committed to memory just yet but he had a feeling he might do soon. Maybe he'd pay his wife back in kind.

'Hello, Mr. Burr', she answered after a few seconds. She always sounded in awe when she spoke to him, like she couldn't believe she actually worked for him. He liked that. A couple of one-to-one's and a vague promise of special career advancement and he had a feeling she would sleep with him without so much as a second thought.

'Ms. Gardener, good morning', he replied, 'I just have a couple of ..'. Before Burr could finish his sentence, the phone line went dead. 'What the hell?' he muttered to himself. After trying the phone a couple more times, he realised it was fruitless and went to check the phone in the adjoining room; the study. He found that line was also dead. 'Goddamn telephone company', he said out loud then shouted at the top of his voice 'Marcia! Marcia!'

Before long, his cleaner knocked on the door and was ordered to call the telephone company from her own cell. 'Tell them I need a line back on ASAP, and don't take no for an answer!' he shouted several seconds after she had closed the door.

After calling Becky back his own cell, he had settled himself back into an undisturbed silence for half an hour or so, when his cleaner reappeared, a scruffy looking engineer standing behind her.

'This gentleman is here from the telephone company',

she announced. Without waiting for an invitation, the engineer strode past her, into the middle of the room.

'We've had some problems this morning with the all the telephones in this area', he confirmed. 'Most are back on but there are several households that haven't come back on-line for some reason. Damn company wants us door to door, checking each and every one, so here we are! Got a hell of a day ahead I can tell you, got another thirty house calls after this one'

'I suppose you have some ID?' Burr enquired, directing his question to neither the engineer, nor Marcia who really should have already checked, in particular.

'Of course', the engineer offered his ID to Burr. Quickly scanning its credentials, it seemed in order.

'So, what do you need to do?' Burr wanted to know. 'Will this take long? I have rather a lot of work to do here'.

'Should only take five minutes or so sir', the engineer replied. 'We just have to check the connections on all the phone lines in the houses that aren't yet back on. Did the original fault occur in here sir?'

'Indeed it did', said Burr irately, cursing the interruption to his work. 'Well, as quickly as you can then', he instructed, waving a cursory hand in the engineers direction and returning his attention back to his work.

The engineer proceeded to check all the phones in the house, first the three downstairs, followed by the two upstairs. Burr didn't really pay much attention, immersing himself back in the upcoming court cases. If he had been more vigilant, even then he would have struggled to notice that the engineer slipped a small device no bigger than a sim card on the underside of a table or chair near each phone receiver, a blink of an eye and you would have missed the planting of each device.

As he made his way back downstairs, the final device

discreetly installed, Nathan Morris couldn't help but be pleased; this had gone extremely smoothly indeed. Each device he laid would enable him to record and monitor all conversations between the caller and receiver. The devices would even pick up the majority of cell conversation, given the right frequency. 'All checked sir', he popped his head back into Burr's office. 'Should be back on in about five minutes; just have to re-boot the system downtown!' Complete fabrication but how would Burr know? Burr didn't even look up from his work and Marcia showed Morris to the door.

'Thank you for coming so quickly', she said. 'He was getting a bit irritable!'

'No problem', he called back, already half way down the drive way.

Just as he'd manually restored Burr's phone lines and was about to climb into his unmarked van a hundred yards or so down from the house, he noticed an AT&T van pull into view and allowed himself a wry smile; that was the actual telephone company responding to the call made by the cleaner. He hoped that Burr and the cleaner would assume that the company had just mistakenly sent two engineers.

He climbed into the back of the van and fired up his communications set up. The Senator hadn't told him what exactly he was listening for, but that he would know it when he heard it.

A couple of hours in, and a few calls made by Burr had confirmed that everything was working. He'd even picked up a call by the cleaner from upstairs telling someone that she would try to fake illness for an early finish. The cheek of it! His cell began to ring. 'Are we set up?' a voice asked.

'Indeed we are', he replied, knowing better than to refer to the caller by name.

'Keep me informed'.

'Of course'. He hoped this favour to Senator Conway would keep him off his back for a few months to come.

45

Well at least the locker hadn't exploded, which was something at least. That had been my first thought when we had eased the locker door open and peered inside, wondering what it contained; whether it held the key to Stella's location or whether it was just another small step towards recovering the poor girl before it was too late. As it turned out, much to my disbelief, it would be both.

Reaching inside, I pulled out a familiar looking envelope, which I knew would contain our next instructions. There was nothing else in the locker though, and I couldn't help but feel a little deflated. I was sure that the locker would have contained something else. But who knows? This envelope could contain the information that would lead us to Stella. Or, in reality, we could be just as far from finding her as we were this morning. All I knew was that we only had The Chemist's word that if we continued to follow the instructions we would find her in time. That was by no means a guarantee though was it?

Closing the locker door, I handed the envelope to Charlie. 'Your turn', I instructed, 'Go ahead, open it'. My partner took the envelope with a grim look on his face; a look that remained once he'd opened it, albeit combined with a look of puzzlement.

'*11am last Sunday, going deeper underground with a Saint in Batman reversed*', he read aloud. 'Well that's very helpful', he added. 'Don't suppose anything immediately springs to mind?'

I shook my head, I hadn't got a clue what that meant. We sat down on one of the benches near the lockers, reading the line over and over, as several children from a school party re-appeared in the locker area, running around excitedly. I'd been stumped several times today, but never more so than now. As much as I hated to admit it, I was completely baffled by that one, and so was Charlie.

'Time to phone it in, I guess', Charlie announced, realising we were getting nowhere. 'Hopefully the guys can decipher this one as well'.

Just as I was about to call in it, my cell rang again.

Having spoken to The Chemist once already today, I wasn't expecting to talk to her again. Not quite so soon anyway. When the LAPD switchboard operator rang me to patch her through, I got a bad feeling immediately. A feeling that maybe she was altering her plans, that maybe she was improvising, and that was most certainly not a good thought. Turned out I was going to be offered a hell of a choice.

'Twice in one day, I'm honoured', I said, putting the phone on loudspeaker so Charlie could be privy to the conversation. Although we now knew the identity of The Chemist, I wasn't giving that away. Not yet. I would play that card when the time was right.

'You should be'. It was the same robotic voice. 'It's not like me to get so up close and personal so frequently, but you should know, you need to know, I'm changing the game'.

As much as I'd guessed this was an unscheduled call, that had been unexpected. I glanced over at Charlie, not quite sure how this was going to unfold.

'I'm giving you a choice'. I was almost holding my breath.

'And what choice is that?' I asked.

'Do you want Stella back?' The question hung in the air, lingering for what seemed like an eternity before I managed to answer.

'Of course we do', I stated the obvious. 'What's the catch?' I knew this wasn't going to be simple.

'You have two choices. Number one; I'll give you Stella back, alive'. Well that sounded alright to me. 'But we begin game number four immediately.'

'What's the second choice?'

'You place trust in your ability to catch me, and pray you do before Stella dies; in which case, we will go onto game number four regardless'.

'I'd like to give that fucker a third option', Charlie growled. 'That we take their ass down.

'Tell Detective Holland that is unlikely to happen'. I didn't need to; Charlie had heard that for himself.

If ever I'd been in a catch-22 situation, this was it. On one hand, getting Stella back would condemn some other poor girl to one of The Chemist's games. On the other hand, we hadn't turned up anything yet on Sarah Caldwell, apart from her name and a link to San Quentin. Our chances of getting to Stella before six a.m. were looking slimmer and slimmer as the hours ticked away. If we took Caldwell at her word, and took option one, at least we would get Stella back and then we would just be in the same situation as we were now, but with more time to get to girl number four. Even so, I shuddered at the thought that we would have to go through this all over again; that we would have to start from scratch chasing yet another victim.

'You have thirty seconds to make your decision, starting now'.

Taking The Chemist off speaker, I looked at Charlie. 'Well it's flip a coin time', he said. 'Either way, we're fucked so far. I say let's get the girl back and go onto game four. In the mean time, let's hope we get something on Caldwell that can lead us to her.' He held his hands up shaking his head. 'What do you reckon Patton?'

'I'm thinking pretty much the same,' I told him. 'So option one then?'

'Yeah, why not? Like I said, either way man, either way'.

Putting Sarah Caldwell back on speaker, I told her our decision. 'Give us Stella. But just so as you know; we're coming for you.' Given what we had on her at the present time, it was an empty threat. I could hear what sounded like laughter down the phone, but given the distortion, it sounded more like heavy breathing.

'Oh Detective Patton', the voice rasped. 'I was hoping you would choose that one.'

Then the phone went dead. Why did I get the feeling we had just made the wrong choice?

46

LAST WEEK

The majority of his work done and satisfied that the afternoons court proceedings would go in his team's favour, Jameson Burr poured himself that well deserved drink. Just the one mind, he'd reward himself with another couple after the day's court session. Despite the interruptions from that pesky telephone engineer this morning, he'd made good time with his paperwork, and had half an hour or so before he had to leave the house. As had often been the case over the last few days when he hadn't been occupied with work, he turned his attention once again to the imminent demise of Senator Conrad Conway. McCrane had procured the Clozapone from an unnamed, yet an assured reliable, source. Burr had provided the individual who would carry out the attack in five days; an individual named Daryl Walls who was one of those rare junkies that remained lucid at all times, no matter what poison he'd injected himself with that morning. An individual that Burr knew he could put in prison at the drop of a hat, no questions asked. He likened Walls to Sherlock Holmes in that narcotics only seemed to enhance his particular line of work; a somewhat different line of work to Conan-Doyle's fictional detective, yet the similarity there remained. Walls had done several jobs for him over the last few years and had never let him down, despite his addiction to class A drugs. He knew that if Walls was given sufficient notice and a specific way to carry out a task, such as injecting someone with Clozapone then suffocating them, he would complete it with ruthless efficiency. As a reward, Walls would receive five thousand dollars and get to keep walking the streets of Los Angeles as an added bonus, at least until Burr and McCrane decided otherwise.

Still, the fact that five days was such a long time away nagged him. A lot could happen in five days; and after looking at the Senator's schedule for this week that he'd also managed to acquire, he thought he spied an opportunity the day after tomorrow, which was a much more pleasing timescale. Conway needed to pay for what he'd done as soon as possible.

Not that he needed McCrane's permission but he thought it best to verify his newly proposed course of action with the DA. He would be pissed if he wasn't at least consulted given the level of loyalty he had shown him in helping him deal with this problem. Even he wasn't keen to add Paul McCrane to his list of enemies.

Picking up the office phone, he managed to reach the District Attorney within five minutes. Not many people in LA could do that!

'Mr. Pacino, a pleasure', greeted McCrane; the Animi's Oscar winner pseudonyms second nature to him after all these months.

'Likewise, Mr. Washington, likewise', Burr responded.

'And what can I do for you, this fine afternoon?'

'I've been thinking about our proposed schedule for our good friend Mr. Brando. I think it should be sooner'.

'Maybe it should', agreed McCrane, 'anything in mind?'

'Well I've been looking at his schedule', Burr continued.

'There is one particular window I can see the day after tomorrow. He's got meetings between seven and ten in the morning but then has a quick nine holes planned between half ten and half twelve. I happen to know that out of habit, he never packs his clubs in the morning before he leaves for the day. I think a while ago, he forgot his clubs on his way out one morning, came back to get them and hit a hole in one that afternoon. He does it now every time out of superstition. That would be an ideal opportunity'.

'Can our man deliver in that time?' McCrane wanted to know if Walls could be contacted and briefed sufficiently with a new time structure.

'I'm sure he can', confirmed Burr, 'never been a problem in the past has it?'

'Mmm, you right there at least. Yes, on reflection I think the sooner the better. I sense you want this thing done and dusted and I can't say I blame you for that. The day after tomorrow you say?'

'I'm sure we can get to him then and I'm sure he will take out Mr. Brando as instructed'.

'Well in that case, I'll leave it in your capable hands, Mr. Pacino. I'll speak to you soon'.

Hanging up to McCrane, but still cradling the receiver in one hand, Burr dialled another number. Walls, after less than a minute answered. 'Hello?' he said softy. It was difficult to tell whether Walls was under the influence of drugs or not, such was his composure when he was high.

'There's been a change of plan', Burr instructed. 'It's going to be the day after tomorrow instead'.

'Cool', Walls responded.

'I'll send you the information in the usual manner'.

'No problem'.

Satisfied with the new schedule, Burr readied himself for court. He would drop the information into Walls on his way home tonight. He looked in the mirror, fastening the top button of his white Armani shirt and straightening his tie. 'Bye bye Senator', he mouthed. 'It was nice to know you'.

A hundred yards or so down the road, Morris thought he'd heard what he'd been instructed to uncover. Conway had told him that any conversation referring to him would be under the pseudonym Mr. Brando. Playing the tape of the conversation back, it was difficult to know what Burr and the guy on the other end of the phone were talking about. The part about taking out Mr. Brando leapt out though as being particularly relevant! He was sure the Senator needed to know about that! Although he knew he'd be here for the rest of the day, cooped up in cramped, hot conditions, he called the Senator with his news.

'It's me', he said 'I think there's something you should hear'. Morris played the tape to Conway over the phone. Even though, in transmission in this way, the quality of the recording lessened, it was more than enough for Conway's suspicions to be confirmed. He had to concede, that had been fast work by Morris.

'Stay on it', he simply instructed. 'Keep me informed'.

Following his conversation with Morris, Conway sat at his desk, shaking ever so slightly, regretting beginning his affair with Burr's wife once again; as enjoyable as it had been at the time. His suspicions seem to have been warranted. The day after tomorrow was it then, according to Burr? He'd see about that.

Picking up his own phone, he dialled the LA Times. After being put on hold for a couple of minutes, a now familiar voice greeted him. 'Britland-Jones here'.

'Green light', he authorised, then hung up. By tomorrow night, the journalist should have some story on Burr and McCrane; something nice and juicy for the media to feed off. Not even Robert Farrington would be able to dilute the story sufficiently for no damage to be caused. As for the day after tomorrow? Whoever they were sending to kill him was going to have a hell of a shock, he guaranteed it.

47

Detective Shawn Axon arrived at San Quentin only a couple of hours after being dispatched by Captain Williams. The Captain had pulled in a couple of favours to arrange express transportation for him, knowing that they didn't have any time to waste, and that every minute that passed, a young girl was potentially a minute closer to her death.

Axon had just been coming off shift as Williams had rallied his department. He'd been in the LAPD for a few years, having transferred from Washington DC on what was supposed to be a temporary inter-state secondment. As one of Washington's most successful members of their Armed Robbery division, he'd naturally been assigned a similar role in Los Angeles. He'd made an immediate impact by capturing a group of bank robbers who'd called themselves 'The Jackrabbits' who had named themselves after the notorious bank robber John Dillinger; a pioneer of the bank robbery during the 1930's Depression era of mid-western America. The Jackrabbits had robbed various banks across the state before Axon, in his first month in Los Angeles, had engineered their takedown, granting him immediate notoriety with the media and his new colleagues at the LAPD alike.

Just like a vast proportion of LA, he'd been following the media's coverage of The Chemist with interest, only with the added insight of being a member of the LAPD. He knew first hand that the whole of the PD wanted The Chemist caught; well he had seen as much over the last few weeks so when news had come through that they might have an ID, despite just coming off a twelve hour shift, he'd been the first to volunteer his services in trying to dig up any information on Sarah Caldwell. Contacting his various sources across the state, with a depressing lack of success, he'd been as frustrated as anybody that Caldwell seemed to be a ghost; that there was no record of her anywhere. When Patton and Holland confirmed a possible link to San Quentin, he'd volunteered once more to take that lead, knowing Patton and Holland both had to remain in LA to play The Chemist's game. Having worked several divisions prior to bank robbery in Washington, he was also more than qualified to take responsibility for this assignment. Williams had verified that Governor Sebastian Tassiker was present at San Quentin that day, and Tassiker had been more than accommodating in granting the LAPD an audience. Williams had been purposefully vague on the phone, never once mentioning The Chemist, Sarah Caldwell or Paul McCrane, only saying that they had a few questions about a former inmate who may now be in Los Angeles. 'See what his reaction is when you mention Sarah Caldwell', Williams had instructed. 'Dig up anything you can, see if there's anything to substantiate what we have from Barnes'.

He'd been waiting outside Tassiker's office for several minutes, going over his line of questioning in his head. He had no warrant that would give him authority to do anything other than question Tassiker; Captain Williams hadn't even applied for one as the information they had was tenuous as best. There was no way one would have been granted so why waste their time? With this in mind, Axon knew how he went about questioning the governor would be the key, mindful of the fact that Tassiker could quite simply refuse to answer any questions and stonewall him if he wanted to.

'Governor Tassiker will see you now', said the pretty blond secretary that oversaw the day to day office amenities. Shame he wasn't local, thought Axon, or he would have tried to get her number.

He was shown into the governor's office, a smile reciprocated by the secretary suggesting that if indeed he'd asked for her number, she might have given it to him. The office itself was pretty much as he had suspected it would be; lots of literature adorned the bookshelves, and several awards both for the prison and for Tassiker personally, hung proudly on the adjoining wall. 'Detective Axon', greeted Tassiker, hand outstretched.

'Governor', Axon acknowledged, shaking his hand then sitting in one of the chairs as Tassiker indicated that he should. 'Thank you for seeing me at such short notice'. Tassiker appeared to be in his early fifty's, silver hair and greying beard, dressed in a made-to-measure suit, he looked every bit as distinguished as Axon had imagined. He looked like an influential man with powerful friends. Was one of them LA District Attorney Paul McCrane, he wondered?

'Not at all', the governor smiled, 'always happy to accommodate the police where I can. After all, we are in the same line of work aren't we?'

'Indeed we are', replied Axon, keen to establish some common ground with the governor, hoping he would lower his guard.

'So how can I be of assistance to you Detective? Your Captain informed me you may have a former inmate of San Quentin in Los Angeles causing some trouble. I must say',

Tassiker continued, looking somewhat perplexed, 'it might have been an idea to tell me who are looking for over the telephone. I'm sure we could have had something ready for you on your arrival!'

Axon had been ready for this question. 'Absolutely', he agreed. 'The thing is, we've only just had confirmation ourselves, literally as I arrived here. Wouldn't want to have wasted your time, I can imagine you have plenty to do,' he flattered. 'The Captain thought it would be prudent to have me in transit, should the confirmation arise, which as I said, it only just has', he clarified. Tassiker seemed to accept this as an explanation.

'So then, Detective', Tassiker leaned closer over his desk. 'May I ask who this inmate is that you are so interested in?'

Taking a deep breath, Axon focussed intently on the governor's face, ready to look for any degree of familiarity when he uttered his next words. 'The former inmate we need information on is Sarah Caldwell'.

48

Even though we thought we'd just struck some sort of deal with The Chemist, albeit on her terms, I wondered whether we could take Sarah Caldwell at her word. I relayed the conversation to Captain Williams, along with the contents of the latest envelope. 'Well I guess we wait and see if The Chemist gives us Stella back', he assessed. 'In the mean-time, until we find her alive and well, then the envelope is all we have to go on, we should carry on following the trail'. I had to agree with him there. What were we going to do? Just stand around until Caldwell maybe gave us Stella back? 'That being said', he continued, 'We need to figure out this latest communication. You guys might as well head back to base until we have. Agent Balfer has just arrived so I could do with you bringing him up to speed. As soon as we figure out where you need to go from here, you go. Until then, I suggest you try and figure out why Caldwell has changed her plans'.

'So are we sure that Sarah Caldwell *is* The Chemist then? Has there been anything from Axon?' I wanted to know.

'He's with Tassiker now, that's all I've got. As for are we sure it's Caldwell? Well how *can* we be sure? It's a name and the circumstances fit, what can I say?'

'Copy that', I replied. 'See you soon Captain'.

'Quantico time', I said turning to Charlie, relaying that Agent Balfer was now at the PD.

It took us less than half an hour to get back to the station. We'd heard nothing during the journey that suggested anyone there had interpreted The Chemist's latest message; our journey being equally as fruitless on that score.

Back in the incident room, there was a buzz as the people there were trying to work out what 'going deeper underground with a Saint' and 'Batman reversed' could possibly mean.

'We got anything yet?' I greeted Captain Williams.

'Not a thing', he shook his head. 'Patton, Holland; I'd like you to meet Agent Balfer from the FBI'.

We duly brought the agent up to speed. He'd been given the outline by Williams, but we filled in the detail, for my part also recounting my suspected link with Sarah Caldwell, and her possible reasons for targeting me. He assured us he was only here to assist us, in any way he could and that he was by no means here to take over the investigation. To that end, he seemed like a stand up guy. I've had cases in the past where FBI involvement pretty much signals the end of your control of the case but that didn't seem how it was going to go here.

'Guys, this is your case; you're the best shot we have of catching The Chemist. I'm here to offer you the FBI's help and if need be, their resources', he instructed. 'Anything you need, just say the word. Quantico estimates that there are about thirty to forty serial killers currently operating in the United States today. We certainly don't need another one'.

I have to say that that statistic blew me away. It was almost beyond comprehension to learn that there could be that many serial killers currently active, un-captured, roaming the various states of our country.

'Fuck me man, what are you guys doing up there?'

Charlie joked.

'Same as you guys down here', Balfer countered. 'We're doing what we can!'

'There is one thing you could do for us', I suggested. 'Run Caldwell, San Quentin and Paul McCrane through FBI intelligence, see if there's any link, anything you can come up with?'

'Consider it done', Balfer agreed. 'Give me twenty minutes, I'll see what I can do', he promised.

'So do you think Caldwell's gonna give us Stella?' Charlie asked as we once again stared at the latest message, having settled into a couple of chairs in the corridor just outside the incident room.

'Who knows?' I responded. 'Something must have happened to make her phone us a second time. I'm pretty sure that wasn't her original intention'. I slumped back in the chair, rubbing my eyes. I was long over the effects of the several beers I'd drunk last night, but there was no escaping the fact that I'd only had an hours sleep the night before. I couldn't even begin to guess when I'd next see my bed. 'Batman reversed?' I asked again out loud. 'Come on, think damn it'. I was talking to myself as much as Charlie. Even with the promise of Stella's safe return, we couldn't take the chance of this trail going cold.

Just as I was feeling my eyes close, with Charlie's voice echoing in my ears, repeating 'Batman' and 'Saints', I heard an unfamiliar voice. 'Excuse me, Detective?'

I looked up and saw one of the station's repair guys hovering expectantly. 'Yeah, what can I do for you?' I asked. The guy looked almost embarrassed to say anything.

'Erm, I overheard you guys talking about Batman, like you had some kind of riddle?'

'Overheard? How you overhear?' Charlie was naturally suspicious.

'They got me up here working on your air-con. Thing's older than I am and I'm getting pretty old', he chuckled. At this point, having had no further communication from The Chemist, I was willing to listen to anyone's ideas. Even one of the contractors.

'Well what you got for us Marvin?' I asked, noticing his name tag on his boiler suit.

'It's just that I overheard you guys talking about Batman reversed and I used to be a big fan of Batman back in the seventies you know?'

'What's your point?' Charlie asked.

'It's just that, hey I read the news you know, I'm no detective but I know you're after that Chemist motherfucker and I know he got you running around in circles. Hell, I watch Farrington news, just like everybody else does. We got TV, even on my goddamn wages'.

'Again, your point?' Charlie repeated, fearing this was just an opportune rant on the part of the engineer.

'Well I got a nephew works down at a school as a cleaner, good kid, takes after his uncle', he was skirting round any point that he may have, much to Charlie's annoyance, but I indulged him regardless.

'And where does he work then Marvin?'

'Well that's the thing Detective. He works down at a school in West Adams and Adam West played the Batman on the TV show didn't he? You want your Chemist, there's your next step. There's your Batman reversed! What you think about that?'

Charlie and I both looked at each other. As much as it pained me to admit; it was as solid as anything that the various officials working the case, us included, had managed to come up with in the last half an hour, and West Adams was about the same distance from Rancho Park as Marina Del Rey was, just in a different direction; the logistics were certainly there.

We stormed back into the incident room, telling Marvin to wait where he was, and commandeered the nearest computer terminal. Charlie typed in 'West Adams' to the LAPD search engine and cross referenced it with 'Saints'. Two matches came back: Mount St. Mary's College and St. John's Cathedral.

'Last Sunday', I repeated. 'The message was about 'Last Sunday'. The college wouldn't be open would it?'

'Must be St. John's then?' it was a question from Charlie as much as it was a statement of belief. 'What do you reckon then Patton? You buying this?'

'We got anything else?' I asked him.

'No'.

'Then I guess I'm buying', I said. 'What about the 11a.m. part?'

'We can check that out when we get there', Charlie said. 'We might as well go and have a look. Caldwell hasn't given us Stella yet has she?'

It only took a minute for us to run it by Captain Williams, who was as embarrassed as we were that an air-con maintenance man might have deciphered the message before we had. Balfer, promising us that although the FBI files had yet to uncover anything about Caldwell, he would be the first to know if they did, was also along for the ride.

Rushing back, past Marvin who was still rooted to the spot, I called back to him. 'Hey, Marv! What do you drink?'

'Jack Daniels, what else?', he shouted, grinning. 'Why?'

Why? Because if Marvin was right, I'd be sending him a couple of bottles when it was all said and done, that's why.

49

If Tassiker had ever known Sarah Caldwell, or if she had ever been an inmate whilst he was Governor, or indeed even if he remotely recognised the name; his face gave nothing away. For a moment, Axon stared directly at the governor, searching for anything that might indicate that Tassiker knew the name. He saw nothing.

After a few seconds, the governor shook his head. 'I'm sorry Detective Axon', he replied, 'the name just does not ring a bell. I'll double check of course', he added, typing the name into his computer at the desk. 'But I'm pretty certain. I like to pride myself on remembering names and faces. I am sure that if Sarah Caldwell was ever an inmate here, certainly during my time, I would remember. Particularly as she's female, far far fewer in number of course than the men'.

Despite what the governor was telling him, Axon had a gut feeling he was being lied to. 'If you could double check sir', he asked. 'After all, I can remember a lot of the criminals I've arrested and locked up in the past but I'm sure one or two names may escape me now, even when pressed. You must have hundreds of inmates here'.

Tassiker sat back from his terminal. 'It's come back with a negative search', he stressed. 'You're welcome to look if you like'. Axon got up and made his way to behind the governor, so he could get an adequate view of the screen. Tassiker typed in the name once more, and Axon saw for himself that the search had returned no results.

'I'm not sure I can be of any more help Detective', said Tassiker. 'You seem to have had a wasted journey'.

'Well while I'm here', Axon pressed on, 'maybe you could tell me about Dave Barnes?' Well, there was no way the governor could deny Barnes had worked for him.

'Dave Barnes?', now Tassiker did look a little surprised. 'Yes, he used to be a prison guard. Had to sack him several months ago. Why do you want to know about him?'

'Oh, it's just that his name has come up with an unrelated incident in Los Angeles, and I thought while I was here ....'

'Well not much to tell really', Tassiker replied, 'He was a solid enough guard, did a fairly good job. Caught him drinking on the job though', he said gravely. 'Not something one can tolerate, especially in surroundings such as these'.

'Quite right', Axon agreed, hoping that the governor would give him *something* he could use. 'Like you say, especially in these surroundings'.

He wasn't getting anything from the governor here that he didn't already know. Patton and Holland were either wrong or the governor could have been a contender for this year's Oscars. Deciding to try one last question, he once again studied Tassiker's face awaiting the response. 'Just by-the-by', he questioned. 'I don't suppose you know LA's DA Paul McCrane do you?'

Once again, nothing on Tassiker's facial expressions changed to convey that he did. 'Paul McCrane? I've heard of him, of course, but as for knowing him? I'm afraid my dealings here are more-or-less restricted to the San Franciscan authorities. Do I know the San Francisco DA,

Jonathan Gray? Of course I do. The LA District Attorney Paul McCrane? No, I'm afraid not'.

Sensing that the governor had closed the shutters on his questioning, and having no evidence to push him further he thanked the governor for his time and leaving Tassiker to wonder why he'd turned up asking about Sarah Caldwell, he made his way back outside, pausing only to wink at the pretty secretary on his way out.

Lighting up a Marlboro, he leant against a wall, thinking desperately. He had to get something concrete. The last thing he wanted to do was to go back to Los Angeles with no more than he left with. It was true that Patton and Holland had that prisoner verification sheet off Barnes, but Williams had said that wouldn't be enough and he was right. It would take far more than that.

Just as he was contemplating lighting up a second cigarette, he saw Governor Tassiker leaving the site at a brisk pace. Well if an empty office presented itself, how could he not take that chance? Seizing the opportunity, after watching the governor leave, he made his way back up to the secretary.

'Hey', he smiled.

'Oh hi there', she beamed back; she looked genuinely pleased to see him.

'I think I've left my cell in the office', he confessed. 'I don't suppose you could check with governor Tassiker could you?'

'Oh, he's popped out for an hour', she said, 'I'm surprised you didn't see him leave, you've only been gone a few minutes'

Axon just smiled and shrugged 'Must have just missed him I guess. Listen, I need my cell, I'm due back in LA soon. Could you let me check?'

'I'm not sure', she looked apprehensive. 'The governor

doesn't like anyone in there when he's not there'. Axon looked at her in what he hoped conveyed a pleading manner with his eyes.

'Oh I suppose I could let you in', she smiled. 'Just don't tell him'.

'As if I would', he grinned back. 'Thank you, honey'.

Once back in the governor's office, Axon knew he didn't have much time. A minute, maybe two tops.

A quick rummage through papers on the desk revealed nothing; but he knew that had been a long shot at best. He heard the receptionist's telephone ring and hoped that if she was otherwise occupied it would buy him a little extra time.

A couple of drawers were locked, and even he would find it hard to justify to a court why he'd broken into them with no warrant and very little hard evidence. After nearly two minutes, he knew he had to get back out to avoid the secretary becoming suspicious. He had to think. He was pretty sure based on what they had back in LA that Caldwell had been here. Why would Tassiker cover it up? What would he do in Tassiker's shoes if he had helped cover it up?

A thought struck him from nowhere. A long shot didn't even begin to describe it. If the governor had covered it up, and then out of the blue a detective from Los Angeles arrived asking questions, the first thing he would do when the detective left was call somebody to let them know that people were asking questions; call somebody higher up in the cover-up chain.

Picking up the governor's office phone, he held his breath as he hit the redial button. 'Hey, you ok in there?' he heard the receptionist's muffled shout from through the walls. The phone stopped ringing and somebody answered it.

'Hello, District Attorney Paul McCrane's office, how may I help you this afternoon?'

'Sorry, wrong number', he replied and put the phone down.

Quickly making his way back out, he waved his cell in the direction of the secretary. 'Got it', he said. 'Underneath the chair!', he added, making himself look just like an idiot that had misplaced his phone and not like a member of the LAPD trying to uncover illicit information from her boss.

'No problem', she grinned. 'Maybe I'll see you again?' Given that he suspected that Tassiker was involved in the cover up of Sarah Caldwell's incarceration and subsequent release, he thought that highly likely.

'Yeah, maybe you will', he grinned back.

Well at least he was leaving with something. Maybe not a major piece of the puzzle, but a piece of the puzzle nonetheless. So the first person Tassiker calls after he'd questioned him about Sarah Caldwell was Paul McCrane, the guy that Barnes swore he saw with Tassiker the day before Caldwell disappeared from San Quentin, and the guy that Tassiker had denied knowing not even ten minutes ago. Surely, that was not a coincidence, was it?

50

About half way to the church in West Adams, Agent Balfer took a call. For about five minutes he listened, practically in silence as someone at Quantico relayed to him what they had found, during which time I cradled the antidote that we had been carrying round all day nervously in my fingers, straining to hear the contents of the call. The movement of the bagged up syringe in my hands became hypnotic, especially given the lack of sleep the previous night.

'Under usual circumstances', Agent Balfer began, jarring me back to reality, 'I wouldn't be telling you this. However, these are far from usual circumstances so I think I can make an exception in this case. What I'm about to tell you is classified, not to be repeated to anyone. You both understand?'

Charlie and I both nodded, wondering what was coming next from Balfer.

'Six years ago, the governor of a maximum security penitentiary in Illinois was at the centre of a major scandal; the details of which are not important. What is important, is that following this scandal, someone from the Whitehouse instructed the Director of the FBI to roll out a program that would keep, shall we say, discreet surveillance on the activities of all of the major US prisons; San Quentin being one.'

'How is that legal?' I asked. As ever, I was sceptical.

'Well it's not something we could use in court, let's put it that way', Balfer continued, confirming my suspicions that it wasn't, in fact, legal at all. 'It's more so the FBI can keep tabs on who moves in what circles. Just a database really of known associates; a pool of individuals interacting with each other.'

'Go on', said Charlie, suddenly more interested.

'Well like I say, it's nothing we can use directly, and at the time we wouldn't have flagged it as anything suspicious. We had no reason to, until now, given the time frame you have regarding Sarah Caldwell's supposed release from San Quentin'.

'What is it?'

Just over six months ago, Paul McCrane visited the governor of San Quentin four times in one week. He hasn't been there at all, since we started tracking, before or since that week'.

I couldn't help but feel a little disappointed. Like Balfer had said, that was nothing we could use, besides which, it was highly circumstantial.

'There is more', Balfer smiled, sensing my disappointment. 'Two things actually: My source down in Quantico tells me that McCrane and Tassiker both went to Harvard together'. Now that was more like it; at least we had a link between them. I wondered how Axon was getting on down in San Francisco.

'And the second?' I asked?

'Well like I said, discreet surveillance was set up, and with San Quentin being one of the more high profile prisons, it had more surveillance set up than most. There are cameras covering every conceivable exit; installed in various structural objects that no-one outside of the FBI knows about. On his last visit to San Quentin, we have photographs of the DA leaving with an unidentified woman. We can't see anything after he left with her, so we don't know how he transported her away from San Quentin, or to where; but my source swears it's Paul McCrane leaving with her.'

'And it's definitely a woman?' I clarified.

'That's what he says', Balfer affirmed, 'A copy of everything he has there is getting emailed to my laptop'.

Just as Balfer had finished recounting what Quantico had uncovered, and just as we pulled up outside the church in West Adams, Captain Williams rang me, telling me what Axon had found out at the prison.

'So Tassiker denied he knew Caldwell or McCrane?' I repeated for the benefit of Charlie and Balfer. 'Yet he rang McCrane's office immediately after Axon left? That's excellent news Captain'. At long last, I actually believed we may be getting somewhere. I quickly repeated what Balfer had told us, and as I did so, I firmly believed we had enough to bring Tassiker in. So did the Captain.

'Trouble is', Williams advised. 'We have no idea where he is at the moment. But we'll stay on it. As soon as we locate him, we'll bring him in'.

'Hey, Patton', spoke up Charlie, who had been quiet, listening intently to all this information get banded back and forth.

'Yeah man?' I turned to him.

'Good news that may be', he said, 'but let's focus on the job in hand. Let's get Stella back'. Once again, Charlie was my anchor. I turned to Balfer.

'Can you co-ordinate what we have with McCrane and Tassiker from here?' I asked. 'Finding Tassiker may now be the key'.

'Of course', Balfer agreed. 'You need me', he said nodding towards the church, 'you know where I am'. The more I was working with Balfer, the more my respect for him continued to grow.

Although we were beginning to get pieces of the bigger picture together, I couldn't help remember my last conversation with The Chemist; with Sarah Caldwell? The Chemist had seemed so pleased with our choice of getting Stella back and that was a very frightening prospect. It was a thought I carried with me as we entered the church.

51

EARLIER TODAY

Even before the Senator had called him with a green light to publish, Britland-Jones knew what story he was going to use. There had been so much information in the file given to him by Conway that the difficulty had been in deciding what *not* to use.

As much as he'd wanted to remain at the garage yesterday and read everything in the file, common sense had prevailed and he had driven back home first. It wasn't the sort of information you wanted to get caught with, and it certainly wasn't the kind of information you wanted to be reading in the offices of one of Los Angeles' premier daily papers, where everyone was always inserting themselves into other people's business! No-one was expecting him back today. In truth he spent very little time at the offices, preferring to be out in the field chasing the news and often typing up reports in the comfort and peace of his own home rather than the cramped conditions and intruding nature of his desk at the office. Today, however, the news had found him.

What Conway's motive was for wanting a story published unconcerned the journalist. Just as long as fifty thousand big ones were his at the end of it, that was all that mattered. As an added bonus, he was about to go to his editor with an undeniable scoop. He'd been so successful over the last couple of years that the editor had long ago stopped asking him where he got his information from; just so long as the paper continued to sell more and more copies. His editor was a bad-tempered, loud and obnoxious individual in his mid-fifty's; Vern Beecher was about as close to the stereotypical Hollywood portrayal of a newspaper editor as he thought it was possible to be. He remembered the joke going round the office when the remake of Spiderman had come out, the guy playing the newspaper editor of Peter Parker's newspaper was almost identical to Beecher.

He was sure Conway had his reasons for wanting Burr and McCrane disgraced but he wouldn't be chasing those for any kind of story. He thought fleetingly about returning to the United Kingdom when this was over; maybe a clean break would be the best thing. Far away from Los Angeles and far away from any repercussions this story might bring.

After reading through the thick file twice, he had decided that the story should be centrally concerned with the two-hundred thousand dollars that Burr and McCrane seemed to have creamed off a housing fund for redevelopment in downtown Los Angeles, the board of which they were both high profile, long-term members. There was no doubt that the news that these two corrupt, public figures had stolen so much money from those so much in need would distress the entire community and that shockwaves would reverberate across the entire state. It was also a story that would highly likely have the police knocking at their respective doors sooner rather than later, just as the Senator had instructed.

Knocking on Beecher's door, he entered to see that his editor was in a customary bad mood. 'You better have something good for me', he barked. 'I've had jack shit off you for over two weeks. What have you got for me?'

Britland-Jones tossed his story onto the desk and without asking proceeded to help himself to a cup of coffee. It was well known around the office that you should wait for Beecher to offer you anything before just helping yourself. He was big on office etiquette.

'What the fuck do you think you're doing?' Beecher was going scarlet with rage.

Calmly, Britland-Jones pointed to the papers he'd just dropped on his editor's desk then raised his cup of coffee in Beecher's direction. 'It's just that good', he said. 'I've just given you the story of a lifetime'.

52

As we circled around St. Johns, I noticed that sometime during today's events, the afternoon sun had subsided and the sky had morphed into an early evening haze with the sun just beginning to set. We'd been on The Chemist's trail today for around twelve hours, yet it felt like only a couple of hours since I'd gotten the call this morning.

Going inside the church, I heard what sounded like a service in progress. 'Perfect timing as usual', I remarked to Charlie, knowing we would have to interrupt whatever holy ceremony was taking place.

'Yeah man', laughed Charlie. 'They're gonna just love us for this aren't they!'

'Sure they are!' I laughed back. The possibility of our waiting for the ceremony to finish never even crossed our minds. 'We need to find out what happened at 11 a.m. last Sunday', I reminded us both. Being a church, the options were probably limited to a wedding or a funeral.

Further to our impeccable timing, several seconds before we entered the transept of the church, the congregation struck up a hymn, which was building to it's

first chorus as we strode in. Marching straight up the aisle, badges out yet again, we made a beeline for the reverend who was taking the service, aware that the hymn was becoming quieter and quieter as more people looked up and noticed our presence.

By the time we reached the reverend, the church had become silent. Even the organist had ceased playing.

'Reverend', I began, 'Detectives Patton and Holland, LAPD. I wonder, could we have a word?' I asked.

'In private', Charlie clarified.

'Can this not wait?' the reverend asked. 'We are in the middle of something here', he said gesturing to the full rows on the pews in front of him'.

'I can see that but I'm afraid it can't', I remained obstinate. 'We are here on a matter of some considerable urgency'.

'Then you better follow me then', he gestured to the vestibule leading off a nearby door. 'I will be back as soon as I have helped these officers with their enquiries', he addressed his congregation. 'In the meantime, perhaps psalms 100 and 149?' he called to the organist. 'And choir,' he added. 'Keep up the fine work!'

We followed the reverend, past the choir who to be honest looked a little pissed off at having an extra couple of unexpected numbers to perform. Once we were a suitable distance from his flock, the reverend turned to us. 'Reverend Jack Riley', he introduced himself, offering Charlie and I his hand, in turn. 'So what can I do for you gentlemen?'

'We've been given information pertaining to a missing girl', I told him. 'And that information has led us here'. I skipped the fact that we weren't entirely sure about that.

'And what? You think she's here? That she's been here?'

'To be honest, reverend, we're not sure yet. But we need to know what your records show occurred here last Sunday at eleven in the morning. The information we were given specifically mentioned that'. The reverend sat down, thinking.

'Let me see, last Sunday? Five days ago? Let me see now'. Out of the corner of my eyes I saw Charlie roll his eyes. 'Ah well yes, of course; last Sunday at eleven o' clock there was a burial service for a gentleman called Theodore Sampson. He died suddenly of a heart attack the week before; only sixty! No age at all really. Was actually a friend of mine. He'll be missed round these parts I can tell you. I performed the service myself. Large turnout as I recall, and rightly so. He was a good man'.

'Did you happen to see this woman attend the service reverend?' I asked, pulling out the photo of Sarah Caldwell we'd been given by Barnes. Riley studied the photograph for several seconds before answering.

'I don't recall seeing her', he said. 'That's not to say she wasn't there', he added. 'My eyesight isn't quite what it used to be you know'.

'No problem', I told him, beginning to think that maybe we'd been crazy to listen to Marvin's theory in the first place.

'We'll need to see the burial site', Charlie informed the reverend.

'Is that absolutely necessary', sighed Riley. 'Knowing Theodore the last thing he'd want is a couple of cops standing over his grave', he chuckled.

'It is absolutely necessary', Charlie replied humourlessly.

'Very well Detectives, very well. Follow me, if you will'.

We walked with the reverend through the church grounds and over to the graveyard, which was relatively small but seemingly, depressingly crowded. After a couple of minutes, the reverend came to a standstill. 'There you go', he gestured. 'Theodore's final resting place'. Charlie and I thanked him, telling him he could get back to his congregation. 'Not a chance', he said. 'You think I want you guys interrupting me in another few minutes. I'll stay with you till you're done'.

Looking at the grave, Theodore had obviously been a well liked member of his community; several floral tributes adorned the grave. Thinking for a minute that maybe Caldwell's next message may be tucked in among them somewhere, we knelt beside the grave for a closer look. As disrespectful as it appeared to the reverend, and his incessant tutting and clicking of his tongue made his feelings on that matter quite clear, we separated each bunch of flowers from the grave, checking the sender; seeing if there was anything from The Chemist. As we removed the final bunch of flowers, once again feeling deflated, that we had gone off course, something very strange caught Charlie's eye, even in the fading light.

'Hey Patton, what the fuck is that?' he said, bringing an even louder disapproving noise from the reverend.

I knelt in closer to see what Charlie was referring to. I had to admit, I didn't know. It looked very strange and definitely out of place given our current location.

Sticking out of the ground, no more than three inches was a small tube, about two inches in diameter. To any passer by and even to any of Theodore's mourners, it would have been well concealed by the flowers.

'Charlie boy', I said standing up. 'Call Balfer. I think we're gonna need him'.

53

I stood staring at the grave, transfixed with the small tube protruding from the ground. I knew what I thought it was I just didn't dare speak the words out loud. It was certainly something I'd never seen before, certainly not coming up from a grave; and I've been to my fair share of funerals over the years. There was only one possible explanation for the tube; ventilation. And that in turn, meant only one thing. Someone was buried in the coffin, alive. Had we found Stella? Had The Chemist led us to Stella?

Charlie was standing at the opposite side of the grave, just as transfixed as I was. I knew instinctively we were thinking the same. He remained silent too, almost waiting for me to say the first words.

'Hey, Patton. Hey Holland', Agent Balfer arrived breathlessly at the grave. 'What have you got?' I guess one of us had to speak.

'Look right there Balfer', I said, pointing at the tube. 'What do you make of that?' Balfer kneeled down, almost squinting in the dusk that had now settled to a dark grey blanket across the sky. Light was fading fast. He stood up, excitement in his eyes, and I could see he'd reached the same conclusion as we had.

'You're thinking the same, right?' he looked at us, alternating between Charlie and I. 'Right?' I just nodded.

'I think she's down there, man', Charlie stated. 'I mean, we all do, don't we?'

Again I nodded, and Balfer followed suit. 'We need to do this very carefully', he cautioned. After the bomb this morning at Sutherland Boulevard which had taken out several of our officers, he was right to want to proceed carefully. 'The last thing we need is for this fucking thing to go off', he added.

The reverend, who had shown his disapproval of us simply removing the flowers from the grave minutes earlier, was looking increasingly alarmed. If he'd thought we'd been disrespectful before, he was in for a bit of a shock very shortly. 'I'm going to need you to evacuate your church reverend', I told him. 'Immediately'.

'Right away', he said, heading straight back to his congregation. Perhaps he had finally grasped the severity of the situation.

'The thing in our favour', I addressed Charlie and Balfer, 'is that we are well within the timeframe of the game. If she's down there, I want her out as quickly as possible; I can't even imagine what's going through her mind but like you said Charlie boy, we need to be careful'. If I had been asked to define Hell, lying alive in a coffin buried underground would be pretty close and the more I thought about it the more I thought we were right. Also, the more I thought about it, the more I wanted to dive straight in and get her out of there.

It took the best part of forty-five agonising minutes for everything to be co-ordinated. The church was evacuated, the necessary sweeps of the parameter conducted, paramedics were on standby and the bomb squad arrived to secure the scene and supervise extraction of the coffin just in case it was booby trapped. As for the exhumation order? Captain Williams simply said 'We don't have the time. I'll deal with the consequences in the morning if I need to. Just get that fucking girl back'. Sentiments we all fully shared.

Nevertheless, three quarters of an hour after the three of us had agreed what we were looking at, we were ready to begin exhumation.

The members of the bomb squad, who quite rightly take their jobs very, very seriously, headed by Carl Kennington, wanted us away from the scene whilst they carried out the job of securing the site and opening the coffin.

'Not a chance', I informed him. Charlie, myself, and to his considerable credit, Agent Balfer stood firm. This was ours. Sensing our determination, Kennington shrugged.

'OK guys, suit yourself up'.

It took us maybe fifteen minutes to dig the ground out from on top of and round the coffin to the requirements of Kennington, who told us whilst we were digging that he needed a clear line of sight around the coffin before we opened it. During the digging, it became clear that the tube was looking more and more like a makeshift ventilation system and a sense of growing excitement grew around the diggers and various police spectators, all of whom were willing Stella to be in the coffin and for her to be alive and unharmed.

We stepped back letting Kennington and his team do their stuff; checking around the coffin, they could see no sign of explosives or booby traps of any kind. Whilst I was happy to let them check it over, there was only going to be one person opening that coffin.

It was dark by now, though the grave was well lit; several portable lights had been rigged, giving a distinctly eerie feel over the entire graveyard. 'Get everyone out of here', I told Kennington. 'Get them well back, just in case'.

He immediately engineered everyone back, twenty feet or so from the grave. Charlie didn't move an inch. He knew that didn't apply to him and he wouldn't have gone anywhere even if I'd told him to.

'Ready, man?' he whispered.

'Yeah I'm ready'.

The coffin lid was heavy in my hands as I lifted it, trying to prise it open, although maybe it was just that all my energy seemed to have drained in the last hour. It had been a physically and mentally exhausting day. Charlie's hands made it lighter, and between us we eased the lid from its base and pulled it open.

54

The first thing I saw was her eyes. Wider than any eyes I can ever remember seeing, conveying a mixture confusion, disorientation, panic and relief simultaneously. Her face was streaky where she had been crying, probably most of the time she had been conscious down there, and I could see tears trickle down her cheeks as she stared back at me.

I put my arms out to gently lift her up, unsure as to how far the Clozapone had advanced through her body. I could see she was struggling to move, but I couldn't tell whether this was due to the drugs or simply from being lying in the coffin for so long.

'You're safe now', I whispered as I cradled her, a sense of relief washing over me; washing over us all. I heard her merely whimper a response. She clearly had no idea what had happened to her or why.

She clung to me, now freely sobbing but still unable to speak; the realisation of us discovering her absolutely overwhelming. 'You're safe now', I repeated softly; I could think of nothing else to say.

The paramedics rushed in to stabilise her; to prep her for her journey to hospital. They had been given the antidote, and I knew they would take great care of her. Anyone could see how fragile she was, we didn't want to damage her any more than she had been. I could only begin to imagine my state of mind if I were to go through the same set of circumstances.

As I relinquished my gentle but firm grasp of her arms, she finally managed one word, which almost broke my heart. 'Mom...' she stuttered.

In finding Stella Edwards, everything else that had happened today had momentarily faded into the background. Only now, hearing her single word, did I realise the devastating news that we would have to break to her soon; that her mother had been killed this morning by a bomb planted at her house by the same person who had kidnapped her. It wasn't news we'd be breaking quite yet; there was nothing we could to do to bring her mother back now, but there was an awful lot we could do to make sure this young girl didn't suffer any more than she had done in the past twenty-four hours.

As one of the paramedics placed an oxygen mask over her face, I could see her eyes still desperately searching for any sign of her mother. 'Shhh', I comforted. 'Close your eyes, try to relax. We'll take good care of you now'.

It goes without saying, that if I wasn't a member of the LAPD, a career in counselling wouldn't be beckoning. Once she was stable in hospital, I would break the unthinkable news to her; it seemed the least I could do; if Sarah Caldwell hadn't been targeting me, Stella and her mother would have been going about their everyday business. Instead, her mother had paid with her life and Stella's world, as bad as it was now, would only get worse when she was told what had happened. I only prayed she would come through it.

My gaze followed Stella, unable to break away, as her vitals were checked and then I watched as the paramedics gently lifted her into the awaiting ambulance. Finally, I turned back to Charlie who had yet to look up from the coffin. 'Hey, Charlie boy', I tried to attract his attention. He looked up, startled, as if he'd been somewhere else for a moment. I looked to where he'd been staring. As soon as we'd opened the coffin, I'd been fully focussed on making Stella's transition back to reality as comfortable and painless as possible; only now did I see the bottom of the coffin for the first time.

Carved into the bottom of the wood in large letters was the word 'Patton'. It served as a stark, harsh reminder that although we had got Stella back, alive, more than we'd managed to do for Keeley and Jennifer, that we were still no closer to catching The Chemist.

'Hey Patton, Holland!' Agent Balfer rejoined us. 'I've got something to run by you guys. Something's puzzling me'.

'What's that?' Charlie asked.

'You said that The Chemist phoned you? Gave you a choice?'

'Yeah', I confirmed.

'Well it seems to me that we'd have found her here anyway, regardless of whether you were given a choice or not'. He was right there. This had been the last step of the game; of game number three anyway.

'So what can we read into that?' I asked Balfer.

'I've been thinking about that too', he told us. 'As far as I can see, there are two options. Either we've got lucky here, breaking the final message before The Chemist thought we would'. That was certainly a possibility; and we had Marvin to thank for that.

'What's the second option, man?' asked Charlie. Agent Balfer's face looked decidedly grim.

'If we've solved number three right on schedule; if we've got Stella back because The Chemist wanted us to get her back, then that means that Sarah Caldwell has already got victim number four'.

55

By the time we wrapped things up at the church, it was well past midnight. Several questions remained; chief among them, how could someone have placed Stella in that grave with no one noticing. Reverend Riley had simply said that the church would have been deserted most nights from nine or ten o' clock. He supposed it would be easy enough for someone who was highly motivated to carry out the necessary work within a couple of hours. We speculated a timeframe that suggested that Stella was buried there just about the same time as Charlie and I had staggered back from the previous evening's beers. It almost went without saying that the church had no CCTV or surveillance equipment installed that could have given us a better idea. 'We have things that are of far greater need to the community than video cameras', Riley had chastised. 'You think my budget stretches to CCTV? Think again!'

We had patrol officers doing a door-to-door on the houses surrounding the church, but I held out little hope; The Chemist was far too clever to have been seen wasn't she? It didn't seem like Sarah Caldwell was going to make any mistakes, so I had to hope that our lead with Tassiker and McCrane panned out and gave us something that eventually led us to her.

The more we talked about Balfer's theory that we would have found Stella anyway, the more I agreed with it; we wouldn't have been far behind Marvin in working out the last message.

We'd had the guys back at the station conduct searches on any young girl who might have been reported as missing, but so far we'd turned up nothing and so far, still no further communication from The Chemist. Part of her last conversation with me; the part about starting number four immediately, echoed in my ears. Caldwell had been operating with such ruthless efficiency so far I was certain that girl number four was already captured and it was only a matter of time before we found out who she was.

Captain Williams told us to go home, get some sleep and to reconvene the following morning. Well, actually in eight hours time, it already was 'the following morning'. As much as it pained me to admit, it seemed like a pretty good idea to me. After almost twenty four hours Charlie and I were spent, and Balfer was also looking pretty drained.

We decided that we'd target how we were going to use the information Balfer had given us about McCrane's relationship with Tassiker in the morning. 'I'm going to have to sleep on that one', Williams said. 'That is a pretty big call to make'. I didn't blame Williams for wanting to tread carefully. One false move and he could very well be Neil Williams: ex-captain. The political sway that Paul McCrane carried in Los Angeles was not to be underestimated. Shawn Axon was to remain in San Francisco on the trail of Tassiker, who, it had appeared, had completely vanished after his conversation with Axon earlier in the day. Williams had already cleared his impending arrest with his San Franciscan counterparts this evening, so if Axon found him, he would have no bullshit red tape to cut through to get him to Los Angeles, which was encouraging.

As I arrived back at my apartment, I realised that the eight hours until we were meeting again was now cut down to around six when you factored in my transit time but nevertheless it was six hours of welcome respite from all that had happened.

I stood in the shower for what seemed like an eternity but in reality it was only around fifteen minutes. As the hot water cascaded over my body, sending me into as relaxed a state as I'd been in some time, I went over the last twenty-four hours, questioning every move we'd made. The deaths of Ferguson, Stella's mother and the other officers at Sutherland Boulevard were weighing heavily on my mind. Looking back, I couldn't see how we could have done anything differently, which even so, was of little comfort. I resisted the temptation to pour myself a large glass of vodka, despite the bottle resting invitingly on the bedside table as I returned from the shower. I had a feeling that I was going to need a clear head today, and for the sake of 'number four', I didn't want to compromise that.

Although I thought I would have a tumultuous rest at best, I settled into a deep sleep almost immediately. I'm pretty sure I dreamed a couple of times that the phone was ringing, but mercifully, for those few hours at least, The Chemist refrained from calling me.

56

TODAY

Paul Britland-Jones sat alone, in an all-night café, just around the corner from his apartment, and only a sixty second walk from the newsstand where he had just picked up a copy of the early edition of the LA Times. He sat, alone, in the corner sipping a cup of coffee and staring at the front page. His latest and greatest story. Admittedly, he didn't have the usual feeling of a job well done, as he hadn't really done much work to get the story. Usually, he felt a sense of satisfaction when one of his stories made the front page; it made the endless chasing of leads and burning the midnight oil to beat a deadline all worthwhile. Today though, he felt more a sense of foreboding, unsure of what lay ahead, unsure of the repercussions across the state that would be felt as a result of his story.

Checking his watch, he sensed that at just after five a.m. it was a little early for the LAPD to have gotten wind of the story but he was sure they would, sooner rather than later. He had upheld his part of the agreement with Conway. There was no way that such a story would bring anything other than arrest, intense scrutiny and possible imprisonment for its two protagonists; Jameson Burr and Paul McCrane. He couldn't quite remember the last time that one such prominent figure had been involved in a scandal of this magnitude, let alone two. That had given him his headline: '$200,000. Two for the price of one?' Underneath the headline, two pictures; one of Burr, one of McCrane; both immediately recognisable. Just in case though, their names were emblazoned underneath, not quite as big a type as the headline itself, but not far off. To anyone who picked up the paper today, or indeed happened to glance at a copy as they walked by, the names were unmistakably prevalent. He was sure that Conway would be pleased and sincerely hoped that fifty grand would be coming his way as a result.

As an added insurance that the LAPD would be fully aware of Burr and McCrane's misdemeanours he had posted all relevant information pertaining to his story at the home address of the Commanding Officer of the LAPD's Criminal Investigation Division, Will Harlow, at just after midnight last night. That would certainly make interesting reading over the breakfast table at the Harlow household this morning and would be more than enough to warrant the immediate arrest of Burr and McCrane. He was sure that Harlow would also want to speak to him, him having broken the story and all. He could be vague about his sources, saying that the information was delivered to him anonymously but he had to have some semblance of background relating to the story, he knew that. That would be no problem though; he could have his facts straight easily enough.

Finishing his coffee, he thought he'd make an early appearance at the office this morning; no doubt his fellow journalists and office minions would be eager to heap their praise on him for breaking such a story; applause that he was always ready to accept with considerable aplomb. He just hoped Senator Conrad Conway was similarly gracious.

57

Captain Williams, Agent Balfer, Charlie and I all arrived back at the LAPD within five minutes of each other. None of us looked particularly refreshed but I felt considerably less tired than I had when I had got home last night, so the sleep had definitely been warranted. The Captain had instructed the rest of the PD not to disturb us for the next hour; we needed to be thinking clearly and clarity of our way forward was now paramount.

The taskforce set up by Captain Williams had been working overnight, with more volunteers having come in last night to investigate Sarah Caldwell. They had nothing more for us, which was a blow but not an un-entirely unexpected one. We'd heard nothing more from The Chemist either, my uninterrupted sleep had told me that much. On the way in I'd telephoned the hospital to find out how Stella was. She was stable, which was good news. It seemed that we had gotten to her in time, although how she would react to the devastating news that her mother had been killed in yesterday's explosion was anyone's guess. Although I'd been planning to break the news to her myself, Captain Williams had other ideas. 'You're needed here Patton', he told me, and he was right once again. I hadn't forgotten that finding

Caldwell was our primary concern and I just hoped that when Stella learned of yesterday's events, she was strong enough to pull through.

Sitting around the table in the incident room, we pulled together what we had so far, eager to draw up a strategy that we could implement; at least until The Chemist contacted us again. It seemed that the only avenue we had was McCrane and Tassiker.

Balfer, over the next twenty minutes, briefed us on what his sources at Quantico had uncovered. He'd had the original surveillance tapes couriered to him overnight. 'You guys must have a far bigger budget than us down here!' Charlie joked, trying to inject his usual humour into the situation. Nevertheless, I sensed he too was impressed so far with Balfer's contribution to the case.

We brought the images up on of one of the screens in the room and watched in silence as we saw Paul McCrane enter San Quentin then leave with another individual from a different exit. There was no denying it was McCrane; we all agreed on that and it was clear enough to me that we could justify questioning him on it. As for whether or not he was with Sarah Caldwell, that was a different matter. Even though we had a photo from Barnes, it was hard to tell if it was her or not. All we could say was that the person leaving with McCrane was definitely female.

Half way through our briefing, Axon contacted us from San Francisco; he'd got nothing new either. He'd spent all night trying to locate Tassiker with no success and figured he'd wait to see whether or not he showed up for work today which seemed like his best chance of finding him. I had to say, Axon's dedication right off the bat to helping us hadn't gone unnoticed.

'So, have we got enough to bring in McCrane then?' I put the question out there but it was directed solely at

Captain Williams. It would be his decision. From the look on his face, it seemed that he'd been pondering this question most of the night.

'I'm not sure, you know', he said shaking his head. 'All we've really got is him leaving San Quentin with an unidentified female. We could do with something else to link him to Sarah Caldwell specifically'.

'We need to bring him in', I countered. I too had been thinking how I'd respond if Williams had decided not to bring him in for questioning. 'He's our only lead at the moment. It's not as if we've got anyone else, apart from Tassiker, even remotely linked with Caldwell'. Williams was quiet for a moment, seemingly playing out the consequences silently.

'Fuck it', he concluded. 'Let's do it. Bring in Barnes first. Get him on record with what he told us yesterday. Then we bring in McCrane. Hopefully in the meantime, Axon will have found Tassiker and can corroborate some of what Quantico has sent us'. Now that was more like it.

'We'll get Barnes now', I jumped up. I doubted whether even he would have started drinking this early.

Just as we were about to go and get him, we were interrupted by an officer whose name I didn't know. 'Captain, I think there's something you should know', he said, virtually ignoring everyone else in the room.

'And what's that?' growled Williams, clearly annoyed that his express instructions not to be disturbed had been violated.

'Something's just happened you really need to know about', the officer continued. 'Will Harlow has just arrested Paul McCrane'. A stunned silence washed over the room. Finally, Captain Williams managed to speak.

'And why would Harlow have done that?' he asked.

'You've not seen this morning's Times?' responded the

officer. He hadn't and quite clearly, no-one else in the room had either. We had been far too preoccupied with what we were caught up in, and rightly so. The officer took our silence as confirmation that we hadn't and tossed the copy that I'd only just noticed he was holding, onto the table, face up.

Upon reading the headline, we all looked at each other, not knowing what to make of it, with the exception of the Captain, who stood up straight away and stormed out, presumably to find Harlow for a fuller explanation. The remaining three of us poured over the story, trying to grasp why McCrane had been arrested.

Finishing the article, I let out a low whistle. Surely the timing of this story couldn't be entirely co-incidental, could it?

'Save's us a job at least', Charlie smiled.

58

Paul McCrane had been enjoying a leisurely breakfast with his family; a truly great way to start the day. He and his wife, Melissa, sat together at the table, enjoying a cooked breakfast, prepared by the housekeeper of course. His days were usually so hectic that he had long ago made the decision that breakfast time was family time. No calls taken and no interruptions.

Around them, their three children rushed around, readying themselves for school. Anna aged seven, Lucy aged eight and the oldest, Paul Junior, ten, all hurried around various parts of the house, looking for clothes, books and various other bits and pieces whilst the housekeeper kept telling them to hurry up; their lift would be here any minute.

Although one of the most powerful men in the state, Paul McCrane liked to keep the common touch in his everyday life. The kids all went to the same public school as he had gone to; The Clover Avenue Elementary School. True, it was pretty much the top rated public school in Los Angeles, but it was a public school nevertheless. This was a fact not lost on the residents of Los Angeles, who held him with such high esteem and affection. His public persona as a tireless worker for several charities further endeared him and his Sunday mornings spent coaching Paul Junior's school softball team was the icing on the cake. As far as the state was concerned, he could do no wrong. If only they knew!

Finishing off his breakfast, he heard the doorbell ring and realised the housekeeper was now upstairs trying to keep the madness in some semblance of order. His wife rose out of her seat, but he stood up, kissing her on the forehead as he did so. 'I'll get it darling, you finish eating'. Never hurt to bank some brownie points!

He made his way out of the kitchen and down the hallway, opening the front door fully expecting to see Paula Martin, the mother of Anna's best friend, who was doing the school run that week. He certainly wasn't expecting a member of the LAPD to identify himself as Will Harlow and then read him his rights.

'Paul McCrane?' Harlow asked, although he would have been an idiot not to already know that.

'Of course', McCrane answered, caught off guard in a major way. What could this be about?

'I'm arresting you on suspicion of fraud and obtaining funds under deception. You have the right to remain silent. Anything you say can and will be used against you in a court of law. You have the right to speak to an attorney, and to have an attorney present during any questioning. If you cannot afford a lawyer, one will be provided for you at government expense'.

Unfortunately for McCrane, the arrest was word-perfect. Over the years he had seen so many cases dismissed simply because the arresting officer had misquoted the Miranda Warning, or missed bits out, or in some cases, not even used it.

The irony of the government offering to provide a District Attorney with a lawyer was not lost on him, and judging from the smile on Harlow's face, it wasn't lost on him either.

59

We picked up Barnes, who had unbelievably been pouring his first drink of the day when we got there, and brought him back to the station, leaving Captain Williams to delve further into McCrane's arrest. We just needed a standard statement from Barnes, nothing more, so it was a fairly quick process. At least we had him on record stating that Sarah Caldwell had definitely been incarcerated at San Quentin and that he had definitely seen McCrane in Tassiker's office. For all that was worth; I knew any defence lawyer in the country could discredit anything Barnes would have to say in any courtroom when they discovered the magnitude of his drink problem.

Just as we were about to find Williams to see what the state of play with McCrane was, my cell rang again. Seeing a familiar number come up, I told Charlie to go on ahead. 'Hey', I said, answering the phone.

'It's me,' came the familiar voice of my ex-wife, Vikki. We'd been married for nine years and divorced for three, but had been together for fifteen years or so in total. It had been pretty amicable, more or less, the divorce. By that time, it hadn't come as much of a surprise to either of us. I'd been working long hours for years, and by long hours,

I mean *long* hours. Sometimes the cases I'd been working on demanded that. What was I supposed to do? Leave on time every day, regardless of where we were up to with a case? I think that was what I had been expected to do, but found that I just couldn't do it. I'd become immersed in a case, and would give it a hundred percent until we caught whoever we were chasing at the time or the trail went stone-cold. I think that was the only way to do my job and I hadn't even tried to change. That, without a doubt, cost me my marriage. Vikki had told me that if I paid as much attention to her as I did the various murderers, rapists and attackers I was chasing, I'd be the world's greatest husband. I'd returned early one morning after another sixteen hours day to find her gone, belongings and all. She'd even taken our only daughter, Katie, who'd been fourteen at the time. In the fairly quick court hearing that had ensued, she'd gotten the house and full custody of Katie. That was pretty understandable given my line of work, and the hours I'd been doing, so it hadn't come as much of a shock. As it was an amicable split and my agreed payments were received by her on time, every month without fail, she allowed me as much access to Katie as I wanted as long as it was agreed with her prior to that. That had been good of her; she didn't have to do that. Again, due to work, it wasn't as much as I'd like but I got to see her every other weekend and maybe four or five nights a month and I treasured every minute.

'Hi Vikki', I replied. 'How are you?'

'I'm fine', she said, although I detected just a note of panic in her voice.

'What's up?'

'Have you heard from Katie? She didn't some home last night', she asked expectantly.

'I've not spoken to her since last weekend', I replied, unsure how to take that news. 'Have you tried all her friends?'

'Of course I have', Vikki said 'You think I wouldn't have tried that?' I hadn't meant to have sounded patronising.

'Well she probably has some friends we don't know about', I placated. 'She's around that age isn't she, maybe a boyfriend we don't know about?'

'You may not know your daughter very well, but I do'. Yep, she had to get that one in, didn't she? 'If she had a boyfriend, I'd know about it. I'm sure she tells me everything'. Although I didn't doubt the bond between Katie and her mother, I doubted she told her everything. I certainly hadn't told my parents everything when I was seventeen, and I didn't think Vikki had either.

'Look, I'm sure she's fine', I tried to calm Vikki. 'She has probably lost track of time and got carried away somewhere!'

'She's never done anything like this before though'.

'Well maybe she's scared to call you then. She'll know you're bound to be angry'.

'I'm worried, I'm not angry'.

'I know you are. I'll have her school checked out', I told her. 'I bet you an extra child support payment she'll be there by the time the bell rings'.

'I hope so', she said. She sounded like she was fighting back tears. 'Can you check now?'

'Of course I can', I reassured her, as Charlie reappeared. 'Look, I gotta go', I said noticing Charlie's expression was ashen, and his eyes were wide with surprise. 'I'll call you when I know'.

'Hey man,' I turned to him. 'What's up?'

'We've had another fax'. For the first time, I noticed he was holding a piece of paper. We had been expecting game number four to start anytime, and it looked like it had, although I'd been holding out for the slim possibility that The Chemist would have mercifully stopped and simply disappeared back under whatever rock she had crawled out from.

'One minute Charlie boy', I said. 'Have to make a call first. Just had Vikki on the phone', I offered by way of explanation.

'No man', Charlie took my arm. 'We need to start this now'. He thrust the fax into my hands, not quite knowing what to say.

I read it once, and fell to the ground as my knees buckled, feeling vomit rise from my stomach. My head was spinning and I felt like I'd just been hit with a sledgehammer. As I knelt on the ground, the fax which I had dropped upon reading landed on the floor, face up. It contained just five words this time. 'Patton, I have your daughter'.

60

'We're sure this is The Chemist and not just some copycat winding us up?' Williams demanded. Upon hearing about the latest fax, he'd dropped what he was doing with Will Harlow and rushed back down to us.

I sat, almost unable to move, back at the table in the incident room; I'm pretty sure that Charlie had helped me up and had steadied me after I'd read the fax. I didn't know why I hadn't thought that Katie might be a target. As soon as I'd figured out why Sarah Caldwell was targeting me, I should have let Vikki and Katie know. And therein lay another problem; should I tell Vikki now? After considerable deliberation, I decided I had to. But I would see what I could get out of McCrane first.

'We'll get her back, man', Charlie did his best to comfort me. 'We got Stella back didn't we? I'm convinced we'd have found her anyway and we'll find Katie in time, man, you mark my words, we'll fucking find her'.

I knew one thing for certain, whether we did or we didn't, Sarah Caldwell had just taken this way beyond personal, and she would face the consequences of that when we met; and we would meet eventually. I was sure that Caldwell wouldn't be satisfied with just Katie, surely she would want me as well? I just had to suffer enough first.

'We're sure it's The Chemist', Charlie replied to the Captain. 'Katie is missing'. Not that we hadn't been given everything we needed to assist us in the investigation thus far, Williams turned to me.

'Whatever you need on this one, you've got it'.

Despite the thought of Katie trapped somewhere similar to Stella, or worse, I knew that the best chance of getting her back was to remain focussed, and try and get whatever I could out of our good District Attorney. 'Thanks Captain. That means a lot', I noted. 'What's Harlow said?'

'He woke this morning to an anonymous tip-off, including a file with all the pertinent material delivered to his house. You've read the story in the Times, it's all there. McCrane and Jameson Burr, who we haven't managed to pick up yet, it seems have pocketed around two hundred grand from a housing fund. There was more to incriminate McCrane than Burr, that's why Harlow went for him first'.

'Fuck the housing fund', Charlie exploded. 'We need to question him about Caldwell'.

'I agree', said Williams through gritted teeth. There was a knock on the door, and Harlow walked into the room.

'Hey Cap', he addressed Williams. 'We're about to start with McCrane'. He paused, noticing Charlie and I at the table. 'Hey Patton, look I'm sorry about Katie', he offered, looking genuinely upset. The news had obviously travelled fast. 'If there's anything I can do man, you got it'.

'As a matter of fact there is', I stood up. 'I need McCrane before you have him. We think he knows who The Chemist is. We think *we* know who The Chemist is. We need to know what he knows'. Harlow for a minute looked like he wasn't going to give us McCrane quite that easily but I think one look at my face told him that I wasn't going to take no for an answer.

'As soon as we're done with him, man, he's all yours', Charlie added for Harlow's benefit. Knowing he didn't really have a choice in the matter, Harlow had to concede.

'Let me know when you're through with him', he nodded. 'I still want to take him down for fraud'. I reached out to shake his hand as a mark of my gratitude. It's never nice when you make an arrest, only to have the suspect taken off you for whatever the reason, no matter how extenuating the circumstances.

'Thanks a lot Will, I owe you one'. I cast my eyes down once more to the LA Times that still lay there from before; front page and story proudly displayed. Seeing the name of the journalist who broke the story, another thing occurred to me; and again it was something I should have already thought of. 'Paul Britland-Jones', I announced to the room.

'What about him?' Harlow asked.

'I'm sure that was the reporter who questioned me after Andrew Caldwell's death'. Not knowing the back-story, Harlow's face was blank but Charlie and the Captain looked like they might know where I was going with this. 'After Caldwell, Andrew Caldwell that is, was killed, he ran a story on it a couple of days later. It strikes me that a reporter doing research on that story would do some background on his family'.

'Makes sense', Williams affirmed. 'Let's bring him in then, see if he can give us anything to help the investigation'. Seeing the despondent look on Harlow's face, the Captain continued. 'You can have him just as soon as we're done with him Will'.

I opened the door, ready to go and question McCrane. 'Just one more thing Captain', I turned back to Williams.

'Like I said, Patton, anything you need'.

'Turn the cameras off in the interrogation room McCrane is in'.

'I'll pretend I didn't hear that', if Williams was shocked at my request, he wasn't showing it. 'You know I couldn't possibly do such a thing', he added. 'However', he turned to Harlow. 'Detective Harlow, would you be so good as to check that the door to the monitoring room isn't open, and if it is could you please lock it? Wouldn't want anyone beating Patton and Holland to interrogation three and turning off the cameras now would we?'

61

Conrad Conway returned from his early meetings to get his golf clubs, as he usually did whenever his schedule permitted. Six months ago, his golf game had been in the lowest rut that he could remember since he'd broken that magical handicap of ten. For weeks his game had remained at that ebb; nothing he hit seemed to go where he wanted; seemingly slicing every shot. He consoled himself that all players of the game must go through spells like that and just hoped his would come to an end soon. In his haste to leave one morning, he had forgotten his clubs and had rushed back to his house to get them in the half hour window he had before his tee-off time. That afternoon, with his first stroke of the game, he had hit a hole in one; and the rest of his game had been pretty damn good too. He had taken the afternoon's kitty of six thousand dollars by three clear strokes; a just reward for his fine performance.

Ever since that afternoon, convinced that somehow the getting of his clubs just before driving to the club had played a part in turning his game around, he now went through the same ritual before each game whenever he could out of superstition. The demands on his time and his often over-loaded schedule meant that this was not always possible, but today, it was.

Jameson Burr and Paul McCrane knew that as well didn't they? That had been the time they'd discussed two days ago over the phone. Well he was prepared for anything they might throw at him. He didn't know if they were watching him; he certainly hadn't been aware of any indication that they were; he stuck to his routine like normal, just in case. Anyone who was watching him, and indeed a certain Daryl Walls *had* watched him leave at just after six that morning, would have seen nothing to suggest that Conway knew about his impending fate at the hands of two of his fellow Animi. The cool, calm and collected card was one that Conway was extremely adept at playing.

Parking his Aston Martin outside his house rather than in the driveway, to give the impression he would be in and out of his house in no time at all, Conway felt a little apprehensive, although the feeling of his Walther P99 against the side of his chest made him feel a little better. As an added precaution, he was wearing a bullet proof vest beneath his shirt and jacket that he managed to lay his hands on from one of his contacts at the LAPD. Well why take any unnecessary chances?

As he turned the key to his front door, he wondered if his potential assailant was already in the house, and if so, where would they be hiding? Whoever had been sent by Burr and McCrane would know how little a window they had to carry out their attack; he was after all only there to retrieve his golf clubs; a two minute task at best.

It was a question that was answered as Conway was half way up the stairs, walking his recently-converted 'hobby' room on the first floor, where he kept his clubs.

Although he'd been looking up towards the landing, and had been expecting an attack of some sort anyway, he was still taken by surprise when a stringy six-foot, pale white male leapt out of the shadows at the top of the stairs, the evil glint in his eyes undeniable.

The psychotic look in the assailant's eyes was confirmed as he launched himself down the stairs towards the awaiting Senator, who could not reach his firearm in time to prevent instant and hard contact from Walls as he collided with him, sending them both tumbling back.

Shaking off the impact and initial surprise, out of the corner of his eye, Conway saw a syringe dangerously close to his neck, and it took all of his strength to manoeuvre himself into a position where he could kick the syringe out of his assailants hands, and landed a powerful strike to the nose of Walls, sending him stumbling back.

Reaching for his P99, he winced in pain, thinking that maybe he had broken a rib or two in the fall down the stairs. It was, however, pain that would pail into insignificance compared to what he planned to inflict upon his assailant momentarily.

Walls stood up, and readied himself for another lunge at the Senator, only to find that he was staring down the barrel of Conway's handgun. As Walls began a charge towards Conway that he couldn't possibly finish in time, his tracks were stopped instantaneously by two bullets from the Senator; the second one killing him on impact as it ripped through several vital organs.

As Walls lay on the floor, an ever expanding pool of blood forming around his body, Conway stood over him, alert to the fact that maybe there was more than one assailant sent by Burr and McCrane. After ten minutes of complete silence, aside from the Senator's harder than usual breathing, he concluded that only one had been sent.

He called 911, sounding far more alarmed than he actually was. Although his ribs still hurt like hell, that was actually a good thing; they would make his story of simply disturbing an intruder all the more plausible and he'd have just enough time to remove the vest from under his clothing; it would look too suspicious if an attending officer was to notice he was wearing one!

Reaching back into his jacket pocket, he pulled out two business cards, which were very rarely given out, taking care only to handle the sides of the cards; one was Burr's, one was McCrane's. Carefully, taking the time to ensure he didn't stand in any blood, he slipped both cards into the corpse's back pocket. The story that Britland-Jones had published this morning was good, very good, but just as an added insurance, let's see if McCrane and Burr can explain what a low-life scumbag, breaking into and attacking the good Senator Conrad Conway, is doing with their personal business cards in his back pocket.

He was looking forward to seeing what explanation they gave for that!

62

I don't think Paul McCrane was expecting me, judging from the look on his face when I opened the door to the interrogation room. I think he'd been expecting Will Harlow again. I must have looked pretty pissed off, as indeed I was, because when he saw me, backed up by Charlie, he looked a little taken aback, although he remained composed. I wouldn't have expected one of the most successful District Attorneys Los Angeles had appointed in recent years to have remained any other way. I didn't bother to introduce myself and luckily for me, there was no solicitor present. I guess maybe McCrane had decided he didn't need one. I simply walked towards him and pushed him off his chair and onto the floor. I felt Charlie's hand on my shoulder; a warning hand, just reminding me not to go too far, which I had no intention of doing. But we needed McCrane to talk, and to talk now. The further McCrane believed I might go, the quicker I thought he would talk.

I picked up the chair and placed it over McCrane's throat, using my weight to increase the pressure, making it difficult for him to breathe. He'd looked shocked initially, but as he lay on the floor, trying to get air into his lungs, the look of shock gave way to a smile. 'You've just signed your own fucking release papers', he wheezed, pointing to the camera in the corner of the room, 'whoever you are'.

'They're not on, McCrane', Charlie informed him from behind me. 'It's just you and us. No-one is watching'. The smile soon disappeared as I leant further forward, piling on yet more pressure.

'That's right', I said. It was hard for me to hold it together, but I thought I was doing pretty well under the circumstances. 'We can make this quick if you like', I told him. 'The Chemist, Sarah Caldwell has my daughter. We know that you know who she is and we need to find her'. I leant back, giving McCrane some respite, and he seized the opportunity to fill his empty lungs with air.

'I don't know what you mean', he began.

'Wrong answer', I told him, leaning forward again, harder this time. The look on his face as the air drained out of him told me that he couldn't take too much more of this. I suspected we could break him fairly quickly. 'We've got surveillance tapes you leaving San Quentin with her' I said, which was more-or-less true. We thought it was Sarah Caldwell at least. 'Where is she now?' I leant back once more, giving him the chance to speak.

'I've got no idea what you're talking about', he spat. I picked him up, the chair falling to once side as I did so, and threw him across the table with enough force that he bounced off the table and landed on the floor a good seven or eight feet from where we were standing. Moving quickly, I was on him again, picking him up once more and landed a solid blow to the side of his head, not hard enough to knock him out but just hard enough to hopefully send him the message that we weren't to be messed with.

'Ok, ok,' he coughed, 'You want to know what I know about Sarah Caldwell?' Charlie and I remained silent, expectantly. 'She was released from San Quentin', he told us 'but she escaped. We don't know where she is now'. After our shock tactics, he seemed to be getting his composure back, and with that, some bravado. 'I do know one more thing about Sarah Caldwell though', he wheezed.

'And what's that?' I demanded. McCrane was now smiling again.

'If she's got your daughter, there's no way you'll be seeing her again', he laughed. 'At least, not alive'. I think he'd still been smiling as I landed a second blow, much harder this time, to the front of his face, which knocked him out cold, immediately on impact.

63

Getting nothing from McCrane, for the time being at least, I was relieved to learn that Harlow had managed to track down Britland-Jones. I'd give McCrane a few minutes to recover then I'd get back in there. If I had to beat what he knew out of him, then so be it. Even if it cost me my job, it would be a small price to pay.

Jameson Burr, in the meantime, had also been located, arrested, and was en-route to the station for questioning regarding the missing two hundred thousand dollars from the housing fund. I wondered, if Burr had worked so closely with McCrane on that, whether he was as close to him in other areas of business. Specifically, the release of Sarah Caldwell from San Quentin.

'Tell you what, Patton', Charlie said. 'I'll take Burr, you take the journalist. Burr might know about Sarah Caldwell but if you reckon Britland-Jones might have done some family research after her brother was killed, he's more likely to have something isn't he'.

The Chemist was being suspiciously distant. Usually, when a game started we'd have something to work with; like the code, but so far we'd had nothing. I suspected this was just to prolong my agony of knowing my daughter had been taken and that there was nothing I could do about it although the one saving grace was that it gave us more time to find Sarah Caldwell herself. I was convinced that she didn't suspect that we knew her identity.

Britland-Jones and Jameson Burr both arrived at the station pretty much simultaneously, Britland-Jones, knowing he would have been pulled in for questioning regarding the story in The Times looked like he had his explanation prepared. Burr on the other hand was looking decidedly more worried; only having just read the article for himself, moments before the LAPD had turned up at his health club to arrest him. I used the time waiting for Britland-Jones to arrive to call Vikki back, letting her know that Katie wasn't at school but stopping short of telling her that she had been taken by The Chemist. There was no point in giving her anything extra to worry about; I'd much rather she thought that she had just gone out and not bothered calling her. I did my best to reassure her that Katie would be fine, knowing that if we were no closer to finding her within the next few hours, I would have to relent and tell my ex-wife the truth; something I was not relishing.

Charlie and Harlow took Burr into an interrogation room and likewise, I took Britland-Jones. It struck me, that across all three interrogation rooms; McCrane, Burr and Britland-Jones, that somewhere in there lay the key to finding Sarah Caldwell and finding my daughter.

Taking two cups of coffee into my room, I sat down opposite Paul Britland-Jones, who recognised me immediately.

'Detective Patton', he acknowledged. 'I thought Detective Harlow was taking this one?' he enquired, maybe a little puzzled as to my involvement in what he thought was only an embezzlement and corruption case.

'He is taking this one', I told him, pushing one of the cups in his direction. 'I need to ask you some questions about something else'.

'Hey Patton, I'm here voluntarily you know', he looked slightly alarmed. 'I've not been read my rights, just to make you aware of that!' He took a sip of the coffee. 'Do I need to call my solicitor?' he asked.

'Relax', I told him. 'You might be able to help me with some research you may have done eight years ago. You remember Andrew Caldwell, don't you?'

'Ah, indeed I do Detective', he said. 'Hardly you finest hour was it?' Well, there was no denying that was there?

'Well obviously not', I agreed. 'You ran a story though I seem to remember, about his family?' Sensing that this was going to be one-way traffic in terms of him helping us, Britland-Jones played the card that I thought he might.

'I did indeed', he confirmed. 'And supposing I assist you Detective and I give you the information you so clearly and so desperately need; after all, you wouldn't be here now if you didn't really need something from me would you? I'm sure Detective Harlow is itching to question me about the story I broke this morning'.

'Go on', I was cautious.

'I sense that there is another story here; an exclusive perhaps?'

'Maybe there is', I said.

'And if I was to furnish you with the information you need, would that exclusive be mine?' If that was all he was asking, it was a no-brainer.

'Of course', I told him. 'You have my word'.

'Well then, Detective, in that case, what do you need to know?'

'He had a sister didn't he?' I already knew the answer, but wanted to hear it from someone else besides myself.

'Yes he did', the journalist confirmed again. 'Sarah Caldwell, I believe her name was. Why do you want to know about Sarah?' I ignored the question.

'Did she come up at all in your research?' I wanted to know.

'Well she was the only relative I could find', he told me. 'Naturally, after your indiscretion whilst chasing her brother, I wanted the family's side of the story. How did she feel that a member of the LAPD had run her only brother off the road? That type of thing'.

'How did you find her?' I pressed. Britland-Jones sat back, looking as though he was trying to remember. 'It was a long time ago Detective, a long time ago. I'll ask again, why do you want to know about Sarah Caldwell?' He was being clever, the bastard. I knew he knew exactly what I needed to know, but he wasn't giving it up for free.

'We think that Sarah Caldwell is The Chemist', my hand was forced. 'And The Chemist currently has my daughter'. The statement hung in the air, as Britland-Jones processed what I had just told him; a mixed look of sympathy, surprise and delight on his face. As much as anyone would not wish to find themselves in my situation, he also sensed that revealing the identity of The Chemist could be the biggest scoop of his lifetime, outdoing even this morning's fine publication.

'So, Mr. Britland-Jones, now you know why we need to find her, how about giving me everything you've got?' He nodded, agreeing to the question.

'She was hard to track down', he told me. 'I only found her after her brother's funeral. I followed her back from there, to a house in Wilton, near Park La Brea. She wouldn't answer any of my questions. She looked more than a little alarmed that I had found her to be honest. I stayed on it for a few days, staked out the place. She'd come and go quite often but after three days I gave up trying to get her to talk. By that time the story was getting old anyway and old news doesn't sell papers'. This was, as far as I was concerned, close to a breakthrough.

'This house in Wilton?' I demanded. 'What was the address?'

'I don't know the address,' Britland-Jones shook his head. 'Like I said, I followed her there but it was a long time ago'. My face couldn't conceal my disappointment, as my head dropped. 'But I can do better than that Detective' I looked up, hardly daring myself to hear his next words.

'I think I can take you there', he revealed.

64

For Shawn Axon, fatigue had set in several hours ago. He just hoped that Tassiker would turn up for work this morning and that he wouldn't be wasting any more of his time looking for him. Captain Williams had instructed him to stay in San Francisco for another twenty-four hours. To say that he was happy about that wouldn't be strictly true, but he was professional enough to have sounded more than enthusiastic when he'd received his instructions.

Williams had also told him that they thought, from what they had put together in Los Angeles, that Governor Tassiker may hold vital information pertaining to The Chemist and what Axon had uncovered thus far indicated that Tassiker may play a pivotal role in helping them recapture Sarah Caldwell.

Even so, after only a few hours rest in the pool car seconded to him by the SFPD which was hardly conducive to a good nights sleep, he was longing for his own bed, and willing Tassiker to show up. When he had called the secretary again yesterday, just before she left for the day, under the pretence of wanting to thank Tassiker once again for his time, she had told him that the governor had called her saying he would be away all day. She had reminded him of an important meeting he had scheduled at ten o' clock the next morning with the parole board, and Tassiker had said he would be definitely back for that. She hadn't, much to Axon's relief, mentioned his second visit to the office to 'retrieve his phone' to the governor.

He should have been here by now though, and Axon was beginning to think that Tassiker was trying to distance himself from the prison, worried that the LAPD were looking into his association and history with Sarah Caldwell and Paul McCrane.

Much to his relief, at five minutes to ten, the governor made an appearance. He wouldn't have spotted Axon staking out the prison entrance. The car was unmarked and a good distance from the main entrance and therefore inconspicuous to any onlooker.

He watched as Tassiker drove past him and into the prison's car park, unaware of the Los Angeles detective waiting to take him into custody. Axon covered the ground between his stakeout vehicle and Tassiker's car quickly, and was more-or-less waiting for Tassiker when he stepped out of his car.

Clearly taken aback, the governor dropped his briefcase and various papers he was holding, when he saw Axon appear out of the corner of his eye. 'Detective Axon', he said, trying to remain calm. 'I assumed you had gone back to Los Angeles. Surely I answered all your questions yesterday'.

'Some things have come to light since we last spoke', Axon said grimly. 'Specifically, governor, your previous and current history with Los Angeles District Attorney Paul McCrane'.

'I told you yesterday', Tassiker stuttered.

'I know what you told me yesterday', Axon interrupted. 'Would you care to revise your bullshit statement?' he produced his cuffs, about to read the governor his rights.

As he tried to raise his arms for his arrest, Governor Tassiker felt a sudden pain in his chest and left arm and staggered back momentarily, his car taking all of his weight as he leant against it. He felt his mouth go dry and his eyes bulged, unsure of what was happening. He collapsed in a heap, and his surroundings became hazy and unidentifiable; everything blurred into one seemingly continuous landscape and he was unable to distinguish one object from another.

As he tried to regulate his breathing, the last thing he remembered before he lost consciousness was Detective Axon pulling out his cell and making an emergency call; reporting that Sebastian Tassiker, governor of San Quentin, had just had a suspected heart attack.

65

Just as we were about to roll out to the house in Wilton, the house Britland-Jones claimed was Sarah Caldwell's, news filtered through that puzzled us all. Senator Conrad Conway had just shot and killed an intruder at his house in Beverly Hills.

What appeared to have been the simple premise of an opportune burglary had been somewhat complicated by the contents of the intruder's back pocket; which had been searched by officers on the scene checking to see if the intruder had keys to Conway's residence. The contents causing so much alarm were the business cards of two of the most prominent individuals in the city; both of who just happened to have been arrested that morning; Paul McCrane and Jameson Burr.

Agent Balfer decided to remain at the station, trying to piece together the events of this morning and whether or not they had any bearing on our investigation. He would also take over from Charlie in questioning Jameson Burr, and from me questioning Paul McCrane. Given that he had supplied us with the covert information from San Quentin's surveillance tapes in the first place, he was as entitled as anyone to have a crack at McCrane and Burr as anybody here. Maybe the presence of an FBI badge would have more of an effect than my fists had about an hour ago.

The ride to Wilton took us around three quarters of an hour; the traffic heavy, even though we had the siren blaring for the best part of the journey. A couple of miles off the directions we were being given, we killed the siren just in case. We didn't want anyone at this house to know we were coming.

During the ride, despite being told repeatedly to shut the fuck up, Britland-Jones fired questions that I suspected were forming the basis of the story he planned to publish. He had signed documents back at the station that prohibited him, or anyone associated with the LA Times from publishing any further story relating to Sarah Caldwell, The Chemist, Paul McCrane, Jameson Burr or Sebastian Tassiker until he received express permission from Captain Williams personally. The legal department had rushed that one through for us. Not that I thought that Britland-Jones would give this story to anyone other than himself; egotistical prick, but we couldn't afford to take that chance. The entire ride, I was imagining Katie in an underground coffin, like Stella had been; how could I not? The images of the previous night were branded in my imagination, and probably always would be.

Britland-Jones directed us through Wilton; with a population of around four and a half thousand, it was one of Los Angeles' smaller towns. Some of the building we drove past remained storm damaged; un-repaired from 1995's El Nino. Levees were broken and roofs remained patchy. The majority of the town, however, a decade on from the disaster, was in sound architectural condition. Like more-or-less every town in the state, it had it's less than habitable areas. We drove through the main hub of the town; a large shopping mall and several adjoining avenues of shops.

'It's just round this corner on the left', Britland-Jones instructed a couple of minutes later, as we pulled onto an avenue, rows of houses on either side. 'Fifth house along on the right, I think'.

We pulled up along side the house that he brought to our attention and took a moment to survey it. It was semi-detached with an overgrown garden; grass was over a foot high and weeds snaked up the fence on the property's border. It also looked suspiciously empty; no curtains, blinds or indeed anything visible from the outside.

We had no hard evidence that Sarah Caldwell either lived, or had ever lived, at this address. Regardless of that fact, we were going in unannounced and weapons un-holstered. We were taking no chances whatsoever. Charlie took the rear, synchronising watches before he went; knowing that in sixty seconds we would both be in position and take down our respective entrances simultaneously. If it turned out that this was a normal house, with normal law-abiding residents then we would be full of apologies; not to mention the LAPD would have to compensate the family for the damage to the doors that we were about to inflict, but what else could we do? We were hardly going to knock on the front door and hope someone answered were we?

Patton, Holland and even Britland-Jones, who had remained seated in the car, were so focussed on the house, and the prospect of it being the residence of Sarah Caldwell, that not one of them noticed a silver Cadillac pull around the corner and purr past them, without once looking at them.

66

Agent Balfer didn't think that his FBI credentials had impressed Paul McCrane one little bit. The District Attorney had remained impassive as he had inspected Balfer's official ID, his face not giving anything away; the bruises swelling up from Patton's earlier interrogation were there for all to see, yet McCrane knew that when push came to shove, the LAPD could simply claim he arrived in that state. If the cameras had indeed been turned off, like Patton had told him they were, they would no doubt claim some kind of bullshit technical failure by way of explaining why the cameras had not captured his alleged beating.

'I don't know anything about the money from the housing fund', McCrane stated as Balfer picked his ID back up off the table. 'I think you will find all the paper work for that particular fund is well in order'.

'I'm not here about the housing fund', Balfer informed him.

'Ah', the look on McCrane's face gave way to familiarity. 'You want to know about Sarah Caldwell then', he stated.

'What can you tell me about her?'

'Well, I told Detective Patton all I know, I can't tell you anymore. And besides, anything you think you may have on me must be circumstantial at best. Otherwise you'd be presenting it to me now wouldn't you?'

Balfer had to admit, McCrane was one cool customer. 'I have one question for you Agent Balfer', McCrane continued. 'Is finding Sarah Caldwell more important than the front page of today's LA Times?' The question lingered, the duality of McCrane's last words easily interpreted by the experienced agent. McCrane almost certainly knew more than he had revealed, but Balfer didn't want to give in to him that easily. Besides, maybe Axon had got Tassiker by now; if they could get Tassiker's statement, documenting what had happened at San Quentin with Sarah Caldwell that would certainly be more than circumstantial.

Without saying a word to the District Attorney, he stood up and left the room. Although he had the authority to strike any deal he deemed necessary, he knew protocol also dictated that he run any suggestions past Williams.

Captain Williams had been watching on the monitors, that had been miraculously restored to working order minutes after Patton and Holland had left McCrane lying on the interrogation room's cold hard floor that morning.

'I can see where this bastard is going', Balfer told Williams. 'He obviously knows more than he's giving us, and wants a deal. He wants this thing with the housing fund swept under the carpet, no questions asked'.

'Yeah I was watching', Williams told him. 'Trouble is, we might not have any other option'.

'What do you mean?' Balfer quizzed. 'Anything from Axon yet?'

'That's the problem', Williams shook his head. 'Just as Axon was about to bring him in he keeled over with a suspected heart attack. They rushed him to the ER but he's in a critical condition. There's not a hope in hell of us questioning him. The ER have said it will be at least a day before he can talk, and that's their most optimistic prognosis'.

'It's a day we don't have though, isn't it?' Balfer was frustrated. Williams merely nodded his agreement. 'Your call Captain', Balfer told him. 'You call the shots on this one. What do you want to do?'

'We can't afford to wait can we?' Williams already knew the answer, he just wanted confirmation he was about to do the right thing.

'Patton's daughter's best chance of survival is if we deal, that's the bottom line'.

'Make it happen, Agent Balfer', Williams was not happy, but with Tassiker out of the picture for the foreseeable future, and nothing else forthcoming, his hands were tied.

Walking back into the interrogation room, the look on his face must have telegraphed his conversation with Williams to McCrane. 'So, Agent Balfer, might there be a deal on the table?'

'Two things', Balfer spat. 'Number one; we arrest Sarah Caldwell and number two; Katie Patton is recovered unharmed'. McCrane contemplated for a second, shaking his head.

'Unharmed', he stated calmly, 'is a little beyond my control. Would you settle for alive? Oh, and until the paperwork is signed, sealed and delivered, I'm afraid I'll be taking the fifth', he added.

67

Even before Charlie and I converged in the house, having covered the ground floor between us, I realised that this house was empty. It wasn't hard figure out; there was no furniture, bedding, appliances or personal effects of any kind. The rooms were bare, and cracks had begun to form in the flaking plaster on the walls. I could see there was damp coming through from a couple of the ceilings and there was a musty smell coming from the carpets where rain had dripped through and soaked the flooring.

'There's no-one here man', Charlie spoke for us both. 'Doesn't look like there has been for a while'. We spent several minutes checking over the house; what we found upstairs was reflective of what we had found downstairs; the whole house looked deserted and un-lived in. Had Britland-Jones been right about the address?

Disappointed and, more to the point, fearful that we still hadn't had any other communication from The Chemist giving us a starting point to try and get my daughter back, we reconvened outside, rain now beginning to fall from the skies.

'What next?' Charlie asked. He too had been praying that this would be a fruitful line of enquiry. 'Where do we go from here?'

'Excuse me, who are you looking for?' a voice came from behind us from the neighbouring garden. We turned around and saw an old man looking at us enquiringly. He looked to be in his mid seventies with a long grey beard, rimmed glasses and wore clothes that he looked like he hadn't changed in a week. Well it was worth a shot. I walked to the fence where he was standing and reached for the photograph we had of Sarah Caldwell, holding it up for the old man to see, close to his face, mindful of the fact that his eyesight probably wasn't the best, even with his glasses.

'Have you ever seen this person before?' I asked. 'Did she used to live here?'

'Who wants to know?' he demanded.

'We're LAPD' I told him, flashing my badge. 'We're here on a missing person case', which was slightly misleading the old man who would assume that person in the photograph was the missing person, and not my daughter, Katie.

The old man almost snatched the photograph from my hands, and held it at arms length, studying it intently, although the photograph was shaking in his grasp.

'Why I'm sure that's Sarah', he said nodding as my heart seemed to momentarily stop. 'Yes, I'm sure of it'

'And she used to live here did she?' Charlie clarified.

'She did indeed', the old man confirmed. 'Well, the whole family did. Tragic,' he said shaking his head, 'absolutely tragic'.

'What is?' I quizzed, taking the photograph back.

'Her parents died a long time ago. Looked like they got into a fight together at the top of the stairs and both fell from the top; both killed', he said, head still shaking. 'Sarah ran away after that, it was the grief I suppose', he continued, not supposing for one minute that Sarah could have been responsible for her parents' deaths. 'Her brother was taken into care not long after that and I didn't see her again until just after her brother's funeral. She stayed here for three or four days then disappeared again until about six months ago'.

'What happened six months ago?'

'Well she reappeared', he looked puzzled. 'Stayed for around a week this time, maybe slightly longer, then left again suddenly. Don't know what happens to the house mind, I suppose she must own it now her family's gone, but it stays empty most of the time.

Well the timeframe would fit. We hadn't known about her parents; well at least Charlie and I hadn't. If Britland-Jones had uncovered that fact whilst researching his story on her brother's death, he hadn't mentioned it to us.

'Do you know where she went?' I asked urgently. 'It's vital that we find her, sir'.

'She's not in any trouble is she?' he asked, suddenly looking worried. 'I wouldn't want to get her into any trouble'.

'Oh no sir, she's not', I assured him. 'We just need her to help us with some routine enquiries'.

'Ah, well that's alright then', the old man looked relieved. 'She did leave me a forwarding address actually, last time she was here. She told me she wouldn't have usually done so but that she was expecting an urgent letter from a friend and that she was going to be too busy to check here as often as she'd like.

'Did you forward it when it arrived?' I asked. That sounded like it could have some relevance.

'I did as a matter of fact. It was just the one', he told us. 'Wait there, I'll see if I can find the address for you'.

It took the old man only a couple of minutes to reappear, during which time both Charlie and I waited nervously. Was this too much to hope for? I wondered what she would need to receive so urgently that she would risk leaving an address with this old man. 'Do me a favour,' the old man wheezed, 'and don't tell her where you got the address from. She made me promise not to give it to anyone and I've known her since she was a child. Think I was the only person she could trust with the address.' he added. 'Sad, sad, sad', he shook his head once more.

I took the address off him, eagerly. Reading it, it looked familiar; like I should know it already, but I couldn't place it. It would be easy enough to check through dispatch though; we'd know exactly where it was in minutes. Thanking the old man, for what was now the best lead we'd had in the month that we had been chasing The Chemist, we walked back to the car. Only then, and even then it was purely chance that I turned my head in the direction that I did, did we notice a woman standing on the opposite side of the road to our parked car, about a hundred yards or so away from us, watching us, smiling.

I locked eyes with the woman, who was swaying slightly; the wind had picked up a little and it was raining harder than it had been whilst we were talking to the old man. Even through the rain, in the couple of seconds after I noticed her, I could see her clearly. She looked to be around a hundred and twenty pounds, maybe slightly more, and was around five foot seven. I could see her smiling, even from here. As I stood staring at her, Charlie followed my gaze to see what I was looking at.

We both knew instantaneously, and with no communication between us, that we were both looking at Sarah Caldwell. And she was looking back at us.

68

I'm not sure how long the stare down lasted, but as we looked at her, the rain started to drive down harder and harder. As I squinted, more to check I wasn't seeing things more than anything else, she stood rooted to the spot, still swaying, almost taunting us; daring us to try and catch her. As my eyes became accustomed to the rain, I began to see her clearly. I couldn't get over how ordinary she looked.

'That's her, right?' Charlie asked, his gaze still fixated on her across the road in the distance. By way of an answer, I started running towards her, reaching for my firearm, sure that it was indeed Sarah Caldwell.

For a moment, she stood and watched as I ran towards her. Even in the driving rain, I could see her still smiling as we crossed the road, dodging the few vehicles that dove past, before she turned quickly and ran; darting into an alley, ruling out the possibility of Charlie following in the car. She must have followed us from the station, there was no other way she could know we were here.

Charlie ran just behind me and I'd thought we'd make up our ground in no time but she was much quicker than I had anticipated, and as we turned out of the alleyway onto a long winding road that led back to the centre of Wilton, we were still a good distance behind her.

The forceful rain had sent the few people that had been on the sidewalks of Wilton darting for immediate cover, and as a result, the road was deserted apart from the three of us. That should have given us a clear line of sight on Sarah Caldwell, but in reality the harsh rain made it anything but. Large drops of water cascaded off us as we ran, soaking us both to the skin. It slowed us down somewhat, but had seemingly no effect on our target, who was pulling away from us a little, if anything.

I pushed myself to another level, despite the weather, the desire to get my daughter back burning inside me. Charlie followed suit, though I could tell from our breathing that we wouldn't be able to keep this pace up much longer.

From somewhere, I found the strength to pull away from Charlie; and within a minute I was right behind her. The speed with which I was running meant that it was difficult to pull my gun without losing my footing but that wouldn't matter; I was literally a couple of feet behind her by now.

Without warning, she made a sharp right into another alley way which caught me by surprise. She made the turn as sure-footedly as I'd imagine it was possible, given the conditions, and I tried to follow her lead.

I kind of half made it. I managed to turn into the alleyway itself but my momentum, combined with the wet conditions underfoot, made me lose my footing and I landed with a hard thud against two trashcans that were overflowing with debris, cracking my head against the floor which knocked me out cold for several seconds.

Charlie, several yards behind, saw us turn off, and slowed his pace accordingly. He must have seen me fall but didn't stop to see how I was; he knew all I cared about was having Sarah Caldwell apprehended. I saw him rush past just before I passed out and I tried but failed to call out to him to be careful.

Though he was carrying considerably more weight than Patton, Holland moved fast and was soon right behind The Chemist as she weaved through the alley, never once glancing over her shoulder to see if he was closing down on her.

She leapt over an abandoned shopping trolley that had been tipped over; probably left there by one of the many hobos that liked to call this alleyway home. As she did so, her foot clipped the handle of the trolley, causing her to stumble but not enough to take her off her feet. That gave Holland the opening he needed; Launching himself after her, he cleared the trolley by several inches, and managed to get a hand to Caldwell's shoulder, spinning her around as they both fell.

The tumble took them both off their feet and they landed in the sticky wet mud that was now running like a river through the alley.

Rising to get his bearings, out of the corner of his eye, Holland saw the bright sheen of a blade glistening, even in the rain which had turned the daylight into a dull grey mist. Rolling sideways out of instinct, he managed to avoid the knife that Sarah Caldwell sliced in his direction, but only just. He swung out with his fist, which connected with The Chemist's temple just as much out of luck as it did out of precision, knocking her over once more.

Rising, drawing his gun as he did so, he didn't see Caldwell lash out with her foot with a vicious strike to his right leg. The force of the strike should have been enough to break his patella, but Caldwell was maybe a couple of inches too far away to get all she could on the strike. Nevertheless, Holland dropped to the floor in considerable pain, dropping his gun as he did so.

If The Chemist had seen where the gun had gone, she gave no indication of wanting it, preferring to bring her blade high up once more and drive it through the collarbone of the grounded detective, who let out a sharp intake of breath and he felt the knife pierce his skin and tissue.

Trying to overcome the pain, Holland lashed out with a couple of wild swings; but the pain had clouded his judgement and the rain impaired his vision. As she stood over him, Holland got his first good look, up close and personal, at Sarah Caldwell. She certainly didn't look how he'd imagined. She was actually strikingly attractive, her natural beauty shining through the mud that had covered her face when she fell. Her eyes shone through; deep blue and piercing and her hair was jet black, tied neatly back in a pony tail, which had remained in place despite their tussle. She smiled at him as she bent down. If he didn't know what she'd done and what she was capable of, she looked just the kind of woman he might ask out for a drink, the stereotypical 'girl next door'. And that terrified him.

Reaching into her coat pocket, The Chemist pulled out another envelope. 'Please give this to Detective Patton', she whispered in Charlie's ear, as his blood continued to pool around them.

69

I stood up, somewhat groggily, my head pounding and my chest aching where the fall had winded me. As I tried to get my bearings, I peered down the alley, looking for any sign of Caldwell or my partner but the rain had severely reduced visibility and I could see no sign of either of them.

I jogged in the direction I knew they had gone, and it took me several seconds to build up my pace again, trying to ignore the pain of my fall, the mud in the alley way making it all the more difficult.

I found Charlie around a minute later; frantically scrambling as he tried to stand, using a discarded wooden pallet to assist his endeavour. I could see immediately that he was injured but couldn't tell how seriously.

'Easy, Charlie boy, easy', I took him with both arms to help him stand, which only made blood stream out of his shoulder wound faster. 'Gonna have to lie you back down, partner', I told him. 'You ok?'

'Yeah man', he winced, as I lay him down, 'She fucking got away. I had her, man, I had her', his eyes looked apologetic. 'I'm sorry, Patton, I should have had her'.

'You got nothing to apologise for Charlie boy', I reassured him. I hadn't fared any better had I? The knife wound looked pretty deep, and I knew better than to pull the knife out of my friend's shoulder. For one thing, the knife itself was going some way to reduce the loss of blood; an open wound would let the blood flow more freely and be susceptible to infection. Secondly, I didn't want to do any more damage by pulling the knife out; for all I knew the knife had a serrated blade which would rip Charlie's insides as I pulled it out. As I lay him back down I pulled out my cell to call the ambulance; Charlie was tough and it looked like the wound was mainly superficial but he would need treatment for it nevertheless; I also knew that if Sarah Caldwell had wanted to kill him, then she would have done so, so in that respect, he was damn lucky.

'She left another envelope Patton', he said through gritted teeth as I lay him back down; it's in my pocket. Even in a great deal of pain, knowing that the rain would soak the envelope through, he had done what he could to preserve it.

I wouldn't open it until I got back to the car, where I could look at it in dry conditions; nowhere in the alley way offered sufficient cover. I also wasn't about to leave my partner just lying here but I knew the ambulance would not take long to get here, so I crouched down, doing my best to shield Charlie from the rain.

'Go, man, go', Charlie urged. 'I'll be alright here'. I shook my head.

'Not a chance', I told him. 'I'm staying right here'. Besides, I knew that Sarah Caldwell would be, by now, long gone and the rain would have washed away any trail she might have left. She could be anywhere by now. I cursed the fact that we had been so close, but I swore that it wouldn't be the last opportunity I had today to take her down.

The ambulance duly arrived, and being too big to drive into the alley, the paramedics had to stretcher Charlie from his position to the ambulance. 'Just patch me up and give me a couple of painkillers', I'd heard him instruct the two guys who had secured him onto the stretcher. Typical Charlie that; he was one tough bastard.

'Not a chance big guy', one of them had replied. 'We're taking you in'. Again, he looked almost apologetic as he was transported into the awaiting ambulance, knowing he'd been taken out of action by Sarah Caldwell, leaving me alone to play her game.

70

It took longer than Conway had anticipated for the officers who attended the shooting at his house to process the scene. He had imagined that it would be more-or-less open and shut; that they would take a statement from him, remove the body and have the blood cleared up out of the hallway and that would be that, but in reality it was somewhat different. They had stopped short of arresting him; after all, the self defence was evident enough; he had several bruises from his fall down the stairs, but the attending officers had insisted on taking his statement on their territory, not his, so he'd had no option but to let them take him in voluntarily.

His hands tied, he accompanied them to the station, the outside of which was already becoming a media circus as the papers and TV stations learned of the arrests of McCrane and Burr. And now here he was, helping with a seemingly unrelated enquiry.

They drove past, relatively unnoticed. Even so, he tried to crouch down in the car, eager to avoid the spotlight. If he had to though, he could play the innocent victim in front of the cameras; just one more statistic of violent crime in Los Angeles. Why should he be different from anyone else? Anyone could be a victim of violent crime. Even him!

He gave his statement to the arresting officer; one which he had been over several times in his head in the car on the way over, and one which was accepted by the arresting officer without too many questioned being asked. That was good; he knew any judge in the state would close any case that may be forthcoming as self defence. Just in case though, he had insisted that pictures of his sustained injuries were taken as evidence, declining any medical treatment. If his ribs were still bothering him tomorrow he'd go and get checked out. He was more eager to learn what charges were going to be brought against his two colleagues who were arrested this morning.

After being told that they would be in touch and he was free to go, and that the Crime Scene Investigators had completed what they needed to do at his house, he declined the offer of a lift back, preferring to call his wife to pick him up. She had been out for the day; shopping once again no doubt, and although she would be relieved that he was alright, she would be less than thrilled that the blood from his attacker that had stained the rather expensive carpet in the hallway. He idly wondered whether his insurance would cover the cost of a replacement.

Walking down the corridor, his ribs still causing him some consternation, he saw, at the far end of the corridor, Paul McCrane being hustled through, accompanied by two policemen, and they were heading this way.

Unable to resist, he quickened his pace towards his Animi compatriot. 'Paul, Paul', he called as he got nearer, playing the concerned friend. 'I heard this morning about your arrest', he shook his head. 'If there's anything I can do?'

The accompanying officers seemed more than happy for him to speak to McCrane, and recognising who he was, actually backed off a little to give the two of them a little privacy, if only for a minute. He brought his head to just behind McCrane's ear. 'Bet you're surprised to see me here', he whispered so the officers would not overhear. McCrane simply looked impassive.

'I am indeed Conrad', he said. 'You haven't been arrested too have you?'

'No I've not', Conway continued. 'I've just given a statement about the intruder I shot and killed this morning'. He searched McCrane's face, which typically gave nothing away.

'Sound's like you've had a lucky escape', McCrane shrugged. 'I just hope that whoever you killed this morning doesn't have any friends who wish to seek retribution', he had recognised the undertones in Conway's voice, suggesting that he somehow knew that the intruder had been sent under his and Burr's instruction.

'I did indeed', Conway whispered, 'I've got no idea, by the way, how the LA Times could have gotten such a story on you, you back-stabbing fuck', letting McCrane know exactly how they had gotten the story. 'Oh, and when you next see him, tell Burr that his wife tastes like a peach', he added, smiling. 'A ripe peach'.

'Like I said', he repeated audibly, for the benefit of the officers who had decided time was up, 'Anything I can do Paul, you just let me know'.

With that, he left McCrane, seemingly passive on the outside, but positively seething with rage on the inside, as the officers continued to accompany him to the office of Captain Williams.

71

I watched as the ambulance departed, leaving me standing alone; the rain beginning to subside. I began to jog back to the car, contemplating how fortunate Charlie had actually been to only sustain the injuries he had, and frustrated at how close we had come to apprehending Sarah Caldwell.

Britland-Jones hadn't moved from the car, but was eager to know what had transpired. He didn't even attempt to disguise his interest as anything other than journalistic.

'You're driving', I demanded, and gave him a brief run down of our encounter with Sarah Caldwell, having to explain Charlie's absence. Although he expressed concern as to Charlie's well-being, I could see he was working out where to slot that into his next story.

Nevertheless, he took the wheel as instructed, and I did my best to shake off whatever wetness I could. It didn't have much of an effect; I was soaked through and covered in mud. I would need a quick change at the station but Britland-Jones was driving for one reason, and one reason only; I had the contents of an envelope to inspect. 'Back to the station', I informed Britland-Jones as I pulled it out of my pocket. Charlie had indeed prevented the envelope from getting wet through, and its contents were well preserved.

'Quick as you can, alright?'

'No problem', Britland-Jones replied. 'Once I've done that, I'm free to go right? I'm a busy man Detective, got things to do'.

'I'll check with Detective Harlow', I told him, 'Just drive'. I ripped open the envelope; would this be my first step of the new game?

British wheels at stationary event tonight

Was it me, or were The Chemist's messages becoming increasingly abstract? It felt strange not having someone to bounce ideas off and I certainly wasn't going to start bouncing them off Britland-Jones. As much as I didn't want the journalist privy to too much information, Captain Williams needed to be kept informed. As usual, they would have every available person there trying to work it out for me. I almost thought about telling him to include Marvin.

'Hey, it's Patton', I said as Williams answered, 'what's new there?' He told me about Tassiker's heart attack and the impending deal with McCrane. 'He's on his way to me now', he told me. 'Just got the paperwork through. Much as I don't want to give him the deal, the son-of-a-bitch, it may be our only shot at getting what we need out of him in time'.

'I appreciate that Captain', I said truthfully. They didn't have to offer him a deal at all, and I bet Harlow would be pissed, but what he said was right; we needed what McCrane knew quickly.

I briefed him on the latest message from Caldwell, which as usual drew the familiar reaction of bewilderment. 'We've broken the rest', he reminded me, 'and we'll break this one'.

News came through that Burr was remaining silent. 'Hasn't said a fucking thing since we arrested him, that's what Harlow has told us', Williams informed me. 'I've also just had the paramedics that took Holland in tell me that he's saying like it or not, he's discharging himself in two hours'. Despite my situation, I couldn't help but laugh. Charlie hated hospitals and was going to be a handful of a patient, I knew that. It also meant that if he was saying that, then his condition wasn't serious, which came as a relief. I had no doubt that Charlie would be back by my side just as soon as he could.

'One more thing', I asked Williams, 'Do we need Britland-Jones for anything else?' The Captain mulled it over.

'Let him go.' he conceded. 'For now, anyway, in the light of the deal with McCrane. If we need anything from him, we can bring him in again. Do me a favour Patton, I know he's signed the damn papers, but just remind him how hard we will come down on him if he violates the terms of our agreement'.

Paul-Britland Jones left me at the station twenty minutes later, with those very words ringing in his ears.

72

I changed in my office. I always keep some spare clothes there, as I do live some distance from the station, especially since Vikki and I split up. There had been times over the last couple of years, usually when I was right in the middle of a particularly taxing investigation, when I had simply slept in the office, knowing that I'd have to be back there in a few hours anyway.

I made my way up to Captain Williams' office, who had just finalised the paperwork for McCrane's deal by the time I got there. 'He's on his way up', he told me. 'Much as I hate dealing with this corrupt bastard, we need him to tell us everything'. I nodded, realising that he didn't have to make that sacrifice on my behalf, but he had anyway.

'Anything with the last message yet', I asked him. He shook his head.

'Well the *British wheels* bit may be a car but as to *stationary event*, we have no idea. At least the message indicates that it's tonight, which give us a little extra time. Nothing from the house I take it?'

In the ensuing pursuit that had taken place after we talked to Sarah Caldwell's neighbour, and in the resulting chaos that chase had produced, I had completely forgotten that we had a second address; one that I'd recognised from somewhere. 'Shit, Charlie's got the new address.' I told him. 'The neighbour had a forwarding address for Caldwell, which Charlie took'.

'I don't suppose you can remember it?' he asked, picking up the phone. I just shrugged, shaking my head. I was trying but I just couldn't remember it at all.

It took Captain Williams a few minutes to locate Charlie in the hospital, and another couple of minutes to ascertain whether or not the paper with the address on was actually there.

'Goddamn it', he exclaimed, hanging up the phone.

'What's up?' I was alarmed. Charlie had the address didn't he?

'Well he's got it alright, thing is; it's been damaged by the rain, it's all smudged; Charlie says it's unreadable'.

'We need to get back onto the neighbour, see if he's got it written down anywhere else', I tried thinking this through. What could we do if he he'd given us the only copy he had? Fortunately, Captain Williams had a suggestion.

'In the meantime, we need to get that piece of paper down to forensics', he said. 'About a year ago I remember they somehow managed to repair and read something that had been completely shredded and burned. God knows how they did it, but they did'.

'They can do that?' I was incredulous. 'Even though the writing is unreadable, you think they can repair that?'

'Well we'll find out, won't we?' he raised his eyebrows as he spoke, letting out a sigh as he did so. 'I'll get a black and white to contact the neighbour and have someone pick up the remnants of the address from the hospital. It might take a while though for forensics to do their thing', he warned. 'We will try and rush it through though, obviously'.

There was a knock on the door, and Paul McCrane walked in, looking happier and smugger than any man in his position had the right to be.

73

That had been much closer than she had anticipated. She had almost been caught, and would have been if it weren't for her lightening quick reflexes in taking out Holland's legs before driving the knife through his collarbone. She had spared his life, though she didn't know why. Maybe she should have killed him, but she was sure she'd done enough damage to him to take him out of today's game.

She had left Detective Holland lying in agony in the alley way and circled back round to her car, knowing Patton would stop to assist his fallen partner when he regained his faculties. She hadn't seen him fall; she had been all too aware that both detectives were closing, but she had heard Patton crash into those trashcans, and the fact that he did not arrive to assist Holland, once she had fallen, meant that maybe he had knocked himself out in the fall. Good; she hoped it had hurt him. It was nothing compared to the pain she knew she was inflicting on him right now though.

She had wanted Patton to suffer; her brother had been dead for eight years now, so why shouldn't Patton suffer? She had initially wanted to start Katie's game straight away, but thought that a few hours of Patton's imagination running riot before she started was the least he deserved, especially after he had found Stella!

The rain and mud, which had soaked her to the skin too, didn't bother her. Very little could now. She had spent years, after leaving home after her parents' 'accident', surviving and enduring the hellacious conditions of LA's streets, becoming almost nomadic within the state, constantly moving around from one area to another; growing increasingly volatile and violent. Her dad had deserved it and her mother had been a pure accident. The guy who pulled up alongside her, a mere two days after she had left home, and made the most obscene suggestions to her for twenty dollars had also deserved it. She had gotten into his car and they had driven to an deserted industrial estate in San Vicente and as he'd undone his flies, she'd grabbed his head with both hands, whilst he'd been looking down, taking him by surprise and rammed his head through the car window, before lifting his head once more and raking his throat down across the shards of glass that had remained. She remembered him rolling over, as the blood drained from his recently slit throat; his eyes wide with surprise and unable to speak. He'd deserved it though. So had the dozens of others over the years, some of which she found herself reliving occasionally, when she got her migraines.

Over the years, before her arrest for a triple homicide anyway, she had become increasingly proficient at evading the authorities and had added various activities to her criminal repertoire, including the ability to con just about anything out of anyone. To this end, she had amassed a substantial amount of money and, now having settled into a small single room occupancy in Pico, whose landlord asked absolutely no questions, she had at least some semblance of a normal existence.

A fire had engulfed the entire building several months later, just around the time she learned of her brother's death. She was told that the fire had been due to faulty wiring that the landlord should have replaced long ago. Although, miraculously, no-one had been killed in the fire, all her possessions were destroyed, including the only photograph she had of her brother; the only reminder of her previous life. The whole building was left a mere husk of a structure, jet black from the smoke damage. She had been relieved that she now had money stashed in various deposit boxes around Pico, Robertson and Manning. With no place to stay, she had returned to her parent's house in Wilton, which had remained uninhabited since her brother was taken into care. A few nights later, she paid a visit to her landlord, who happened to be eating an evening meal with his wife and sister-in-law when she visited them. She broke in easily enough and was on her landlord, Oscar Rodriguez before he'd finished chewing what he had in his mouth, twisting his neck and killing him instantly despite the substantial weight advantage he carried; the look of surprise was still etched in his face when he stopped breathing. His wife and sister-in-law were too shocked to move, so they had been easy too; taking out her knife she had made short work of the pair of them. To this day, she didn't know if neighbours had reported a disturbance, or if the police had just happened to be in the neighbourhood, but they had been outside the house and saw her run from the residence, with blood covering her arms and hands. Unable to out manoeuvre three police officers, and unable to fight them off, despite her considerable strength, she had succumbed to their arrest, crying for her brother as she did so.

74

'I take it everything is in place', Paul McCrane remarked to the room in general, as he walked into Captain Williams' office. His anger at finding out who had leaked this story to the press remained bubbling under the surface but he realised that this deal he was about to sign would take care of that. He had no option but to give the police most of what he knew. If The Chemist was caught, then he would face no charges relating to this morning's front page of the LA Times and there would be no arraignment on anything to do with corruption forthcoming. Once he'd gone about putting those charges to bed, he would have to pay Conrad Conway a visit and seek a little retribution. He had indeed been surprised to see Conway walking the halls of this very station, for he knew exactly the window of opportunity that Daryl Walls had been given to carry out Burr's instructions, and that window had now long since passed. He hadn't had the chance to find out exactly what had gone wrong, but he feared that Conway had got the better of Walls in the struggle, maybe even killed him. Maybe he could get something out of Captain Williams.

'My good friend, Senator Conrad Conway was downstairs as I was coming to your office Captain. I trust he's ok?' he enquired.

'He shot and killed an intruder at his house this morning', Williams replied looking directly into the eyes of the District Attorney.

'My word', McCrane replied, 'Sounds like he had a lucky escape. Do you know who the intruder was?' It wouldn't hurt to make a seemingly concerned enquiry.

'He's been identified as Daryl Walls', Williams informed him. 'He was already in the system. As soon as we got his prints, we had him. Curious thing though', he continued. 'He had both yours and Burr's business cards in his back pocket. But you wouldn't know anything about that, would you?'

'Indeed I would not', McCrane genuinely told him, leaning back in the chair, thinking quite rightly that Conway must have planted them on the body to try to further incriminate himself and Jameson. 'I couldn't begin to think where he might have got them from', he added. The tone of Williams' last question had clearly implied he suspected either himself of Burr knew the attacker.

'Anyway', Patton inserted himself into the conversation. 'You've got your deal. Tell us what we need to know'. McCrane was not about to rush himself for the man who had beaten him earlier this morning.

'If I may inspect the proposal?' he held his hand out and Williams grudgingly handed him the document lying on his desk.

It took McCrane several minutes to fully digest the proposal, checking its legalities and legitimacy. He could have done it in half the time but he quite enjoyed seeing Detective Patton grow more and more impatient, the longer he took. Finally, satisfied that the deal was as advertised, he reached into his breast pocket and pulled out a pen, signing the document with a flourish.

'So then', he smiled. 'Now that we are happy the deal is in place, how may I be of assistance?'

75

The Chemist left Wilton satisfied that she had done the right thing by following Patton to her former address, even though she had come close to being caught. She had been right about Holland too; he moved much quicker than his frame suggested he could, and had been very strong during their brief tussle in the alley way. She hadn't planned to follow them, but couldn't resist when she'd seen them leave the station. She recognised the reporter with them too, even though it had been eight years since she'd last seen him. Paul Britland-Jones had been sniffing around asking questions after her brother's funeral, and had actually alerted her as to the circumstances surrounding his death on the Windsor Hills. She was sure he worked at the LA Times.

She drove from Wilton; following Patton and Britland-Jones back to the station, and then after a brief stop, on to Montebello, where she was holding Katie. Although she had used Clozapone on all the previous girls, in her excitement to start Katie's game straight away, she hadn't found the time to find an additional courier at such short notice; therefore the Clozapone would have to be forfeited, for now anyway. Not that it really mattered, the end result would be the same: The death of Katie Patton, which would leave her father regretting the day he ran Andrew Caldwell off the road during a high speed pursuit, forever.

She pulled up to the small house in Montebello, which she had rented under a false name around five months ago. She hadn't cared to see what it was like inside. Her only prerequisite had been that it had to have a cellar, which was surprisingly difficult to find nowadays. The house was run down, with paint peeling off every wall, and vermin could often be seen scuttling across the floor in the moonlight that shone through the back window. Quite often, gunshots could be heard to ring out across the night sky, penetrating the hum of traffic from the freeway half a mile from the house. It was a neighbourhood where everyone minded their own business and no-one asked any questions; which was of much more importance to Sarah Caldwell than anything as menial as a well-maintained building or pleasant surroundings.

She parked the Cadillac a good distance from the house as she usually did, preferring to walk the rest of the way. The car might attract unnecessary attention, sticking out in such a neighbourhood. In fact, the only time the car had been anywhere near the house was when she had taken Katie there yesterday, and even then, it had only been outside the house for maybe ten minutes. She would have to pull the Cadillac around the back in a few minutes, but wanted to check on Katie first.

Getting to the house, she made her way to the cellar trapdoor, moving the rug and table that covered it; unless you knew about the cellar, no-one would suspect one existed. She hadn't wanted to take any chances there, you never knew in this city when the police would be in the right place at the wrong time! In a neighbourhood where crime was rife, particularly at night, it wouldn't do for the police to take a random interest in the house as they went about their business.

The house was set as such that no-one who happened to be walking by could see any of the goings on inside; the windows were higher than foot level and hadn't been cleaned in quite a while, which added to the murkiness that surrounded the house in general. Not that if anyone happened to peer inside, they would see anything suspicious but it didn't hurt to have precautions like that in place.

Pulling open the cellar door, she could hear muffled, frightened cries that told her Katie was conscious. She hadn't been back to check on Katie since initially bringing her here yesterday afternoon; it had been around five o' clock by the time she had gotten her back here yesterday and she had still being unconscious from the chloroform used in her abduction. She still hadn't come round whilst The Chemist had tied her to the strappado-like pulley that was a fairly crude replica of the medieval torture device. She had read, whilst incarcerated in San Quentin actually, of the Spanish Inquisition and the various methods of torture they employed. The strappado appeared to be a favourite, where the individual was hoisted up on a rope with their arms behind their head, causing dislocation and internal nerve damage. She had gone for a more subtle method, whereby the arms were above the victim and not behind; therefore dislocation was less likely, but she had wanted to preserve Katie in pretty good condition; for now. She wanted Katie to suffer just as much as her father; she could only imagine what the last twenty-something hours had been like for her, strung up there, imagining what fate may lie ahead. She had also placed a hood over Katie's head which would not only make it more difficult to breathe but would also substantially heighten her sense of fear.

A quietness overcame the frightened girl as she sensed someone was in the room with her. She was visibly shaking, which made her sway back and forth on the pulley, the ropes digging into her wrists and ankles, which delighted Sarah Caldwell.

'Who, who's there ...' she called, stuttering her words. 'What do you want with me? Why am I here?'

The Chemist moved slowly towards her, like a creature stalking its prey. Stopping inches from Katie, she was sure that the girl could hear and feel her breath as she approached. Almost mesmerised, transfixed with Patton's shaking daughter, she lifted the hood from the girl, and couldn't help but smile when she saw the fear in her face. Her mascara had run from where she had been crying, which only served to seem to make her more frightened, more afraid. Her eyes were wide and became focussed as she adjusted her vision to the light.

Sarah Caldwell said nothing, but merely stared at Katie, watching as her eyes darted around her environment, watching as she realised the trouble she was in. Finally, Katie's gaze fixed on her captor, remembering how she had been abducted on her way to the library yesterday afternoon. She couldn't believe what was happening. She had only stopped to help the woman with directions. When the woman had smiled at her she had thought there was no harm in helping her. She looked the same now too, although she had a welt on her cheekbone which was turning blue that she didn't think was there yesterday.

'Fuck you', she spat, and as she did so a globule of spit landed on Sarah's forehead, and trickled down over the bridge of her nose. Ah, so maybe she did take after her father then? Saying nothing, and showing no sign of shock at Katie's actions, The Chemist merely stuck out her tongue, capturing drops of the spit as it dripped over her lips, and laughed as she finally raised her hand to wipe away the remnants of the saliva.

'Oh Katie', she smiled, 'you're so much like your father'. Like lightening, she swung a clenched fist across Katie's face, knocking her back into unconsciousness and drawing blood, which trickled from a cut across Katie's eyebrow. 'Oh yes', she repeated as she placed the hood back on her victim. 'So much like your father'.

Katie would have to keep, for now. She had something in the back of her Cadillac that required her immediate attention; something she hadn't planned on until about an hour and a half ago, but it was certainly a wonderful addition to the game. And something that would give Patton another big surprise.

76

'So who was responsible for releasing Sarah Caldwell?' I asked McCrane. 'We know it's not just you and Tassiker'. I suspected that even though the deal was in place, the more he thought we knew, the more forthcoming he might be.

'You know that do you?' he asked. 'And who else do you suspect might have been involved then?'

'Why don't you tell us McCrane?' Williams chimed in. 'You've got your deal, but if we don't get Katie Patton back alive and if you don't give us anything that leads us to Sarah Caldwell, your deal's not worth shit'.

In truth, although Paul McCrane really didn't know much else apart from the fact that he and Burr had engineered her release from prison and that she had subsequently killed the two guards and disappeared. He had been piecing together bits of the puzzle himself.

What eluded him the most was how she could just simply disappear. Between them, he and Burr had pulled in favours all across the state trying to track down Sarah Caldwell. She must have had assistance from somewhere, otherwise he was sure that they would have located her by now. They had been looking for her for the best part of six months.

Williams brought up the surveillance tapes of him leaving San Quentin with her. 'That's you and Caldwell, right?' he stated. Well there was no point in denying that was there?

'As you can clearly see', McCrane retorted, 'that is indeed me, and that is indeed Sarah Caldwell'.

'Where did you take her after that?' Patton wanted to know.

'Well there's little point in denying that Jameson Burr, who you no doubt have in an interrogation room somewhere assisted me in extraditing her from San Quentin', there was no harm in giving them something they had already probably worked out. 'She was taken to a government safe house in Florence. We placed two guards with her who thought she was a witness to a mafia hit. Perfectly plausible'.

'And she escaped?' Patton continued for him. 'Where did she go?'

'That I cannot say, for I do not know Detective Patton', he was thinking on his feet now. Someone close to him and Burr must have known. He had thought that they had been the only two people, Tassiker aside, who had known about their operation.

'One thing I want to know', Williams asked, 'is why you released her in the first place?'

McCrane wasn't about to divulge the existence of the Animi; certainly not to those as undeserving of the knowledge as a LA Police Captain and one of his detectives. At the thought of the Animi, another thought hit him from left field. Could one of the Animi have known about Sarah Caldwell before they had told them at the last meeting?

'Did you have no means of tracking her?' Patton asked, firing another question at him. 'Surely you realised how dangerous she was?'

Tracking her? Of course they had, as they usually did. Caldwell hadn't been the first prisoner they had recruited to do their bidding over the years. Burr had taken care of the tracking implant himself, at the safe house. Caldwell would have been unconscious for the implanting wouldn't she, so how would she have known she was implanted with a tracker? More to the point, why had he not thought of this before?

As far as he was aware, the only individuals that knew of the implanting process were the members of the Animi. It dawned on him that the only way Sarah Caldwell could have known she was implanted with a tracking device was if she had been told. He hadn't and he was pretty sure his colleague who had been arrested this morning hadn't either. That only left a pretty short list of possibilities. Who had told her?

'I need to speak to Jameson Burr', he announced, standing up. From the look on Patton and Williams' face it didn't look like they were going to accommodate him.

'Five minutes', has added. 'I need to clarify something important with him'.

'Tell us what', Patton demanded.

Having no other choice, McCrane complied.

'I might be able to give you the individual that has helped Sarah Caldwell since her escape from my custody'.

77

By the time he was marched down to the interrogation room where Burr was being detained, he'd gone over several different scenarios in his mind. He thought he had worked out who had aided Sarah Caldwell, possibly hiding her as McCrane and Burr had pulled in their respective favours all over the state, failing to locate her. He was annoyed with himself for not working it out sooner.

He had hoped that Patton and Williams would have given him time to speak to Burr in private, but they weren't taking the chance that Burr might pass something onto McCrane that would not be reciprocated in their direction. As they entered, Burr looked up in surprise, alarmed to see McCrane was now sporting several bruises since he'd last seen him.

'Five minutes has started', Williams instructed. Seeing that they weren't going to get any privacy, McCrane hoped Burr would pick up his signals and try to get himself a deal. Regardless of whether Burr did or didn't however, he still needed to clarify something with him.

'Jameson', he began, 'I've been forced to help these gentlemen with their enquiries regarding Sarah Caldwell'. Burr looked startled. What had McCrane done that for?

How had they known about that in the first place?

'I need to clarify something regarding the implanting of the tracker', he continued. 'Something only you can verify', he added, hoping that Burr would pick up on that. Thankfully, it worked.

'I'm happy to help', Burr announced turning to Captain Williams, 'however, I sense that my good friend Paul McCrane here has struck some sort of deal with you gentlemen, and my assistance with your investigation into Sarah Caldwell would of course be subject to the exact same terms'.

I turned to Captain Williams myself, aware that one deal on the table was more than he needed to have offered. Two deals would certainly be pushing it.

About thirty seconds passed whilst the Captain mulled it over, finally nodding his head. 'You'll get your deal but you talk now. Non-negotiable; take it or leave it. I find you've held anything back from us, I'll null and void it and you'll be looking at a minimum of ten to fifteen from what I've seen in this mornings papers'.

'In that case, I'll take it.' Burr practically snapped his hand off. 'Now then', he turned to McCrane, nodding in silent recognition of how his friend had engineered his deal. 'What exactly do you need to clarify?'

'It's about when you implemented the tracking device', McCrane re-stated.

'Ah yes, well as usual, we ...'

'As usual?' I interrupted. 'You mean you've done this before?' I couldn't believe what I was hearing. That was a slip up McCrane hadn't been expecting, but he was quick to act.

'Whether we have or we haven't', he said immediately, 'Neither scenarios pertain anything relevant to us releasing Sarah Caldwell', he stated imperiously, 'and are therefore irrelevant to your case'. He turned back to Burr. 'What I need to know is if you followed our discussed implanting procedure to the letter?'

'Of course I did', Burr said indignantly.

'So you're positive that Sarah Caldwell was unconscious when you implanted her with the tracking chip? You were alone? There's no way she would be aware of the procedure?'

'No way at all', Burr confirmed. 'She was certainly unconscious and I was alone. The guards remained outside until I went; they wouldn't have known anything'.

McCrane stood up. 'Thank you Jameson', he shook his friend's hand. 'Your deal will be delivered, will it Captain?'

Unsure as to the relevance of the information Burr had just given, Williams nodded 'Subject to the two conditions being met'.

'Conditions?' Burr enquired.

'That Sarah Caldwell is caught and that Katie Patton is alive when found'

'Ah, she has you're daughter', Burr directed at Patton. 'Well I hope for my sake, you get her back', he almost laughed.

Whilst Patton and Williams hadn't understood the pertinence of the information just confirmed by Jameson Burr, Paul McCrane did. He knew that only three people were aware of the tracker implanting process when Sarah Caldwell escaped; and he now knew who must have assisted her.

Certain now that one member of the Animi had known about Caldwell's release before they were told about it at the meeting a few days ago, McCrane turned to Patton and Williams.

'I'm not sure how or why', he informed them, 'but I'm fairly certain that one individual may have assisted Caldwell on the outside. Maybe even still is'. He knew that aside from himself and Burr, only one other person, prior to the

Animi's last meeting, had known how they were going to track Sarah Caldwell once she had been released from San Quentin. That person was the individual who had suggested implanting their subjects with the tracker in the first place, the first time it was needed. Neither Patton nor Williams spoke. The next question they would have both asked blindingly obvious.

'And I think that individual is Robert Farrington'.

78

Not particularly wanting to return to the scene of this morning's incident quite so soon, Conrad Conway did so under considerable duress from his wife who had seemed mildly annoyed that her early afternoon coffee with her friends at some swanky restaurant on Melrose had been interrupted by her husband shooting and killing an intruder at their home that morning. To his not entirely unexpected surprise, she had ranted the entire duration of the mercifully short journey from the police station where she picked him up to their home in Beverly Hills that the luxurious carpet she had picked out for the hallway eight or nine months ago during one of her not too infrequent house restyles had better not be ruined. Not that he'd been paying too much attention, but he was sure she had asked about the state of the carpet before his well-being!

Reassuring her that by the end of the day, Los Angeles' finest carpet cleaning company would be there to assess the damage, he turned his thoughts to how his plan to take McCrane and Burr out of the picture was proceeding. They had both been brought into custody this morning, and McCrane had looked positively livid for a moment when they passed each other before in the corridor of the police station. The fact that McCrane now knew he had masterminded his arrest must have come as a double-whammy of a shock when he'd realised that the plan to kill him had been thwarted.

His cell rang and seeing the number that it screened, he knew this was a call that required a certain level of privacy to take. Leaving his wife to flap around the blood stained carpet in the hall, he strolled through to the kitchen and out into the spacious garden, which even on a cold November's day such as this one, retained a certain degree of warmth, with flush green grass and blooming flowers cascading throughout. Their gardener did a splendid job, no doubt about that, but on the money he paid him every month, he damn well should do! He winced slightly as he lifted his cell to his ears; his ribs, although not broken as he'd first suspected, were bruised and despite the couple of pain killers he'd taken, were still causing him some pain. Not that he was about to go and get any medical advice, he had other matters to attend to today.

'What have you got for me?' he demanded as he answered his ringing cell. The caller was Steve Bridges, one of his several informants within the infrastructure of the LAPD. Bridges worked as an administration clerk, and was also often used as the 'go-to' guy between certain departments. Conway had telephoned him, along with all his other informers, from a payphone on the corner of 6th just after he had left first thing this morning, instructing him to call if he should hear of anything pertaining to the individuals named on the front page of the Times this morning. Bridges was an astute individual, who Conway kept on his extremely unofficial books with a couple of hundred dollar-a-month retainer. Not earning a particularly great deal in his current job, it was a couple of hundred bucks that Bridges was always happy to receive.

'Just thought you should know', Bridges answered, 'that McCrane struck a deal about an hour ago. I don't know exactly what he's giving them but all charges relating to the housing fund are being dropped'. Conway almost dropped his cell in surprise.

'Dropped? What the fuck do you mean, dropped?' he exploded.

'Just saw the file now', Bridges stated. 'I had to take it up to the Captain straight from the legal department, about an hour ago. It's not quite done and dusted but it's not far off'.

'What do you mean?'

'The deal seems to hinge on two conditions being fulfilled'.

'What fucking conditions?'

'Well', Bridges recalled, 'the first one is the apprehension of someone called Sarah Caldwell; don't know who she is though, never heard of her before'.

'And the second one?' Conway enquired. He certainly knew who Sarah Caldwell was, even if Bridges didn't.

'The safe return of Katie Patton', Bridges informed him.

'Know anything about that?'

'I do as a matter of fact, yeah', Barnes enlightened him. 'We got a detective here, Patton, had his daughter abducted either last night or this morning. Not sure which. What I also know, well have heard through the jungle drums anyway, is that Patton laid one on McCrane this morning, roughed him up pretty good too'. Ah yes, that would explain the bruises on McCrane's face when he'd seen him this morning.

'What about Burr?' Conway wanted to know.

'Pretty sure he's getting the same deal but I've not seen that one yet. Word is that they'll both walk today while Patton's investigation takes it's course, then apprehended again if either of the conditions are not fulfilled'.

'Can that happen?' Conway wasn't happy to say the least. 'I mean, can they just walk?'

'What can I say, they must have some powerful friends or some pretty big fucking influence themselves, I guess'. Well there was no denying that. Technically, he knew he shouldn't have been released so easily after this morning's shooting but they'd had no evidence that it had been anything other than self defence. The yet to be confirmed, but predictably forthcoming arraignment on that score would be a formality.

'Well once they've given the LAPD what they need, all the information they have to assist in fulfilling those two conditions, they're not going to want to be detained whilst the case plays out are they?' Bridges clarified.

'Can you find out what time they will be due to leave?' Conway wanted to know, an alternative plan already beginning to form in his mind. One that he maybe should have used in the first place, even though there was a great deal more risk that he could be tied to what he had in mind.

'More than likely', Bridges stalled.

'You get me an accurate time and you get another thousand this month'. That, it seemed, was all Bridges needed to hear.

'No problem, I should be able to do that', he confirmed.

'I'll need to know at least an hour in advance', Conway warned.

'I'll sort that for you', he was assured.

Conway searched through his cell for another number, and seeing the name Leon Reno dialled the number.

'Hello', came a lazy drawl after several minutes.

'You know who this is?' Conrad asked.

'Yes I do', Reno replied after a brief hesitation.

'I'm going to need a favour from you'.

79

The revelation that Robert Farrington could be in contact with Sarah Caldwell, perhaps even helping her, rendered both Captain Williams and I speechless for several seconds. Farrington owned the third biggest television network in the country, just behind Fox and CBS, and was on the verge of going global. He had built his media empire up from a small cable network, starting over twenty years ago, and by all accounts operated his business with a ruthless efficiency and aggression rarely seen in today's business arena. Rumour had it that he'd worked sixteen hours a day; maybe more on Sundays and that he cursed sleep for depriving him of the opportunity to expand his empire even further. He moved in the highest of circles, often seen on his own network rubbing shoulders with various members of the Whitehouse and A-List celebrities, who all seemed gracious that he'd taken the time out of his busy schedule to give them the time of day. I remembered seeing one newsbyte a few months ago where he said if he'd appeared on The Apprentice, he'd be firing Donald Trump. He'd been laughing at the time but the look in his eyes told me that he was probably serious. If there's one thing I knew about him, it was that he had an ego to match the size of his network.

I glanced at Captain Williams, who was digesting McCrane's speech, looking deep in thought. That was fully understandable. Giving McCrane, and now Burr, a deal was a big call that he had made, giving me his full backing. Going after Farrington was an equally big call; one false move and we would be splashed all over the television from Thanksgiving to Christmas, and beyond. And not in a particularly flattering light at all. Added to that, how did we know that McCrane was telling us the truth? Our only saving grace was that he did genuinely seem to want the housing fund charges that would be forthcoming nullified, and getting my daughter back and capturing Sarah Caldwell was the only way that was going to happen.

Nevertheless I was still sceptical at McCrane's revelation. Robert Farrington was a powerful, highly respected member of the state. It didn't make sense that he would be involved with this, at any level. 'You need to do better than that', I shook my head. I knew Williams would never let us go after Farrington with little or no evidence; merely the word of the District Attorney who was now trying to dig himself out of a sizable hole and would no doubt say anything to help him do this. 'You need to convince us', I added.

McCrane sighed and bowed his head slightly, almost as if he'd been half expecting us to require an explanation. 'Off the record?' he enquired. Williams nodded silently in agreement.

'There is a group of powerful individuals,' McCrane began, 'of which both Jameson and I are members; as is Robert Farrington'.

'What kind of group?' Williams demanded. McCrane looked at him as if the question was too demeaning to require an answer, almost as if we weren't worthy enough to know. McCrane looked directly at me.

'Your daughter does not have the time for me to fully

explain what kind of group', he retorted, 'but I will say this; From time to time, we require certain kinds of individuals to carry out work on our behalf. Sarah Caldwell was one of these individuals. Needless to say, it is imperative that we keep track of these subjects to ensure we monitor their location at all times'.

'And you implant them with a tracker?' I clarified.

'Exactly. Now it important you realise that only *three* members of our group knew about the tracking process; Myself, Mr. Burr and Mr Farrington. We implant the tracker into the big toe of whoever we need to monitor. Farrington was the one who came up with the process initially, the first time we carried this out'.

'So what makes you absolutely sure Farrington is linked with Caldwell?' Williams was keen to drive this point home.

'After Sarah Caldwell escaped', McCrane responded, 'we received her severed big toe by courier. Now as I've said, only three people knew about where we implant the tracker, and two of them are sitting in front of you. I'm certain that the only person who could have informed Sarah Caldwell about the tracker and helped her extract it, so to speak, is Robert Farrington as neither of us did and no-one else knew about it'.

'Why just the three of you who knew about the tracking procedure?' I wanted to know. 'What about the other members of your group?'

'Well it keeps things simpler', McCrane shrugged. 'The less people who know about the specifics, the less can go wrong. At least that was the principal', he added.

I sat back thinking for a moment; taking in what McCrane had just told us. Was he telling us the truth? I reconciled my doubts with the fact that I was certain McCrane wanted the housing fund fraud dealt with in such as way as to preserve his freedom and standing within the state.

'Believe me Detective', he spoke again and it almost seemed like he'd been reading my thoughts. 'I want the housing fund shit gone almost as much as you want your daughter back and Sarah Caldwell caught'. He spoke with a venom in his voice that suggested that he actually believed that equating my daughter's life to some bullshit fraud charge was on some kind of level plane. I resisted the temptation to knock him out again, just for that.

'What I've told you is the absolute truth and nothing less', he added, almost as an afterthought.

Just as I was about to address that, the interrogation door flew open and a relatively new officer, just out of the academy signalled to me and the Captain, an excited look in his eyes.

We followed him to outside the room to one of the grey, poorly lit corridors that I have become so accustomed to over the years, and he could hardly contain his excitement. 'What is it son?' Williams demanded.

'The guys upstairs sent me to get you both right away, Sir', he seemed quite nervous, but then if I was addressing an experienced detective and the Captain when I was a rookie, I'd have probably been the same. 'They think they've deciphered the latest message from The Chemist'.

The rookie was left standing, without a response, as both the Captain and I left McCrane and Burr sitting in the interrogation room wondering what was going on and rushed urgently back upstairs, praying that we were a step closer to my daughter's safe return and wondering how exactly Robert Farrington fitted into this increasingly expanding puzzle.

80

Leon Reno had only interrupted inhalations on his well-used crack pipe to take the Senator's call. He'd been lucky he'd heard it ring at all. His equally high friend, Brett Silverman had heard a ring emanating from the back of the dogged sofa where they sat in the squat that they had long ago commandeered, in one of the most run down areas of Los Feliz. Not far from Silver Lake, where The Chemist had been improvising the previous day with her opportunistic murder of David Ferguson of the LAPD.

Both in their early twenties and both from backgrounds that foretold their descent into crime and drugs, they both dropped out of school early on, although officially it was a lot later than any of their teachers probably realised, so seldom was their attendance.

Spending their days running the streets instead of focussing their attention on their education, and turning to increasingly bigger and better crimes to fund their expanding drug habits, it was not long before both were disowned by their respective families, leaving them both to fend for themselves in the dangerous territory, rife with other drug users, dealers and hoodlums.

Before long, it was not uncommon for them to hold up

a liquor store once or twice a month. There were plenty of them everywhere, so to them it was an endless supply of both money and booze. Dangerous yes, but a couple of hold-ups a month was better than lots of smaller robberies, and gave them more time to drink and get high.

It was as they were fleeing from one of these hold-ups about a year ago that they almost got caught. A cop had happened to walk into the liquor store they were holding up, purely by chance and things had gotten fairly intense pretty quickly. Silverman had instinctively cracked the cop across the head with the butt of his shotgun and they had both fled the scene, taking what little money they could. The cop, who recovered quickly from his assault, and his partner who was outside, gave chase. As Leon and Brett were both high at the time, they didn't have the co-ordination that sobriety would have otherwise have brought, and as they ran, both of them were sure they were going to be caught. As they rounded a corner, with the cops in pursuit, an expensive Aston Martin had pulled up, and a stranger had told them to get in quickly, and that he wasn't a cop and they could trust him. They had both done so, not knowing who it was, but sure that it wasn't one of the cops who was chasing them at least, and that had been good enough. The stranger had asked them where they lived, and it had taken them a few minutes to describe to him where they were squatting.

The stranger dropped them home, finally introducing himself as Senator Conrad Conway, and telling them that from now on, whenever he needed a favour, if they were asked, they would accommodate him, no matter what the circumstances. If they didn't, then he could find them and have them sent to jail. He also said that for every favour they successfully completed, they would get enough crack for a week, which seemed like a great deal to them.

They had done him a few favours in the last twelve months, each rewarded as Conway had promised, with a healthy supply of drugs. None of the favours they had carried out were on the magnitude of the favour Conrad Conway had just asked of them, but once again, it was a favour they found themselves unable to refuse.

81

'What have you got then', I demanded, as I swung the door of the operations room open, where Williams' task force had been working on the latest message from Sarah Caldwell. I prayed that whatever they thought they had was accurate and that it was something I could use to get Katie back.

'We think that *stationary event* means The Staples Centre', said one of the tech guys, 'There's a rock concert on today; Masters Of Puppets, that's what they're called', he informed me.

'Never heard of them', I shrugged, indifferent as to who was playing. 'Is there anything else it could be? I mean *stationary event*? The Staples Centre is that all we've got? That's our only option?'

'That's all we've got', confirmed the tech guy. '*British Wheels*, well that probably refers to a British Car doesn't it?'

'The bad news', another tech guy continued, 'is that the Staples Centre has a twenty thousand capacity and it's sold out. It also has four thousand car parking spaces, and the event has already started. It's not just Masters Of Puppets playing, there are another five bands on; it started around an hour ago'.

'And that means that most people are already there', I concluded. 'That most cars are already there. It's not like we're going to be able to check each car on the way in to see if it's British'. It was dawning on me that the scale of trying to find a British make of car, never mind the right car, was going to be a huge operation.

'How many parking lots?' Williams wanted to know.

'There are twelve, including Olympic West Garage, which is currently under construction', the first tech guy told us, pulling up a plan of the parking structures on the screen for us to see. It was a massive area for us to be searching for something that needed to be found quickly. There were two freeways passing by the Staples Centre; the Harbor freeway and Santa Monica freeway, giving easy access to the twelve parking lots. Even with concert-day level traffic, it would be easy for anyone to get to. I felt slightly downbeat; even with several teams combing all the lots, it would be like looking for a needle in a haystack and we'd need more than a little luck to find what we were looking for.

Over the next fifteen minutes, I assigned all the available officers that the captain had allocated to this case to the various lots, as well as a couple of officers to review the CCTV footage of all cars arriving at the Staples Centre over the course of the day. Even though we'd been chasing Sarah Caldwell through the alleys of Wilton earlier today, for all we knew, this step could have been implemented by her anytime before or after that, so although we could probably rule out the time we had been chasing her, and maybe forty-five minutes either side, it was still a hell of a lot of footage to check in such a short space of time.

As always, Captain Williams kept me optimistic. 'Patton, if the car is there, we'll find it. It's only a matter of time'. Although he was right, I just wondered how much time we actually had. I very much doubted we'd find Katie in the car, but part of me didn't want that. There was no way, I thought, that if she's in the car we're supposed to find, that she would have been left alive. That wasn't The Chemist's style now, was it?

Aware that in McCrane and Burr, he still had a couple of very high profile individuals being detained, Captain Williams opted to remain at the station to oversee events there and also to work out what part, if any at all, Robert Farrington was playing in this ever-expanding web of deceit.

82

If any of the officers hadn't realised the scale of the operation and thought that we'd find the car after a few minutes of casually searching the Staples Centre, their wake up call came as we pulled off Santa Monica Freeway, getting a view of the massive Staples Centre arena, and its surrounding complex for the first time.

There were hundreds of lines of cars surrounding the arena, split, as we knew, into twelve lots. Some of these lots were underground, which only compounded the sheer enormousness of the task in hand. We could see several latecomers to the gig, running towards the area, eager to catch as much as they could of the day of rock, no doubt wanting to get value for money for the hundred or so dollars tickets would probably have cost.

Each lot had been assigned a varying number of officers, depending on the size of the lot. One officer remarked that there may well be several British cars over the twelve lots and how would they know if it was the right car? Given my experiences with The Chemist, I could only answer that they would know if it was the right one when they found it. Something in or on the car would let us know; I was sure of that.

The officers split into their teams and I took my team to my assigned lot, which also happened to be one of the biggest; West Hall Parking. I had to put my faith in the other teams and that their searches would be thorough and efficient and that they would not miss anything they were supposed to find. Agent Balfer had rejoined me and was supervising another team in the second of the biggest car lots, South Hall Parking, so I was confident he would conduct his team with the required professionalism. I just had to trust that the other teams, who were made up out of a lot of officers I'd never worked with, would be similarly dedicated. Two officers were also dispatched to the Staples Centre security offices to try and review car park footage from earlier in the day to help narrow our search but I didn't hold out any hope that they would find anything there. I've done my fair share of reviewing hours of CCTV footage, and it's easy to miss vital clues as after a while, it all tends to blur into one continuous stream.

Whether the car we were looking for was British in make or whether it would simply have British plates attached, we had no idea, but we began the arduous and somewhat monotonous but necessary task of checking each car; splitting the lots into sections and each officer taking a section. Each team were under the clear instruction to radio me immediately if they found anything that looked like it was a possibility or saw anything suspicious. Was Sarah Caldwell here again, watching, just like she had at the house in Wilton? I didn't think so personally, but it wasn't something I could discount. She'd had her look this morning and I didn't think she'd need a second one today. I was pretty sure I'd be seeing her again soon, in any case.

83

Paul McCrane and Jameson Burr had watched as Patton and Williams had left the interrogation room, giving them a chance to speak in private for the first time since they had been arrested earlier that morning, although they spoke at a level that would not be picked up by the interrogation room's surveillance cameras.

'Conway leaked the story', McCrane spoke first, venomously, 'and he knows that we tried to have him killed this morning', he continued, bringing his friend up to speed. 'But don't ask me how he knows but he does', he said, pre-empting Burr's first question. 'He also knows we know about him having an affair with your wife, Jameson'.

'I can't believe Farrington has known about Caldwell. How the fuck could he know in the first place?' Burr had been listening to McCrane address Patton and Williams intently and recalled Farrington looking more shocked than most at last week's Animi meeting.

'I don't know', McCrane mused. 'I can only speculate that he must have intercepted an email or phone call or something between you and I that contained some specific details pertaining to her release and our plans for holding her at the safe house. One thing that puzzles me is why he would want to assist her in the first place. Any ideas?'

'I cannot imagine', Burr shook his head. 'Are you positive Conway leaked the story? Could that not have come from anywhere else? Though I do agree with you that Farrington must have been responsible for helping Sarah Caldwell escape'.

'Well Farrington is the only one that it could possibly be', McCrane was also sure. 'He was the only one of us, you and I aside of course, that knew how and where we were implanting the tracking device. None of the others knew this prior to us revealing it at the meeting the other day, so how could Brittles, Brindle, Hague or Conway have helped Sarah Caldwell if they had no knowledge of where the tracker was going to be implanted in the first place?'

'Agreed', Burr accepted. 'And Conway leaking the story?'

'Well I passed that motherfucker in the corridor, and trust me; he knows we tried to have him taken out and he insinuated very strongly that he was responsible for breaking the story. He knows that, well, certainly you have motive for wanting him killed. Maybe having us arrested for fraud was his way of trying to take us both out of the picture'.

'Well I think we should certainly pay him a visit', Burr suggested. 'I think it's time I finished this once and for all. What time do you think we'll get out of here? I take it the deal you have in place entitles us to our freedom whilst Caldwell remains un-captured?'

'Of course it does', McCrane said. 'Well they should just need to process us both out – couple of hours maybe. After which, my friend, I think you're right; a little visit to Conrad Conway might be in order. Although I think maybe our first port of call should be Robert Farrington; assuming the police haven't brought him in of course'.

'There's going to be a media shit storm when we get out', Burr remarked. Their arrests were big news and every paper and TV channel in the state would be taking a major interest.

'Leave that to me', McCrane advised. 'We'll go out the front door like we have nothing to hide. I'm sure I can swing it so everyone believes we have been set up by an ambitious rival'.

'I sincerely hope so McCrane', Burr stated. 'And you did the right thing by giving them Farrington, you had no choice'.

'Indeed', McCrane nodded. 'I just pray that Farrington can give them nothing new on us once he *is* brought in. After all, we can avoid this housing fund thing if we handle it right, but who's to say Farrington couldn't give them something else? If he knew about Sarah Caldwell as he evidently did, then there's every reason to suspect that he is privy to other certain operations we have conducted without his knowledge'.

'If they arrest him, or bring him in for questioning, could we get to him in here? Have him taken out?' Burr wanted to know. McCrane took a moment to mull the question over before answering.

'I'm pretty sure we could', he said. 'And what's more, that could be our only viable option'.

84

It took, as McCrane had suspected, another couple of hours for the necessary paperwork to be processed, allowing the release of himself and Burr whilst the LAPD's investigation into Sarah Caldwell took its course. Officer Bridges kept himself apprised of the situation, which was a big talking point all over the station, so that hadn't been particularly difficult. As Conway had requested, he kept him updated with the time he thought McCrane and Burr were being released.

During that time, both Captain Williams and Patton who was still searching the Staples Centre wondered how they could bring in Robert Farrington and justify holding him for questioning regarding the whereabouts of Sarah Caldwell. It was another career gamble if they brought him in for Captain Williams, so he had to tread carefully, mindful of Farrington's ruthless reputation.

'Find that car Patton', Williams instructed, 'I'll see what else I can find out here. We're going to need more than speculation and hearsay to bring Farrington in'.

He went back to the interrogation room where McCrane and Burr had remained, and as much as it pained him to let them go, albeit temporarily, the deal had been engineered in such as a way as to ensure their freedom.

'It goes without saying that if we fail to bring Sarah Caldwell in with the information you've given us, that I will be prosecuting you to the fullest extent', Williams almost spat. McCrane was almost smiling.

'I'm sure Robert Farrington will be able to provide you with the rest of the information you require to secure her capture', he said. 'I take it we're free to go?'

Williams said nothing but held the door open and stood aside, indicating that they were. Nevertheless, he walked them down several corridors and two flights of stairs to the main entrance of the station, where a media-frenzy awaited. He didn't see the need to offer either of them transport.

'So you're not giving us any phone call?' Burr enquired, not overly keen to face what awaited outside, even with McCrane there to back him up. Figuring that just by bringing them in, he'd already made an enemy out of the pair of them, he had nothing else to lose by telling them exactly what he thought.

'You guys like playing games don't you?' he smiled. 'Well I can play too. No phone calls, no transport. But just like your deals state, gentlemen, you are free to leave this station'.

McCrane leant a little close to Williams, who was taller than him by a good three or four inches. 'I'm sure when this little matter of The Chemist concludes, Captain, I can have a little chat to some friends of mine and well, maybe you won't be Captain for too much longer?'

Williams simply opened the door, causing the awaiting reporters and journalists to surge forward. 'Get the fuck out of my station you piece of shit', he snarled. 'Both of you'. That had felt good to say, at least.

Burr and McCrane eased themselves into the awaiting throng, with McCrane appealing for silence as he was happy to give a brief statement; an appeal that was largely ignored by the majority of reporters. Across the street, Leon Reno started walking towards them.

85

We'd been searching the various lots of the Staples Centre for around an hour, with no success. We hadn't even had sight of a British car or British plates, never mind found the actual vehicle and I was beginning to think that we were completely misguided in our translation of the message.

A couple of the smaller lots had been fully checked, although my team and Balfer's team were only about a third of the way through ours. I was urging my men to check faster, aware that time was ebbing away. Who knew though, if we were where The Chemist wanted us to be? Were we on the right track? Not for the first time since he'd sustained a knife injury earlier today, I wished Charlie was here to bounce some ideas off. I'd spoken to him briefly about half an hour ago and he was in the process of trying to convince the doctors to discharge him, swearing that if another hour passed, he would do that himself. My cell went off again.

'Hey, Patton'.

'Charlie boy', I greeted him. 'What's the update partner, how you doing?'

'Any luck finding that car yet, man?' he wanted to know, ignoring my question.

'Nothing yet, but we've still got a lot to check', I told

him. 'How's the wound?'

'Well I'm on the way man, couple of hours max', he sounded pretty well actually, all things considered. 'It's against their advice', he told me, probably referring to the doctors, 'but hell, it's gonna take more than one knife wound from that psycho bitch to keep me down, man'.

'Look, you take it easy', I stressed. 'There's nothing you can do anyway until we find the car. If that's what we're supposed to find'.

'I'll leave you to it for now, but I'm call you when I'm on the way', Charlie said. He wasn't taking my advice, which didn't surprise me in the least.

'Ok man, only if you're up to it', I knew when I was beaten and when I was wasting my breath. Not that his help wouldn't be more than welcome, but I didn't want him to aggravate any injury.

'We'll find her Patton', he assured me, before hanging up. I was trying to remain optimistic but as time marched on, I knew that every minute I didn't find Katie tipped the game in Sarah Caldwell's favour.

In the distance I could hear a muffled drone of music coming from the Staples Centre which began to grate on me as the search continued over the next half an hour or so. I stepped up my search team, double time, and we were nearing the completion of our search when my radio crackled into life.

'Patton, hey Patton, come in. Over'. I recognised the voice as that of Jon Walsh, one of the officers searching the Cherry Street garage, which was the lot situated on the edge of the Harbor Freeway.

'Walsh, its Patton. What have you got?' I prayed he had something.

'We've got a battered Pontiac here, real piece of shit rust bucket', he sounded excited. 'But here's the thing; it's got

British plates. They're definitely British plates'. It sounded promising, but my knowledge of cars is virtually non-existent. For all I knew Pontiac could also have a British manufacturer and this car could be genuine. I didn't think the type of people who were watching Masters Of Puppets were the type of people who could afford the high-end car range. I voiced these opinions to Walsh, who cut me off mid-sentence.

'There's one more thing, Patton', he told me. 'The plates are on upside down. This *has* to be the car'. Taking that information into account, I had to concede that he was probably right.

86

I left my team to complete the remainder of the search in our lot, and I radioed Balfer to leave his team to do the same, and to rendezvous with me in Cherry Street garage, where Walsh was under explicit instructions not even to approach the car that we suspected was the one left for us by Sarah Caldwell.

Strictly speaking, the bomb squad should have got their second call from me in as many days to secure the scene, but I didn't have the time for that. I knew that if they had to secure the scene, I would lose vital time that might cost my daughter her life. I also held off telling Captain Williams that we had a possible vehicle sighted, just in case he felt the need to over-rule me on the bomb squad call. Not that I would have listened. There wasn't a man on earth that would be able to keep me from inspecting that car before the bomb squad arrived, so if that was what Williams would tell me, it would be futile. Although he'd had my back throughout, well not just the last couple of days, but the entire time we'd been chasing The Chemist, he'd still be riled if I purposefully disobeyed a direct order from him. I was keen to avoid that entire scenario if possible.

It was still daylight outside, with dusk still a couple of

hours away. The sun had begun to lower, but it was bright, and the rain from earlier in the afternoon had long since subsided, leaving just traces here and there of the downpour that had swept through the city earlier today.

The brightness of the sun disappeared in a flash as we entered Cherry Street garage, which descended to the bowels of the Staples Centre foundations. It was well lit, as you would expect, but was a sharp contrast to the daylight outside.

I ran towards the team searching this lot, radio to my right ear as Walsh gave me directions to where they were standing. It was a deceptively large lot, which had looked fairly small from the descending ramp but still, it took me a few minutes to find Walsh. I could hear rapid footsteps echoing behind me, which I presumed was Agent Balfer, although it could just have been my own footsteps bouncing off the walls as I ran.

Finally, I reached Walsh, who had kept the remainder of his team searching, but he stood transfixed, watching the stationary car, which was parked in the far corner of the lot. The light directly above it had been smashed, making that particular corner considerably darker that the rest of the lot. It had also been smashed recently; I could see, even from where I was standing, fragments of the glass glisten as what little light there was made them shine like diamonds. Walsh hadn't, as I had instructed, approached the car and he was motionless. He looked almost in awe at the Pontiac, as if he knew this was a significant piece of The Chemist's puzzle; which I believed it was.

He was also right about the plates. They were certainly British and certainly on upside down. I knew this was the car.

Balfer arrived just behind me, and giving the car a quick glance just looked at me and nodded. 'Your call', he told me. 'What do you want to do?'

I drew my gun without saying a word and Balfer followed suit. Slowly, I approached the car, the inside of which was not visible due to the angle it had been parked at and the darkness that the smashed light provided, like an umbrella over the car.

As we got nearer, I couldn't make out anything significant in either the front or the back seats. I circled the car, twice, Balfer staying close behind, after which I stopped at the passenger side front door. I put my hand to the handle and glanced at Balfer, who nodded again. Gently, I pulled the handle and opened the door.

The car parked next to the Pontiac was parked as such that I couldn't fully open the door as much as I would have liked, to enable me to see inside, but Balfer provided adequate cover and had secured the inside of the car almost before I had pulled the door open as far as it would go. And more to the point, nothing had exploded which was as much a relief to Balfer as it was to me.

I circled round the car again, by which time Balfer's head was back out of the car. 'Nothing', he said, shaking his head. 'We'll get forensics down here but there's nothing in here'. He stood fully upright again, as we both instinctively made our way to the rear of the car.

'Trunk?' Balfer said, and I merely nodded again. Was Katie in there? My blood was pumping round my body far faster than I could ever remember. I almost didn't want to open it, just in case. Balfer must have seen the fear in my eyes because he took the lead.

I heard a click, as the latch opened and Balfer slowly lifted up the trunk to reveal its contents. Balfer turned away instantly and I thought I heard Walsh, who had come to stand just behind us, wretch as his stomach heaved.

Mercifully it wasn't Katie, and even as I stood, looking into the trunk in horror, I said a silent prayer thanking

God for that. It's safe to say, however, that even if you had given me a hundred guesses as to the contents of the trunk, I wouldn't have even come close.

87

Leon Reno was breathing hard, perhaps fully comprehending for the first time what he had been instructed to do by Conrad Conway. He didn't so much ask him as tell him, and he knew better than to refuse. Leon had once seen the senator lose his temper with a vagrant on the street who had been harassing him for change. It had been one of the rare times Conway had ventured into their neighbourhood, unable to contact them by phone. He had beaten the unfortunate beggar to within an inch of his life. For all they knew, he could have died from the injuries he'd sustained at the hands of the volatile politician. That wouldn't have surprised Leon one little bit. If the vagrant had survived he had spent the next several weeks, maybe months, in excruciating pain, he knew that much.

The kafuffle that surrounded McCrane and Burr as they exited from the police station was still quite a distance away but despite it being busy, with traffic whirring by at a steady rate and several commuters walking on by, he covered the distance quickly, not knowing how long his window of opportunity would last. Brett Silverman watched him at the wheel of a recently stolen car, procured especially for this occasion half an hour ago. Brett kept a discreet distance behind his buddy, although his vision was slightly blurred due to the vodka he had drunk to steady his nerves for the senator's bidding, just after they had received his telephone call. He had sunk around a third of a bottle but it hadn't impeded his driving to the degree of attracting too much attention. Not yet, anyway. He was ready to collect Leon when the time was right, which should be any time now.

Leon, drawing closer to the gathering outside the station, watched calmly as the reporters fell relatively silent as one of them, either Burr or McCrane; he didn't know which, settled himself in to address the news people, giving an authoritative speech, which he could hear clearly as he approached the back of the gathering.

'Let me be the first to denounce the appalling lies', McCrane stated, 'that were reported today in the LA Times'. Several flash bulbs went off as he spoke. 'It goes without saying that both myself and Mr. Jameson Burr are offended by this ridiculous slander and will be looking to take appropriate legal action in due course', he continued, now into his stride. 'Both Mr. Burr and myself have worked tirelessly as board members of this fund for the past several years, and have not only donated our time and money to ensure it's success but have also been instrumental in obtaining large charitable donations from organisations such as the Farrington Network in order that this fund may operate to it's full capacity, carrying out sterling work throughout the entire city. Helping and housing the impoverished, needy and desperate'. McCrane paused for a moment, letting the reporters digest that last part. If he said so himself, that had sounded world class. Particularly name-dropping the Farrington Network. He was sure that Robert Farrington would be watching and although he had passed Farrington's name to the police, he was keen to appear to still be supporting his colleague to avoid arousing suspicion.

'Not only will we be seeking substantial legal damages, which we will be donating to the housing fund itself', oh what a nice touch that was, 'but we shall be seeking a full and unreserved public and front-page apology from Mr. Britland-Jones and the editor of the LA Times, Mr. Vernon Beecher, ensuring that these ridiculous allegations are retracted'. Burr was nodding his approval throughout, echoing McCrane's sentiments through his body language, appearing together as a united front.

Leon had heard enough. It was easy enough to make his way through the gathering, who had been jostling for position anyway, and as he eyed his escape route he saw Brett pull around. It would be difficult to make his way back through the reporters; he would have to be quick. He was pretty sure that in about ten seconds time everyone around him would be too stunned to react. He prayed that was the case.

He couldn't get quite as near to the front as he would have liked but that didn't really matter, he had a clear line of sight from where he was standing. He edged himself a few feet to the left, just to give him that extra leverage to his escape route, whilst maintaining his line of sight on the targets. Satisfied with his position, he reached into his waistband and pulled out his revolver. If anyone had seen it, they gave no indication; they were all far too absorbed in the speech that was being given and trying to get the best picture or the best position for any questions that might be taken afterwards.

The guy giving the speech saw the gun first. He didn't quite stop speaking before the first shot was fired, but his speech certainly slowed down as he realised that amongst the microphones and cameras that were pointing towards him there was also a fully loaded firearm. Leon simply squeezed the trigger once, shooting his target in the face from a distance of maybe seven feet. He could have shot him anywhere, but why take the chance that he would survive?

The shot immediately sent everyone into a mass panic, no-one quite sure where the shot had come from; not even the people standing close seemed sure. Only Leon himself remained calm and focussed as people hit the ground, scrambling around trying to protect themselves. Jameson Burr simply looked horrified; covered in blood from McCrane, whose body lay on the floor, almost on top of Burr who had instinctively crouched down with everyone else when the shot had been fired.

People began to run, afraid they might be next, but Leon had Burr in his sights and squeezed off another two rounds, killing him instantly. He still didn't think that many people, if anyone at all, realised he was the shooter, but mission accomplished he tucked the gun away again and sprinted to his awaiting getaway vehicle.

'We did it man, we fuckin' did it', he announced triumphantly as he jumped into the passenger seat'. No-one was running after him, he noticed as he glanced back, which was definitely a good sign.

'Fuckin' A right we did', Brett shouted back, hitting the gas as he spoke, just as eager as Leon to put some considerable distance between themselves and this police station. 'We fuckin' rule Leon man!'

Whether it was the vodka he had consumed earlier, or the eagerness to get away from the scene of the crime, or whether it was the sudden feeling of invincibility that came with the successful completion of their mission, or maybe a combination of all three of these factors, who could say? But a hundred metres or so from the station, where the two politicians now lay dead, Brett ploughed the stolen car forward, ignoring a the stop sign, directly into the path of a speeding Hummer, which collapsed the driver's side door on impact, breaking both of Brett's legs immediately. The stolen car flipped over three or four times as the driver of the Hummer slammed on the breaks, trying to avoid going over themselves.

The Hummer came to a screeching halt, the driver miraculously unscathed, bar some minor scratches and bruises, extremely shaken, but otherwise unhurt. As the getaway car flipped over for the final time, Brett plunged headfirst through the windscreen, shrieking in agony as his broken legs were wrenched forward and he was instantaneously lacerated by the thick glass which shattered as he was launched onto the sidewalk.

The initial jolt of the impact had snapped Leon's neck back hard, breaking it, and his head hung at an awkward angle as he struggled for breath. He was vaguely aware of people running towards them, but his vision was fading and there was blood everywhere. Someone opened the door and a man's voice spoke urgently.

'Hey, guys, you ok? You alive? Hey, can you hear me?'

Hear the man speaking? Yes, he could just about, but he couldn't speak himself, to answer.

'Woah, fuck man! You guys shot McCrane and Burr!' the stranger exclaimed.

Leon could just about make out his gun, still tucked in his waistband, despite the accident. He couldn't look up at the stranger, he knew his head couldn't move and aware that he had seconds, not minutes left of his life, he knew the one thing he to do.

'Yes we did', he managed, gasping for breath, harder and harder. He resigned himself to the fact that his next words would be his last. 'Conrad Conway ordered the hit'.

88

Even as I stared at the beaten and mutilated body of Paul Britland-Jones in the trunk of the Pontiac, I could see the envelope, although my gaze quickly reverted back to the dead journalist. I didn't envy the M.E. on this one.

His body was naked from the waist up, and I could see a multitude of deep cuts all over his torso. I lost count at around thirty, unsure of which cuts and lacerations I had already counted, they all seemed to lead into each other. His face remained untouched. I supposed that this was so I could identify him as soon as we opened the trunk; a clear message from Sarah Caldwell. I shook my head, aware that his death had almost certainly not been quick or painless, and couldn't believe that I had only been talking to him a few hours ago.

His throat had been sliced from ear to ear; the final cut from The Chemist's knife I suspected, but it was clear that he would have suffered an incredible amount before The Chemist finally took mercy and ended his life.

My immediate thought was that Sarah Caldwell must have somewhere fairly close in order to carry out what she had done within the timeframe I knew we had. What she had done to Britland-Jones was something that required more than a little privacy and not one quick action like yesterday with Dave Ferguson that could be carried out quickly on the street, going unnoticed. That, at least, might narrow the search area. She would have had to have moved pretty quickly in order to abduct him, kill him and then deliver him here in time for us to find him, not knowing when we would break her last message and find the car.

Britland-Jones' murder also had to be opportune on her part as well though. There was no way she could have predicted his involvement at this juncture when she had been planning her games. I cursed, once again, our missed opportunity earlier today when we had been chasing her through the back alleys of Wilton.

I moved a little closer to retrieve the envelope. I didn't want to touch the body and strictly speaking, I should have waited for forensics before I even picked up the envelope, but I was no closer to finding Katie now than I was before we found the car, so that didn't even cross my mind.

As I gently picked up the envelope, which had gruesomely been placed in Britland-Jones' hands, almost as if he was delivering the envelope to me himself, the body rolled over slightly and I could see that his back had even more cuts on than the front. I also notice for the first time, taped on the underside of the trunk hood, another pager; virtually identical to the one Sarah Caldwell used yesterday to detect that we had opened the email. We had no tech guys or CSI on the crime scene yet of course, but I fully expected that they would confirm that the pager had been triggered when we popped the trunk. Yet again, Sarah Caldwell would know exactly where we were up to in her game.

Balfer had regained his composure, which was more than could be said for Walsh, who had put some distance between himself and the Pontiac. That was understandable. I didn't know how much experience Walsh had, and I know for me that it didn't get much easier seeing my hundredth dead body than it was for the first.

'She must have followed you guys back to the station', he concluded. 'That's the only way she would know where he was, she can't have had long to do this'.

It made sense. We had lost her in Wilton and I hadn't paid much attention to the rear-view mirror as Britland-Jones had driven us back. Maybe if I had, he would still be alive.

'That's a hell of a nasty way to go', Balfer added, shaking his head. 'I've tried to count how many cuts are on there but I keep loosing count'.

'Me too', I said quietly. Should I have seen that we were being followed back to the station from Wilton? All my attention had been on the last message from Caldwell.

'Hey', Balfer pulled me up. 'What's done is done. Just you focus on getting your daughter back, that's all that matters. Open the envelope'.

Nodding, I looked down at the envelope which was dripping blood onto the floor and it was almost soaked through. I hoped that this hadn't soiled its contents, leaving a vital communication from The Chemist unreadable.

I opened the folded sheet of paper it contained, and as I did so, a newspaper clipping fell to the ground. I bent down to pick it up and saw that it was a cutting from the LA Times, from around eight years ago. It was reporting on the circumstances surrounding Andrew Caldwell's death, and my picture central in the report, circled in a red marker. I read what the sheet of paper said once. If all the other messages and codes had needed an army of tech guys, and one goddamn maintenance guy, to figure them out, I had this one myself and it only took me a couple of seconds to figure it out.

Patton, go back to where it all began. Alone.

Where it had all began? Well this had began with me running Sarah Caldwell's brother off the road hadn't it? Looked like I was going back up to Windsor Hills to where the car had spun off the road sending Andrew Caldwell to his death two hundred feet below.

I was sure Sarah Caldwell would be waiting for me. I could only speculate as to what she had in store, but given the events of the last couple of days, I knew it wouldn't be easy.

I called Captain Williams, who grimly informed me that all hell had broken loose outside the station several minutes ago.

During a week where nothing was really making sense and that had seen more bloodshed and carnage than I cared to remember, the assassinations of Jameson Burr and Paul McCrane shouldn't have been as much of a surprise as they were.

I was slowly getting the picture that several of the state's top politicians were operating with their own agendas, and when Williams told me that there had been a report that Conrad Conway had ordered the hit, this only served to confirm my suspicions.

Two junkies had been killed when their vehicle, speeding away from the assassination scene, had collided with an oncoming Hummer. The one in the passenger seat had told the first person to check their vehicle that Conway had ordered the hit. This information made me wonder about the events at Conway's house this morning. Was the intruder in Conway's house there under instruction from Burr and McCrane and were their murders this afternoon retaliation for that?

Regardless of my natural interest, after all, these were people that were directly linked with Sarah Caldwell, all my attention had to be on Sarah Caldwell herself and the return of my daughter, Katie.

I quickly told him of the findings at Cherry Street garage and he, like me, had trouble digesting the continuing and rising body count and was at a loss to second-guess what may lie in store up in Windsor Hills.

'One thing I do know', he growled, 'is that there is no way you're going alone. Does this sound like the end-game to you?' I had to admit that it did. Windsor Hills would be a natural place for Sarah Caldwell to end her game. Was she planning on killing me? Planning on killing my daughter? Or maybe even both of us? Was I supposed to go now?

'Patton', Williams instructed, 'I've got a shit storm here. I need to go. I've got Lee Brindle on the other line wanting to be briefed on what's gone down here'.

'Who's he?' I asked.

'Works in the Whitehouse. He's a big deal. Think he's the joint Chief of Staff or some bullshit title. I need to take the call. Listen, Patton, this bitch is responsible for killing some of our own as well as those two poor girls. Ferguson, the guys yesterday at Sutherland and Charlie, well an inch to the right and he'd be dead too.

I stayed silent. I knew what was coming.

'Nobody wants her more than you, I know that', Williams said 'but I've lost good guys, guys that should still be here. There's no fucking way you're going alone. I'm not losing you too'.

'What do you want me to do?'

'Go there with Balfer but give me ten minutes to brief SWAT. I'll have them up there with you. I want to take this bitch out'. My first reaction was one of defiance – I had to get there now, but then I reconsidered. The pager meant that Sarah Caldwell would know we had found the car. There would be no element of surprise on our part. Maybe SWAT was my best chance of taking her out.

'No problem', I told Williams. Have SWAT meet me on the corner of 12th and main. I'll brief them personally.

If Sarah Caldwell wanted me she could wait a little longer, couldn't she?

89

Things were going according to plan, and that pleased Sarah Caldwell a great deal. Paul Britland-Jones had been the icing on the cake as far as she was concerned. She had found herself becoming increasingly adept at altering her plan in a heartbeat, and couldn't resist adding the journalist to her plans when she had followed him and Patton back from Wilton earlier today.

It hadn't been her original plan to have anybody in the trunk of the Pontiac she left at the Staples Centre, but what a sight that must have been when Patton, well she presumed it would be Patton, opened the trunk to discover Britland-Jones holding the next, and final message for him.

It had taken her around half an hour to inflict all the cuts to Britland-Jones, and he had been conscious when she had done so. She had driven back to the house in Montebello with him, checking on Katie's condition at the same time. She hadn't been entirely sure if she'd have enough time, but the police wouldn't break the latest message that quickly, so she took the chance.

She hadn't dragged Britland-Jones down to the cellar as she wasn't sure she would have the strength to get him back up the stairs, but had carried out the mutilation in a back room of the house, taking the precaution of lining the floor with the kind of sheets painters and decorators use which was a prudent decision; there had been a lot of blood, which had been so much easier to clean up as she just had to fold the sheets away.

His hands and legs had been bound but she had refrained from gagging him. He yelled and screamed a lot and she had enjoyed that. Besides, no-one would hear him anyway. Finally, he had begged for his life and she had actually told him that she would spare his life. The look of relief in his eyes had been the best part of all and it was a look that changed considerably when she had sliced his throat a second later.

She had watched, smiling, as he thrashed around on the sheets, trying desperately to breathe, bringing his hands to his throat to try and stop the blood from flowing out, but less than ten seconds later, he was dead. She only wished that Katie could have watched this with her, giving her a taste of what might lie ahead.

Checking the time, she knew she now had to move fast. The Pontiac with the British plates was parked, well hidden, about half a mile from the Staples Centre. She would now have to drive there, with Britland-Jones' body and transfer vehicles, before delivering the Pontiac to the Staples Centre car park. One of the underground garages would be best, she decided.

However, she was a little behind schedule, taking into account her latest improvisation. So perhaps she better take Katie now as well then after she had parked the Pontiac at the Staples Centre, she would run back to the Cadillac and then drive up to Windsor Hills for the final stage of the game.

She loaded the dead journalist into the trunk of her car, which took more effort than she thought it would and commended herself for refraining from taking him down to the cellar to kill him. She then walked back down the cellar steps to where Katie was hanging, looking more frightened than ever. Maybe she would have heard the journalist's screams as he begged her for his life?

'Hello again, Katie', she smiled, cutting her down. The girl landed on the floor with a thud, crying out in pain as she did so. 'I think it's time we both went to see your father, don't you?'

90

Conrad Conway watched the news with interest. He was still at home, sprawled out on one of the several leather sofas and sipped on a large cognac as he gleefully relished the newsflash that was unfolding under his very eyes. He'd sent his wife back out, telling her that she'd had a shock and that some therapeutic shopping might do the trick. That had certainly calmed her down and had silenced her incessant bleating about the damn carpet.

It seems that his two street soldiers had been successful. Both Paul McCrane and Jameson Burr had been assassinated by an as yet unidentified shooter, from the middle of the crowd that had gathered outside the police station when they had been released. Lighting a cigar to accompany the cognac, he reflected on his actions, wondering if there was an alternative path he could have chosen. He decided that there hadn't been; McCrane and Burr had left him no choice. They had hired some scumbag to try and take him out this morning so he'd had no option but to take them out in return. He had been successful where they had failed. It sure had been a hell of a day. He wasn't worried that Cyprian Hague would figure out that he had been behind the hit on two of the Animi. Even if he did, there was nothing he could do about it was there? In fact, his actions today put him in pole position for head of the Animi. They would need a couple of new members of course, he laughed, but there were several candidates he could think of. Maybe Ashley Davies, an upcoming politician very much in the same mould as himself. Or maybe Victor Antrobus, a successful property mogul who already carried considerable political sway? Well there would be plenty of time for that. He'd have no problem in convincing the other members he should take charge, and from there, well, who knows?

All of a sudden, Conway's feeling of superiority gave way to one of uncertainty, as the mug shots of Reno and Silverman appeared on the screen. He listened intently as the newscaster spoke.

'And this just in from our man on the scene', the anchor announced. 'The police have identified these men, Leon Reno and Brett Silverman as the individuals responsible for this afternoon's shootings. It's believed that Reno was the shooter and Silverman the getaway driver. Both men were killed when their getaway vehicle collided with an oncoming Hummer, the driver of which escaped with only minor cuts and bruises'.

Conway almost dropped his cigar and knocked over his cognac in surprise. What the fuck had happened down there? Were they really both dead?

'An unofficial police source', the anchor went on, 'has told us that they believe the shootings of McCrane and Burr this afternoon to be a hit of some sort. That Reno and Silverman were 'guns for hire', if you will. As yet, there has been no official word from Captain Neil Williams, but he is expected to hold a formal press conference within the hour. We'll bring you more of this story as we have it, right here, on Farrington News'.

He stared open mouthed at the screen, his mind racing at a thousand miles an hour. Was that just guesswork about Reno and Silverman being hired by somebody? How could they know? Had one of them told somebody before the hit? What about after? Maybe one of them spluttered it to an onlooker as they died? Was there anything in their squat that could link him to them? So many questions that all came back with the same answer; it didn't really matter.

He picked up his cell again, and thought for a moment. Who would be the best person to call? Who owed him big time? Reno and Silverman weren't the only criminals he had in his back pocket. Deciding finally on Sam Bower, a small time hustler who worked the streets of LA scamming and conning, one quick phone call added arson onto Bower's list of specialities. Conway gave him the address of Reno and Silverman's squat and instructed Bower to leave nothing standing.

Even if Reno or Silverman had given somebody the information that he was behind the hit on McCrane and Burr, there was nothing to tie him to either of them if Bower did what he had been told to do. Apart from his cell! How could he have nearly forgotten that? He had a spare SIM card with all his numbers stored safely in his lock up at Korea Town, so he could retrieve any numbers that he didn't know by memory, or get from his office, from there. Quickly, he jotted down Bower's number, in code; reversing every other number, so that should anyone search his house, they would have a completely different number; but it would be easy for him to work out to check that Bower had completed his assignment. He removed the SIM card and tossed it onto the fire, watching as it crackled for several seconds before burning and shrivelling up completely until you couldn't even see the remains. Well that was that. Nothing that could link him to them now.

No sooner had he done that then there was a knock at the door. He casually strolled to the front door to find two uniformed police officers standing, apprehensively, outside.

For the second time that day, he was driven to the same police station only this time, he had been read his rights.

91

Part of me almost didn't want Sarah Caldwell's game to end. As long as it didn't conclude, then I thought Katie would still be alive. I didn't think it was in Sarah Caldwell's nature to be forgiving and let my daughter go free. I sensed that her game ended with me suffering for the rest of my life; grieving over the loss of my daughter that I could have avoided, if only Andrew Caldwell hadn't been run off the road eight years ago. If only I hadn't run her brother off the road eight years ago.

The accident, well at least it had been an accident on my part, had occurred on one of the highest roads in Los Angeles, never mind one of the highest roads of Windsor Hills, which is an affluent area of the state to say the least. The residents of that area, which I believe to be around eight to ten thousand, hadn't exactly welcomed the attention that I'd attracted to their area when I'd run Andrew Caldwell off the road and down the cliff side to his death. Not that crime was non-existent in Windsor Hills, far from it. But it always enjoyed near top-of-the-table status when annual figures were published, proclaiming it to be one of the safest places in Los Angeles to live. That was an accolade that I brought into question when I'd brought reality into their lives during my pursuit of a drug dealer through their streets. I remember that several residents wrote indignant letters to papers, politicians, local TV; you name it. How dare I put them in danger by pursuing a criminal who had fired upon police officers through their safe little streets?

I remember the day of the pursuit, having an uneasy feeling as we had unsuccessfully tried to pull Andrew Caldwell over, as we had sped round the lower streets of Windsor Hills, trying in vain to stop him. That feeling was exacerbated as I realised he was taking the road that led to the top part of the Hills; a dangerous road at the best of times made all the worse for the icy winter conditions that day.

I had never been back since, but can picture that day as clearly as I can just about anything else. The winding road took us a couple of hundred feet up over just under three miles; tall trees adorning one side of the road, a safety barrier the other. I remember reading, after the incident, that the road we had taken was a notoriously dangerous one; and despite the barriers had averaged two fatalities per year for the last decade. Granted, these were mainly drunks, vision and reactions dulled by the alcohol; doing little to increase their chances of survival, but the danger nevertheless remained just as prevalent for any sober driver taking that path.

If memory served me correctly, I couldn't remember any buildings or anything other than trees near to where Andrew Caldwell had fallen to his death. There would be nowhere really for Sarah Caldwell to hide. Was this really the final stage of the game? Or was I supposed to think that it was? It had to end there didn't it? Or would I simply find something else there, more instructions?

Balfer agreed to accompany me, with no hesitation whatsoever. It took around forty minutes to drive to my rendezvous with SWAT from the Staples Centre although we didn't say much during the journey. He didn't push me either. Perhaps he saw the look in my eyes. Even if I got Katie back untouched and unharmed, Sarah Caldwell had kidnapped my daughter and I knew that the only acceptable way this could end would be when she had stopped breathing. It struck me, only minutes into the journey that this was probably similar to how Sarah Caldwell had felt towards me when she learned of her brother's death.

When we got to the corner of 12th and Main, only the SWAT unit Commander, Carl Orton, was waiting for me. He told me that Williams had briefed him as to the possible location of Sarah Caldwell and he had dispatched his team to that position five minutes ago. It seemed that the drive here had been enough time for SWAT to check the schematics of the location, allocate positions and tactical manoeuvres. Whilst I was slightly surprised, I really shouldn't have been. SWAT is renowned for their ruthless efficiency when it comes to putting together an operation such as this at short notice.

'We'll have your back Detective', he assured me. 'I know she has your daughter', he continued, seeing me about to speak up. 'I'll be in communication with my guys at all times. When one of them has the shot, I'll give him the green light. Your daughter won't be at risk. Not from us'. Orton oozed confidence, although that gave me little comfort. It wasn't SWAT I was worried about, it was Sarah Caldwell.

'Agent Balfer', he continued. 'I'm led to believe you will accompany Detective Patton in the car?'

'That's right', Balfer confirmed.

'OK then', Orton handed him an earpiece 'I'll tie you into our communication channel. Any change in status I need to know about then just speak up'.

It took a couple of seconds for Orton to confirm his

team was in position. 'We're good to go. You guys ready?' he asked. I didn't answer, I just nodded. I'd been ready for a long time.

We took the drive up to where Andrew Caldwell had crashed through the barrier slowly; taking the time to survey any area where she might be lurking, but we didn't pass a single person or car as we made the near three mile drive up. I hadn't really expected to see her. She would be exactly where her brother had gone over the cliff side, wouldn't she? Once, I thought I saw something but on closer inspection it turned out to be nothing; just my overactive imagination wanting to see something that wasn't there.

As we pulled round the corner to our destination, I saw a bunch of flowers lying on the side of the road by a safety barrier. Looking at the barriers you would never guess the number of fatalities this road had claimed over the years. There were scuffs here and there on the metal where a car or two had scraped along side them, and I noticed that these barriers were substantially more reinforced than the one Andrew Caldwell had crashed through.

Telling Balfer to remain out of sight, I ground the car to a halt, and stepped out, only a few feet away from the flowers. Although I knew the flowers were for Andrew Caldwell, I suspected that the card in them that I could see from here was for me.

92

Conrad Conway looked untouchable as he sat across from Captain Williams, whose telephone call with Whitehouse Joint Chief of Staff Lee Brindle had only served to make him more pissed off than he had been all day. And that was saying something. Brindle had asked questions that Williams hadn't had the answers for, and Brindle suggested, fairly forcefully, that those answers had better be forthcoming before the close of play today. No excuses.

Unbeknownst to Williams, Brindle was naturally concerned that two of the Animi had been gunned down. For he too was no wiser to the fact that McCrane and Burr's warning at their meeting last week that The Chemist was seeking revenge on all Animi members was in fact, largely fabrication. A cover story for their attempted hit on Conway himself.

Nevertheless, Williams knew that when any member of the Whitehouse staff thought it necessary to call you personally, what they had to say mattered a great deal, and unaware of Brindle's Animi connection, was keen to appease this formidable individual.

Conway had taken the backseat ride to the station in silence. Going over in his mind what the police might know, or what they thought they knew. But what could they prove? Even if Sam Bower was slow to carry out his instructions, he doubted the police would ever find the squat that Reno and Silverman had occupied and he was also fairly certain that there would be nothing there to tie him to either of them in any case.

He declined to ring his lawyer, knowing that this would send a message to Williams. He knew they had nothing on him, so why bother contacting his lawyer for nothing? He could see the look in the police captain's eyes which told him as much. 'So tell me, Captain Williams', he smiled, 'why have I been arrested?'

Williams flipped two pictures onto the table; mug shots of Reno and Silverman. 'You know any of these two men?'

Conway gave him the pretence of looking intently at the photographs for a couple of seconds. 'Never seen either of them before in my life', he stated, matter-of-factly.

'You sure?' Williams continued, 'Take another look Senator, please'. Conway glanced down again. 'Well, I mean, I've seen them on the news', he said. 'Just before you came to arrest me actually. But other than that; like I said, no never before'.

'How well did you know Paul McCrane and Jameson Burr?' Williams continued.

Conway shrugged, 'Obviously I knew Paul and Jameson well', he said. 'Our paths crossed on a weekly basis as we conducted our business; some weeks more than others. I might even go so far to say that they were friends of mine'.

'I have to say', Williams pounced on that last statement, 'that you don't seem particularly upset that two of your friends were gunned down outside this very station less than two hours ago and are both, as we speak, lying in the mortuary awaiting post-mortem'.

Conway shrugged again. 'Let me just say that my

particular line of work demands that I don't show my emotions; that I never let people see what I'm thinking by facial expressions alone. If I did, I wouldn't get very far now, would I?'

'And what are you thinking now, Senator?' That was a loaded question and one which Conway declined to answer truthfully.

'I'm thinking, 'what the fuck am I doing in this police station, Captain Williams?".

'Well what would you say if I told you that just before Leon Reno died of the injuries sustained in the crash as he fled from the scene where he had just shot and murdered, in cold blood, Paul McCrane and Jameson Burr, he told a member of the public that you had ordered the hits on them both. That you instructed him to carry out their murders?'

Conrad Conway, as confident as he'd felt all day, leant back and shrugged once more. 'I'd say 'prove it!".

93

As I picked up the card that lay tucked in the flowers, I glanced around nervously. There was an eerie silence that was only broken by the birds and the wind rustling through the trees. I wondered again if she was watching. I had full confidence that SWAT would remain undetected. Those guys are the best of the best. The elite. I knew they had our backs.

The card threw our plan into disarray; something which none of us had prepared for. I read it a couple of times, realising it meant that SWAT were not where they needed to be. Shit. I'd been sure she'd be here – right where her brother crashed to his death. The card just said 'Keep going – one mile. Go now', with an arrow pointing further up the road, which veered round to the left.

I discreetly flashed the card to Balfer, who nodded and I heard him communicating with Orton. My head was spinning. I knew I couldn't wait for SWAT to reposition before making my move. I knew I had to go immediately with Balfer as my back up and just pray that SWAT repositioned in time to take her out.

It was beginning to get dark now too, which didn't stack the odds any more in my favour; the element of surprise almost certainly belonged to Sarah Caldwell and I'd be lying if I said I didn't feel sick to my stomach. Although at least, as it got darker, it would be easier for Balfer to remain undetected.

We got back into the car and drove another three quarters of a mile or so, before we both got out and continued on foot.

Slowly, I began the walk, trying to give SWAT all the time I could to relocate. Balfer used the trees on the opposite side as cover, to mask his presence. My gun was drawn. Should the opportunity present itself, I would have no hesitation in shooting; and shooting to kill.

Apprehensively, I turned the corner and standing a hundred yards or so in front of me, near the safety barrier, only a couple of feet away from a sheer drop of at least two hundred feet, was my daughter, Katie. Behind her, with what can only be described as a maniacal glint in her eyes that I could see even from where I was standing, was Sarah Caldwell. I couldn't help but notice that she had picked a spot that provided her with substantial cover and that directly opposite where she was standing with my daughter the cliff rose up again, meaning it would take SWAT even longer than I had first thought to address their new tactics and reposition.

I could also see that Katie's mouth had been gagged which prevented her from crying out to me, but the look in her eyes as she saw me relayed her relief beyond any words she could have uttered. I could also see that there was a syringe that had been implanted into her neck, the plunger of which had mercifully not been pressed down. Not yet, anyway. If I'd had to guess, I'd guess that in keeping with her moniker, Sarah Caldwell had filled the syringe with Clozapone.

As much as I was relieved to see my daughter, even in this precarious, dangerous position, I knew that all my attention had to be focussed on Sarah Caldwell. It was the only way I was going to save Katie.

As I got a little closer, I saw that Caldwell also had a gun, cradled in her left hand. Her right hand was hovering over the plunger; her thumb and forefinger resting on the syringe itself. That meant that although she couldn't use her hands and arms to physically restrain Katie, she very much held all the cards.

'Detective Patton', it was the first time I'd heard her voice without the digitiser and she sounded almost normal, almost human. Maniacal glint in he eyes aside, she looked normal too. If you walked past her in the street you would assume she was an ordinary, every day type of woman and not a stone cold killer masking a dark existence. Her previous crimes also indicated that she was a lot stronger than her build suggested. 'I must say that you have made excellent time with my game'. She paused. 'And you don't look entirely surprised to see me', she noted. 'So you knew who I was before I left you the clipping in Mr. Britland-Jones' hands?' I ignored the question.

'Sarah, you have to let Katie go', I pleaded, edging closer, trying to buy some time. 'I ran your brother off the road, not her. It's me you want. I killed Andrew'.

'Don't you dare fucking speak his fucking name!' she snarled. Well she certainly sounded more like a killer now and I realised I'd just made a mistake. Who knows what she would do instinctively if I riled her even further? She saw me glance at the syringe, and regained her composure, smiling at me.

'I'm sure you can guess what's in the syringe Detective', she laughed. 'But I must warn you, the concentration of this particular little cocktail is enough to kill instantly'.

'Just take it easy, please', I tried to sound calm and relaxed which under the circumstances was proving nearly impossible. Where was SWAT? Had they had time to reposition themselves?

'You have until the count of three to drop your gun, otherwise little Katie here will find out just how concentrated that Clozapone is'. If there's one thing I knew about Sarah Caldwell, it was that it wasn't in her nature to make threats she wouldn't carry out. I didn't even give her the chance to start counting. I wasn't going to take the chance and tossed my gun a few feet in front of me, raising my hands in the air.

Suddenly, she raised her gun in my direction and fired off two shots which whizzed past my left shoulder. Her other hand never left the syringe, and I heard Balfer cry out in pain behind me.

'You disappoint me, Detective, you disappoint me. Did I not tell you to come alone?' My natural instinct was to check on Balfer, but I remained focussed on Sarah Caldwell who was only a few feet away. At least it seemed that she thought Balfer was my only back up. She didn't know about the SWAT team that I prayed now had her in their sights.

'Would you have come alone if you were me?' It was all I could think of and I saw her smile once again.

'How is Detective Holland by the way?' she laughed. 'I can't help but notice he's not here tonight!' I suspected she thought she'd done more damage to him than she actually had.

'Like I said,' repeating myself, 'it's me you want. Nobody else was responsible, only me'. I held off using her brother's name.

'Oh I do want you, Detective Patton. I want you to suffer like I've been suffering for eight years'. I didn't like where this was going. Balfer was down, the fact that SWAT hadn't taken a shot indicated they weren't ready, I wasn't armed and my daughter's life was now solely in the hands of Sarah Caldwell.

'After today, for the rest of you're life, you will see me every time you look in the mirror and every time you visit your daughter's grave you will know that I was the one that was responsible for her lying in the ground, rotting, decaying'.

I knew I was going to have to make my move soon regardless, and that the chances of me making it to my weapon before Caldwell could inject my daughter full of lethal Clozapone was slim; but the way she was talking, it seemed like she would be doing that in a few seconds anyway. I looked into Katie's eyes for a moment, almost seeking her approval to make a move.

Without warning, Sarah Caldwell staggered back a little, seemingly in a great deal of pain. Her hand came away from the syringe and up to her temple; her face screwed up in agony. For a split second I thought SWAT had made the shot, but I hadn't heard any weapon being fired. That was immaterial. I knew this was my chance.

'Katie move!' I yelled, diving for my weapon. This would be the only opportunity I would have to end this.

I don't know if I'd startled my daughter or if the events of the last twenty-four hours had simply been too much for her, but she only moved a little; not enough for me to get a clean shot off; and Sarah Caldwell quickly regained her upper hand.

The migraine that had come at the most inopportune moment had thankfully only lasted a couple of seconds, but it had been right up there with the worst of them in terms of pain. As soon as she realised what was happening she knew Patton would use that opportunity to move, so even though the migraine had come with no warning at all, she knew instinctively what she had to do and as she staggered back, she let go of the syringe and grabbed Katie by the scruff of the neck.

Both of them fell backwards, towards the safety barrier at the edge of the road and Caldwell acted quickly. She violently jerked Katie back and hauled her over the barrier, having to drop her gun in the process, which sailed over the barrier and over the cliff side; she needed two hands to prevent Katie from falling to her death. Katie would be dead soon anyway, she just needed to make sure that she had a way out of this alive before plunging the girl to her death, in the same way Patton had her brother all those years ago.

Katie was over the barrier and Sarah Caldwell had positioned her grip just right before Patton even made it to his gun. Migraine now subsided, she realised she still had the upper hand. She glanced at Katie, who's muffled screams through the gag penetrated the silence. Her arms and legs flailed in the air as she tried desperately to get a foothold or a grip on something, sure that this crazy woman would drop her to her death on the rocks that lay all that way down.

'What you going to do Detective?' she laughed, looking down the barrel of Patton's gun. 'Shoot me and Katie dies. But you want to shoot me so badly now don't you?'

Despite her bravado, she realised that her current situation didn't favour her as much as she had first thought. Patton was edging ever closer. If he got too close, he might be able to get a hand to his daughter and still get a shot off. One thing was for certain, Sarah Caldwell couldn't die today. She had so much more left to do. She knew she had to make a decision and make it quickly. She turned to the girl, who was becoming heavy, the lactic acid in her arms beginning to burn. The girl was still struggling, eyes wide with terror as she tried in vain to hold onto something. 'Bye bye Katie!' Sarah Caldwell even blew her a kiss as she let go, turning and running as fast as she could, knowing that Patton's first priority would be his daughter. She had an escape route planned anyway, in case something unforeseen had cropped up, and it had. She knew she could be far away, fairly quickly.

I was six or seven feet from the barrier when I knew what Sarah Caldwell was going to do. She was right of course; if I shot her, she would drop Katie. I saw she was going to drop her anyway and had no option but to dive from where I was in the direction of my daughter and pray to God that I got there in time.

The next second played out in slow motion, certainly in my eyes, and it's a second I never want to relive again. As I leapt, arms outstretched I saw Caldwell turn. She would have to wait. I could hear Katie's muffled screams go up in pitch as she realised she'd been let go.

I'm not sure whether she managed to grasp something momentarily, which delayed her fall, but somehow, I managed to grab her wrist as she was falling back. I crashed hard into the barrier, and thought for one horrific second that the reverberations of my collision with the barrier might loosen my grip on my daughter's wrist. I struggled to tighten my grip, and it took me a few seconds, which were definitely the scariest seconds of my life, to grab her arms securely with both hands. As I pulled her up, back over the barrier, I was shaking almost as much as she was. I briefly, for one moment, looked over my shoulder and saw no sign of Sarah Caldwell at all.

Quickly, I pulled out the syringe from Katie's neck, thankful that Sarah Caldwell had not been in the position to inject her from where she had been dangling her over the barrier, and I removed the gag from her mouth. The tears that were streaming down her face were now accompanied with sobs as I took her in my arms, both of us collapsing on the side of the barrier.

I looked up and saw Agent Balfer beginning to rise, and he gave me the thumbs up, letting me know that he was alright and that I could just concentrate on my daughter.

As she lay in my arms trembling and sobbing, all I could do was to whisper that I was sorry in her ears. Over and over again.

94

The ambulance picked us up, including Balfer, who had fortunately only sustained minor injuries at the hands of Sarah Caldwell. To my eternal relief, Katie seemed alright too. I didn't press her too much on details of what she'd been through, she would tell me when she felt able to. She did tell me though that she had no idea where she had been held and that she didn't remember arriving there and had been blindfolded this afternoon when Caldwell had moved her from a cellar into a car.

I was hoping that Katie would have been able to give me more than that, but I was just glad to have her back. She would go to the hospital for the usual checks but I was hopeful that she would only stay overnight. I called her mother, again not telling her about The Chemist. How could I do that over the phone? That was something I would have to do face to face, and I knew Vikki would blame me unreservedly for what had happened.

I blamed myself too, and hated what I had put my daughter through in the last twenty-four hours. Katie whispered that it wasn't my fault and it was all I could do to stop myself from crying with her. I could live with Vikki blaming me for this but if my daughter didn't then that was more than I had any right to ask for.

The area surrounding our showdown with The Chemist was being combed by a team of officers, who had so far uncovered nothing. I spoke briefly with Orton who told me that SWAT hadn't had time to reposition to the new location. The terrain had been too mountainous to scale in such a short time. Aside from the bunch of flowers lying at the side of the road, there was no sign that Sarah Caldwell had ever been here. Was that it for now, or did she have more for me? Did she have an alternative plan, just in case this one didn't work out? To me now, catching her came secondary to ensuring the well-being of my family, and after Katie has whispered that she didn't blame me, the rest of the journey was silent as I held her in my arms, looking up to the heavens and silently thanking God on more than one occasion.

When we arrived at the hospital, Vikki was already there, frantically pacing up and down, looking mortifyingly worried, even though I'd assured her Katie was alright. The look that she gave me as Katie was helped from the ambulance spoke volumes, and it was a look that did not subside as I sat her down and told her, from start to finish, the events that had unfolded in the past two days.

She chastised me for not telling her in the first place this morning, and was horrified to learn that Sarah Caldwell had evaded capture.

'This is what you do. This is the one thing you're good at', she yelled at me, 'and you didn't catch her? How could you not catch her?' I refrained from telling her that I thought saving Katie had been infinitely more important. She already knew that.

Her anger eventually subsided into audible relief, and she too lay in my arms, sobbing quietly, as she realised how close our daughter had come to being one of Sarah

Caldwell's victims.

'Is she done with you? With us?' she asked in between cries. I had no choice but to tell her that I didn't know.

A doctor came found us and told us that Katie appeared to be fine. Shaken and bruised, but fine. They would keep her in overnight as a precaution and discharge her the following morning. That was what I'd been praying to hear, and thanking the doctor profusely, I couldn't help the tears that finally came.

95

The events at the station couldn't have been further from my mind as I sat by the end of Katie's hospital bed, watching her sleep. She was exhausted and frightened from her ordeal but looked at peace as she slept. Vikki sat next to me in silence, still blaming me for our daughter's predicament, but her look had softened somewhat when she realised that Katie hadn't sustained any real injuries and that she was going to make a full physical and mental recovery. An officer had been placed on the room's door at my request. Until Sarah Caldwell was caught, she remained a target. Not that I was planning on going anywhere until she was discharged tomorrow morning.

I felt a hand on my shoulder and looked up. Charlie stood behind me, smiling. 'Hey, man', he greeted me as I stood up.

'Hey', I reciprocated, giving him a hug. 'How's the shoulder?'

'Like I said, it's gonna take more than that to keep me down, man', he grinned. 'Katie's alright, thank God', he acknowledged. 'Hey Vikki'.

'Yeah she is', I nodded. 'But it was a close call'.

'Hi Charlie', Vikki spoke quietly.

'Just been speaking to the Captain', he told me. 'Still no sign of Caldwell, it's like she's just completely vanished'. I shook my head, disappointed, although if there had been any news of her capture, I would have been the first to know.

'But the good news', he informed me, 'is that we need to get our asses back to the station. Williams says forensics have had some luck with that address we got from the old guy in Wilton. He should have it any minute'.

Ever since we'd had that address, so much had happened that I'd actually clean forgot that we'd had it, much less that it had been sent to forensics to see what they could repair from the damage the rain had caused. This was not over. If we had a lead, we could potentially get to Sarah Caldwell. Maybe then, we could all get some sleep. I looked at Vikki, not needing her permission or approval to leave but sensing that it would be a well-received gesture on my part. If she didn't want me to go, then I wouldn't.

'Go, if you have to', she said 'It's alright. Go and do what you do but just do me one favour'.

'What's that?' I asked.

'Make sure you make sure you take that bitch down. Dead or alive, I don't care which'.

I stood up, not answering her, but gave her a quick hug.

'One more thing', Charlie said, gesturing to his bandaged shoulder.

'What?'

'You're driving, man', he laughed. 'You're driving'.

96

We made our way back to the station, and as we jogged up to the office of Captain Williams, virtually everyone I passed gave me a message of support for my daughter. I nodded in response, but I was eager to see what Williams had for us. With Katie now accounted for, despite the lack of sleep and the emotional strain that The Chemist's personal game had placed on me, I was ready to go. I needed to go.

Williams himself shook my hand, telling me how much of a relief it was that Katie had survived unharmed. When you put it in the context of what had happened to Keeley, Jennifer and even then Stella, I agreed she had been fortunate but I couldn't help remember how close it had been to an entirely different outcome.

'I've not had a chance to tell you,' Williams began, 'but we brought Conway in this afternoon for questioning over the shootings of Burr and McCrane'.

'Who's taking it?' I questioned.

'Harlow', Williams answered it. 'Seemed the least I could do after I took McCrane off him this morning'.

'Anything on him so far?' I wanted to know. Williams shook his head.

'Nothing as yet. Even had a crack at him myself before

Harlow took him. Smug bastard knows we haven't got much'.

The phone rang, and after taking the call, Williams looked up smiling. 'That was forensics. They're ready for us'.

After having to listen to two of the forensic guys tell us, in more detail than we cared to know, how they had managed to do what they had done, we had the address and were waiting for the computer, which seemed to get slower and slower every day, to return any results. They told us several times that to do what they had done in the timeframe they had was next to impossible, but I guess on reflection, the forensic guys are often the unsung heroes of the police department. Without them, our conviction rate would be nowhere near as high as it was, just the same as it was for every police department across the country.

I thought the computer network had stalled as it seemed to be taking longer than usual, and I had little patience to begin with. Just as I was about to vent my frustrations, the day's events had left me wanting Sarah Caldwell more than ever, the computer returned the search with just one match.

'That who I think it is?' Charlie exclaimed as we stared at the match it had returned. I just nodded as I stared at the screen. The address given to us by the old next door neighbour of Sarah Caldwell was that of Robert Farrington.

97

The revelation that the address was Farrington's was a surprise to us all. None of us could get a handle on why someone with such standing, power and presence would be linked with someone like Sarah Caldwell. The address seemed like a cast iron link for some reason. We just didn't know what that reason was and we all agreed something wasn't quite right here. Did Farrington have something to hide? How would Sarah Caldwell have gotten that address in the first place? Captain Williams picked up the phone again.

'Get me all you have on Robert Farrington', he barked. He looked up as me as he spoke, aware that once again we were going to have to tread very carefully indeed.

Five minutes later, clerical had delivered us the file, the contents of which were massively disappointing. To say that there wasn't anything pertinent in the file relating to Farrington was an understatement. According to the file, Robert Farrington hadn't received so much as a parking ticket in the last fifteen years.

'His wife died a couple of years ago', Charlie noted as he thumbed through a section of the file. 'He's got a son, Daniel Farrington. His only son, in fact. Thirty-one'.

'Worth taking a look at the son?' I asked. 'Maybe the address relates to him and not Robert Farrington?' I was reaching and we all knew it. Williams shrugged his shoulders.

'Why not?' he nodded, picking up the phone once again.

If the first file that clerical had brought us didn't have much we could use, then the second file, the file on Daniel Farrington, was an entirely different proposition.

By the age of thirty-one he had racked up a string of DUI's including one only six days ago where his blood-alcohol concentration had been 0.11. Well above the maximum legal ration of 0.08. He had been bailed but was looking at doing time after his arraignment took place in just over two weeks. According to the arresting officer's report, he had hit another motorist whilst driving intoxicated. The driver of the other vehicle, a young woman called Tina Holt, had only sustained minor injuries but that, taking into consideration his previous DUI's, should be enough to ensure a custodial sentence.

I flicked over the report to reveal Daniel's fingerprints and booking photograph. Looking over the background information that the file contained I was so startled I almost dropped the file. Charlie and Captain Williams were surprised by my reaction.

'Hey man', Charlie asked, 'you ok? What's up?'

I was unable to speak but passed the file to Charlie who looked over the file before making his proclamation. 'Well I'll be damned'.

'What have we got?' Williams demanded. It didn't take me long to tell him that the next of kin in Daniel's file was not listed as Robert Farrington, it was Anne Caldwell: deceased. The address for Anne Caldwell was the same address we visited in Wilton earlier today.

'So you're saying that we think Sarah Caldwell and Daniel Farrington have the same mother?' he was incredulous.

'Exactly', I told him. 'And I can't help but think that if they have the same mother, then maybe they have the same father'.

'Robert Farrington', Williams finished for me, almost smiling.

The next hour was a flurry of activity as we decided the best way forward. We now had a cast iron link between Sarah Caldwell and Robert Farrington. Williams was confident that he could get a warrant first thing in the morning but I knew we needed more. Farrington wasn't going to just roll over was he? I tossed an idea out to the room which both Charlie and Williams agreed was our only option. For this idea to work though, we needed to speak to Daniel Farrington.

We were able to confirm that Daniel was not at home but we knew he could return at any minute. We had to act quickly.

'If he co-operates, can we lose the DUI thing?' I asked Williams. 'It's our best card to play. It may be our *only* card. He'll want that null and voided, I guarantee it'. Williams thought for a moment before giving me his response.

'We can keep him out of jail'. I nodded my approval. That should be enough.

'Let me sit on the house, man', Charlie growled, popping a couple of Tramadol for the pain his shoulder was giving him. 'He comes back man, I'll get him on side. Let me do this for you'.

As much as I didn't want the big man flying solo on this, the emotional strain of Sarah Caldwell abducting my daughter was overwhelming me and I finally gave in.

'Do it for all of us', I told my partner. This might be our last roll of the dice and I prayed it would pay off.

98

Daylight had already broken when the search warrant came through for Farrington's house. Captain Williams had naturally wanted any case that might be forthcoming to be watertight and not leave us wide open for prosecution by taking any short cuts. He'd woken up one of the most senior judges in the city, Judge Martin Tyrell, at six o' clock and it was a call that, even given the circumstances, Williams hadn't relished making. Nevertheless, the early hour of the morning aside, Tyrell had been more than accommodating once he'd heard what we had, and the warrant had been rushed through. He agreed there was definitely enough probable cause for the warrant to be issued, although he had stopped short of agreeing with Williams that these were exigent circumstances. Farrington's standing within the state had probably played a part in Tyrell's decision. I'd wanted to go in with the warrant unannounced but under Tyrell's ruling, had to abide by the standard 'knock and announce' procedure. In the end I hoped it wouldn't make a difference but I wasn't about to jeopardise any case we could make against Farrington by disregarding the Judge's wishes.

Charlie had sat on Farrington's house last night until Daniel had returned at around one in the morning. He had taken Daniel for a ride and made him our offer. Charlie seemed to think we were in business but we both knew that we had no way of knowing for sure.

We drove up to Farrington's house, which was coincidently only about a mile from Conway's, although it was far greater in stature. Farrington had obviously spared no expense as his lavish three storey mansion and acres of surrounding land attested to. It also had state of the art security cameras that meant we couldn't arrive unannounced. He would almost certainly be aware of our presence before we had the opportunity to knock on his door and present the warrant.

Williams was adamant that we should have substantial back up. Given that we had linked him to Sarah Caldwell, whose bomb at Sutherland Boulevard yesterday had injured and killed several officers, not to mention the two girls she had successfully killed, that was understandable. Although I'd had no backup apart from Balfer directly behind me yesterday in Windsor Hills, I had no such restrictions now.

Six black and whites followed us to the mansion. Charlie and I led the way, driving us right up to the door, which took over a minute from the entrance; such was the expanse of Farrington's land. When we officially made our presence known, Robert Farrington answered the door personally, giving us the impression that he already knew we were here.

'Good morning', he greeted, almost smiling. He was calm and unruffled by the unsociable hour of our arrival. He was dressed in a silk dressing gown and held a fat Cuban cigar in his left hand. Not a hair was out of place, though the bags under his eyes were perhaps signs of a restless night. He didn't look surprised to see us one bit. I wondered if he was simply an expert at not revealing his hand, or if someone had tipped him off as to our impending arrival. I prayed my gamble was going to pay off but at that moment I wasn't sure it would at all. 'What can I do for you gentlemen on this fine morning?'

When I identified myself as Detective Patton, his eyebrows raised slightly; his first indication of surprise perhaps? 'You're Detective Patton?' he repeated. 'The same Detective Patton who is on the news? The same Detective Patton whose daughter was abducted by The Chemist?' He took my silence as an affirmative. Maybe he saw the answer in my eyes. I held the warrant up.

'We have a search warrant for the house and grounds', I informed him. Once again, his eyes didn't give anything away.

'Well then, you'd all better come in', he gestured to the officers from the black and whites who had gathered behind us during my brief exchange with Farrington. The officers rushed in, leaving Farrington alone with Charlie and I. 'May I ask what this is about?' he enquired.

'We're here to talk to you about Sarah Caldwell', I informed him 'You're daughter', I added, looking him in the eyes to gauge his reaction. Several seconds passed, waiting for him to respond, before he finally looked down, nodding. It was almost as if he'd been weighing up a decision whilst he was thinking.

'Detective Patton, may we speak in private?' he enquired. 'Well, not quite in private actually', he added, 'but without any other law enforcement present?'

I paused for a moment, before finally agreeing. 'Why don't you oversee the search Charlie boy?' I turned to my partner who understandably seemed reluctant to leave me. 'It's ok', I told him. 'I've got this'.

As Farrington led me into his study he was seemingly impervious to the surrounding chaos the search was already producing; the officers, and now Charlie, were leaving no stone unturned in trying to find any evidence that Sarah

Caldwell had been here. 'Please be seated Detective', he gestured that I should sit in one of the chairs by the fire. 'I have something I need to tell you', he told me, 'but if you'll give me a couple of minutes, I'll be right back'. I nodded my response.

He was gone for no more than ninety seconds. When he reappeared, he wasn't alone. 'Detective Patton', he introduced, 'this is my son, Daniel Farrington'.

I shook Daniel's hand. He was tall and slim and he had his hair tied back in a pony tail that reached his shoulders. He wore small rimmed spectacles that he took off when he sat down. He looked younger than thirty-one and far from the heir to the Farrington Network that I knew he was. I sat now, waiting expectantly.

'Let me begin by saying, Detective Patton, I assume you are not wired?' he raised a quizzical eyebrow, 'Because that would be entrapment you know, as I'm no doubt you are fully aware?' I shook my head.

'I'm not wired'.

'And son', he turned to Daniel. 'I can only hope you can forgive me for what I'm about to tell you'. For the first time, I saw real emotion in Farrington's eyes; almost pleading. Daniel remained silent and Farrington began.

'May I ask what led you here, Detective?' Farrington enquired.

'We know about Anne Caldwell', I responded. There was no harm in letting him know we knew that.

'Ah yes, Anne', he began. 'Well son, I'm not proud to say that in the earlier years of my marriage I wasn't a hundred percent faithful', Daniel remained as impassive as his father had when we announced our arrival. 'That's not to say I didn't love your mother, Daniel, I loved her very much, but...' he trailed off, maybe knowing there was no justification for his actions.

'My wife, Detective, was unfortunately never able to conceive but she wanted a child more than anything else in the world. Daniel is adopted. Well, I say adopted; it is true to say that he is biologically my son'. I could tell from the lack of reaction on Daniel's part that this was not news to him.

'I began an affair with Anne Caldwell, who worked for me in one of my offices. She fell pregnant, entirely unplanned by both parties, in the spring of seventy-eight. This came as a shock of course, but upon reflection, I saw an opportunity to give my wife exactly what she wanted. Anne's husband was in the middle of serving a two year stretch in County and Anne was fearful of having an abortion in case it led to fertility complications. I confessed to my wife, who I was able to convince that this was a one-time indiscretion on my part, and convinced her that we should take Daniel as ours once he was born'.

'And Anne was happy to just hand him over, was she?' I questioned.

'Ah well she was more than compensated for that', Farrington continued. 'Besides, how was she going to explain the addition of Daniel to her husband upon his release? Anyway, we took Daniel the day after he was born and my wife loved him like he was hers each and every day. We both did'.

'If you don't mind me saying, he doesn't seem entirely surprised by these revelations', I noted.

'We told Daniel they truth about his real mother just after his seventeenth birthday', Farrington clarified. 'What you don't know, son', he turned to Daniel, 'is that my affair with Anne Caldwell resumed and she fell pregnant again the following year. This time, I didn't even consider the route I took the first time; my wife would never have forgiven me a second time and Anne's husband had been released'.

'So you never stayed in contact with Anne then?' I questioned.

'I saw Anne and my daughter once after Sarah was born', Farrington stated, then saw neither of them again. Anne did send me letters and photographs but I never answered one'. I detected a note of remorse in his voice. 'I think she wanted me to save her', he said. 'I knew her husband beat her …'

'So if you didn't keep in contact, how did you know that Sarah Caldwell was actually your daughter?'

'I intercepted a file from an email between Burr and McCrane, as I often do to keep tabs on their activities; a file detailing their plan to free Sarah Caldwell from San Quentin. The name of course struck a chord, so naturally I took a closer look. I knew Anne had named her child Sarah from the letters she had sent me but I knew I could not allow myself to keep in contact with either Anne or Sarah for the sake of my marriage, so I had no idea what had become of Sarah until I intercepted this file. The file, Detective, had a complete history of her life – including the address of her childhood residence. An address I knew well. The address in Wilton. At first I tried to dismiss it, I really did. But I couldn't. I just couldn't. There was a computerised sample of her DNA in that file on the email so to put my mind at rest and be a hundred percent sure, I had some tests run'.

'What kind of tests?' I asked.

'Well I have an independent contractor who does me favours of that kind from time to time and I had him run what was on that file against my own DNA. There were matching strands and from there, well, finding her was easy enough'.

'I now knew what she had become', he continued 'The file had everything in there. I knew about the triple homicide that she was convicted of. I don't know; I felt *responsible* somehow. I knew I couldn't let her fall under the control of Burr and McCrane, I had to help her. I thought I could help her. I thought I could save her. A bit late I know but ...'

'How did you think you could save her?' I asked.

'I was going to have her placed securely, anonymously at a private psychiatric hospital; the best money could buy. She'd have been safe there. She'd have been saved'.

'When was the last time you saw her?' I wanted to know.

'Well I approached her at the safe house. She'd already killed the two guards by the time I got there'. His face was ashen as he recalled what he'd seen. 'I'm not sure she really believed that I was her father to start with but I had the letters and photographs from her mother. I was soon able to convince her of the truth. She stayed here for a week or so before she fled. She overheard me arranging something with the hospital', he almost laughed at the absurdity of the situation. 'But she telephoned me last night and said that I could do one thing for her'.

'And what was that?'

'She told me all about you. She told me how you ran her brother off the road eight years ago and that if ever you were to come knocking on my door, asking questions, then maybe she was dead. That if you came here Detective, then I should deliver you a message'.

'And what is that message?' I demanded, trying to comprehend what I was being told.

Farrington almost smiled. 'The message is, Detective Patton, that even if she was killed during the course of your recent investigation, she had taken the precaution of setting up another game. 'One that would be executed by one of her *followers*' was how she put it'.

I sat in the chair, too numb to speak or move at the thought that this was going to continue, somewhere, somehow. Farrington turned to his son, who had remained silent throughout.

'Son, can you forgive me?' Farrington looked at Daniel who began to slowly nod. 'I'm sorry Daniel, I'm so sorry'.

'Do you think mom would forgive you if she was alive?' Daniel's voice was soft, almost a whisper. 'My real mom, I mean, not Anne Caldwell'. Farrington looked a little surprised at the question, but answered it, nevertheless.

'I'm, I'm not sure she would', he responded honestly. 'I'm sorry'. Farrington looked like he'd unburdened himself of a weight that he had been carrying. Maybe not only since he found out what his daughter, Sarah Caldwell, had become, but for many years.

'In that case', Daniel replied as he reached into his jacket pocket, 'I'm not sure I can forgive you either'.

He pulled a small tape recorder out of his pocket and silently passed it to me and I let out a huge sigh of relief. He'd gone through with it. Whatever Charlie had said to him last night had been enough.

Farrington stared open mouthed as I checked the tape recorder. I looked at Farrington and smiled. 'You asked if I was taping our conversation', I told him. 'You didn't ask if Daniel was'. Farrington had no reply, his mouth wide open, trying to take in the betrayal of his only son.

I was about to read Farrington his rights, when a question that had been burning for the last few minutes rose to the surface. 'One thing I don't understand', I told him, 'is why you would do what Sarah Caldwell asked of you. Why would you put yourself at risk, taping aside, by telling me all that? Why incriminate yourself?'

Farrington looked up again. 'If I'd known my only fucking son was taping me', he couldn't hide his anger, 'then of course I wouldn't have. But she asked me to and she's my daughter. If there's one thing that you should understand, Detective, given all that you have been through in the last two days, is that we, as fathers, should do everything in our power to honour our children's lives and wishes'.

He was right. I understood that only too well and for a moment, I almost sympathised with him. 'No matter what they have done', he added. Whether he was talking about Sarah Caldwell's actions or Daniel's betrayal, I wasn't sure. Not that it really mattered. I read Robert Farrington his rights, charged him with aiding and abetting a known felon, then called for Charlie to assist me with him to our car.

99

THREE MONTHS LATER

Judge Charles Walker watched as the twelve members of the jury filed back into the courtroom silently. He cast a look over the courtroom, which was packed to the rafters. Everyone was waiting on the verdict the jury would be delivering shortly. He could only begin to guess the media circus that lay in wait outside for all concerned, no matter what the verdict. One by one the members of the jury sat down and, as he always did, he tried to read the verdict from their faces. They weren't looking at the accused but what did that matter? Many would have you believe that if a jury doesn't look at the defendant on the way back into court then they have reached a 'guilty' verdict. His years of experience presiding over trials such as this had shown him that wasn't strictly true. He'd had some high profile cases during his fifteen year tenure in his position but none more so than this one. He waited until everyone was seated before he spoke.

'Would the foreman of the jury please stand', he asked. Walter Kordinzki stood up, all too aware that all eyes were now on him. A respectable middle aged businessman, used to holding his own negotiations in the board room, he had been a natural choice for foreman and had received no opposition to his proposal that it should be him. In truth, when he'd looked around his fellow jurors on the first day, he doubted whether any of them had the balls to step up to this position with this case being so high profile. 'Have you reached a decision?' Kordinzki cleared his throat.

'We have, your Honour'.

'Very well', Walker nodded. 'Would the accused please stand?'

Senator Conrad Conway stood up, exuding confidence and charisma, confident of the jury to his right delivering the correct decision. Ever since Burr and McCrane had been assassinated by Leon Reno, the scumbag that had given him up as he lay in the road dying, Conway's life had been almost intolerable. There had been nothing substantial to link him to the murders except the word of a low-life, drug abusing loser and a couple of other minor, circumstantial pieces of evidence, yet all this time had been wasted trying convict him of ordering the hits on Burr and McCrane. Conway smiled as he looked at the judge and cast a sideways glance at the jury, and the foreman in particular. Well there was no reason for Conway not to feel confident was there? Only two days ago, Kordinzki had accepted thirty thousand unmarked US dollars to steer the jury the way they needed to go. Not that he'd had any direct contact with any of the jurors himself, but two of his associates had found Kordinzki easy enough to turn. They hadn't even had to threaten to harm his wife and two children if the wrong decision was made, although they would have been more than happy to make that threat on his behalf. Nevertheless, until Conway heard the words spoken, he couldn't be one hundred percent.

'For the charge of 'conspiracy to commit first degree murder', do you, the members of the jury, find the defendant guilty or not guilty?'

The courtroom was silent. It seemed as though no-one was even breathing. Everyone was waiting with baited breath for the foreman's next words which, to Conway at least, he seemed to take an eternity to speak.

'Not guilty, your Honour'.

The courtroom erupted with cheers from Conway's supporters, of which there were many, and jeers from his detractors, of which there were almost as many. Conway himself simply sat back down as he shook his council's hands one by one, more relieved than anyone else that those words had been spoken.

Fearing his courtroom was on the verge of descending into chaos, which he would never tolerate no matter what the circumstance, Walker brought his gavel down hard, several times, appealing for order. As the courtroom became silent for the most part, the Judge spoke once again. 'Senator Conway, you are free to go'.

Three hours later, having fulfilled all his media commitments, Conway found himself in his study and poured himself a large glass of scotch. He smiled as he recalled how he played the 'innocently accused' card when he had walked onto the steps of the courthouse to the awaiting media frenzy. 'I will always have my detractors', he had announced. 'Those who seek to discourage and discredit me'. The media had lapped it up. 'However, this afternoon I rejoice at justice prevailing and can assure you that I can now turn my attention back to business with my full focus, now this nonsense has been exposed for just exactly what it is. *Nonsense*'.

His private line rang and he picked up the receiver, confident that it wouldn't be a journalist after a quote or anything of the kind. Only his closest friends and most respected business associates had this number and it wasn't a number that could be easily found or traced.

'Conway', he answered.

'Congratulations on the verdict, Senator', a voice spoke. It was a voice Conway had only heard three or four times before, but he knew who it was.

'Thank you, sir', he replied.

'A most pleasing outcome', the voice continued. 'However, the events of the last few months have left us with a problem'.

'I know', Conway affirmed.

'The Animi must be allowed to continue their work', the voice said. 'But McCrane, Burr and Farrington are now out of the picture. As *you* almost were, Senator'.

'What would you like me to do?'

'I am sending a list of suitable candidates for their replacement by the usual means. You are free to suggest any candidates you might have in mind'.

'Thank you'.

'And if I might make one suggestion, Senator?'

'Please do'.

'If you could refrain from sleeping with any of their wives, it would be very much appreciated'.

Conway nodded, aware that this is what had started Burr and McCrane's vendetta against him in the first place.

'Of course'.

'In that case, we will speak again once you have had time to vet all the candidates *Chairman* Conway'.

Conway hung up the receiver, laughing. His, and indeed The Animi's, work was just beginning.

100

I hadn't gone to Conway's trial myself, preferring to take a personal day, the afternoon of which I was planning to spend with Katie. She had made a full and speedy recovery, for which I was eternally thankful. She had received counselling for six weeks after the event but had returned to college part time four weeks ago, having shown no lasting mental effects of her abduction. She had felt ready and the counsellor agreed. I can't begin to describe how relieved and happy that made me.

The events that had unfolded during my daughter's abduction by Sarah Caldwell had uncovered Conway's involvement with Burr and McCrane but nothing concrete to link him to Sarah Caldwell herself. I suspected he was involved somehow but we had unearthed nothing that could prove that.

When news filtered through of the court's verdict that morning on the news channel, I can't say that I was entirely surprised. I'd been monitoring the case closely and had thought that what evidence there had been to tie him to Burr and McCrane's deaths had been circumstantial for the most part.

Nevertheless, Conway was now on our radar and I was certain that our paths would cross eventually; that I would find out to what extent he had known about Sarah Caldwell one way or the other. For now, I was satisfied that Robert Farrington had just begun his four year stretch in California State Prison for aiding and abetting Sarah Caldwell. I had no doubt that his wealth and stature would ensure that his time there would come with more privileges than most, but he was there at least and in all honesty, that was the best that I could have hoped for. For me, the priority was finding Sarah Caldwell again. Farrington's warning that another game had been set in motion by one of her followers still echoed in my ears. However, as the days after her escape from the cliff top in Windsor Hills passed, I knew the chance of finding her was passing with them. Now, three months on, I suspected that the next time I would see or speak to Sarah Caldwell was when she decided it was time, and not before.

The phone rang, and I momentarily hesitated, just as I had every time the phone had rung since Sarah Caldwell had evaded our capture. Was this the call? Was this the time?

'Patton', I answered.

'Hey, Patton, it's Jonny Devine'. Devine was a fellow detective and a good friend. He worked vice out of San Fernando Valley and we'd helped each other numerous times when our investigations had sometimes crossed paths.

'You seen the news?' he asked. 'Goddamn walked'.

'Yeah I've seen it', I told him.

'Hey how's Katie doing?'

'She's doing fine', I looked up and silently thanked God as I often do now. 'Picking her up in half an hour as it happens'.

'Hey man, that's good to hear. I'll catch you later'.

I hung up the phone thankful that it hadn't been Sarah Caldwell. I knew that until she made contact again, not a day would go by that she did not haunt.

In that respect, even though I'd got my daughter back safely, maybe Sarah Caldwell had won her game after all.